RUSSELL JAMES

DEMON DAGGER

This is a **FLAME TREE PRESS** book

Text copyright © 2022 Russell James

FLAME TREE PRESS
6 Melbray Mews, London, SW6 3NS, UK
flametreepress.com

US sales, distribution and warehouse:
Simon & Schuster
simonandschuster.biz

UK distribution and warehouse:
Marston Book Services Ltd
marston.co.uk

Publisher's Note: This is a work of fiction. Names, characters, places, and
incidents are a product of the author's imagination. Locales and public names
are sometimes used for atmospheric purposes. Any resemblance to actual
people, living or dead, or to businesses, companies, events, institutions, or
locales is completely coincidental.

Thanks to the Flame Tree Press team.

The cover is created by Flame Tree Studio with
thanks to Nik Keevil and Shutterstock.com.
The font families used are Avenir and Bembo.

Flame Tree Press is an imprint of Flame Tree Publishing Ltd

flametreepublishing.com

A copy of the CIP data for this book is available from the British Library
and the Library of Congress.

HB ISBN: 978-1-78758-695-6
PB ISBN: 978-1-78758-693-2
ebook ISBN: 978-1-78758-696-3

Printed and bound in Great Britain by Clays Ltd, Elcograf S.p.A

RUSSELL JAMES

DEMON DAGGER

FLAME TREE PRESS
London & New York

For Christy.

Thanks for all the support you give that makes
this author thing possible. Sorry if this story ruins
theme park characters for you.

CHAPTER ONE

A warm Pacific breeze blew in the scent of eucalyptus and blooming oleander. Sage lent its sweet fragrance to the mix. Greg Wolter inhaled the intoxicating floral bouquet that whispered promises his concrete city could never keep.

Somehow during the early mornings in March, Los Angeles could still smell wonderful, despite hazy air and homeless encampments along the dirty streets. As the day progressed, the belch of diesel engines and the stink of broiling dumpsters would soon foul the air, but for this brief moment, Greg closed his eyes and imagined the paradise this place could have been.

He opened them to the city's reality. He sat in his wheelchair on one of the sidewalks that snaked through poorly maintained MacArthur Park. The park was a square island of green surrounded by the city's tight-packed grid of buildings and streets. A large lake took up one corner of the park, and a few forlorn trees dotted the area. The builders' early 1900s vision of an urban oasis had not been fulfilled. Handsome beaus did not escort their well-dressed betrothed along manicured paths. Instead, the impoverished from the local area lounged on patchy grass. The tents of the homeless hogged the shade under the trees. Young men in leather and tattoos did a furtive business exchanging small plastic bags for wads of cash.

But Greg wheeled himself here in the mornings because he could catch that glorious LA scent and bask in the SoCal sun better than through the window of his tiny apartment. And despite the park's high crime statistics, no one had ever messed with the old man in the wheelchair. He figured that even the most callous thugs thought it beneath them to rough up a geezer who appeared to have nothing worth stealing.

He spent the time watching people pass by. He looked at them from the waist up, never from the waist down, never at their shadows. The decades had taught him it was less stressful to keep secret the status of strangers' souls.

The sidewalk in front of him curved downhill to where Wilshire Boulevard cut through the center of the park. The road had been built in the 1930s, proving that city government had been committed to cars over people since the earliest days. Vehicles did a slow roll in the morning traffic and bicycles whizzed by the cars.

Then Greg saw, walking in the crowd, what he feared the most. His mouth went dry.

It walked along the sidewalk on Wilshire. Its humanlike head appeared charred, like meat left on a grill for far too long. A blackened, pointed nose stuck out over a wide mouth and elongated ears swept to points top and bottom. Dots glowed red within deep, black eye sockets. Atop its head, twin horns swept out to the sides and then curled inward. A demon.

Its grotesque body proportions made the demon even more repellent. A wide torso tapered to a narrow waist. The skin on the torso was opaque, and beneath it writhed indistinct shapes. But Greg knew just what they were.

Its blackened arms and legs seemed impossibly thin, yet somehow its legs supported its body. The creature's hands only had three bony fingers and a thumb, with sharp black claws at each tip.

The people around the demon didn't run, didn't scream in terror as they should. Because the gift/curse that the old man had was that only he could see the demons as they truly were. The rest of the population just saw the human being the demon had possessed after its escape from Hell. So it walked through the pedestrian crowd unnoticed, just another person on the way to work.

Greg's bladder seemed to swell to twice its normal size and he fought the urge to pee himself. His age-weakened heart slammed in his chest at a rate it hadn't reached in decades. Because this wasn't just any demon walking through MacArthur Park. He recognized the demon as Nicobar.

He dug his nails into the wheelchair's armrests. Almost thirty years ago, he'd helped end this abomination's hunt for human souls and sent it back to Hell. Memories he'd long repressed came flooding back. Paralyzing terror, sickening bloodshed, soul-crushing loss. If that creature had returned, it would bring chaos and death to the City of Angels again.

Suddenly, Greg's wheelchair spun to the right. A golden retriever barreled past, dragging a small boy behind him at the other end of its leash. Greg fought to balance his chair as it leaned downhill.

Then a woman grabbed the armrest on his left and steadied the chair. It went still and the humiliated face of a young Hispanic woman looked down at him.

"The dog," she said. "It is too much for my boy. I am so sorry!"

She released the chair, and for a second kept her hands inches from it, as if it might jump out of control again on its own. When it didn't, she ran downhill after her son without waiting for Greg's absolution.

Greg looked back to where the demon had been. It was gone. Lost in the crowd, a crowd that had no idea of the evil that walked among them.

He and his demon-hunting partner had beaten Nicobar before. The fight had left his partner dead. Greg had survived, but his injuries had sapped the strength from his legs. That experience had boiled away his courage to hunt down a demon again. He'd wondered afterward, if they had known Nicobar's true strength, would they have even considered taking it on?

A much wiser, and much, much older Greg knew facing down a demon now would be suicide. What was a disabled old man going to do all alone against evil so monstrous that it was supposed to be banished from ever walking the Earth? He felt utterly helpless.

He prayed that somewhere out there, a new generation had stepped up to do what he'd once done, that right now they were executing a plan to get that abomination off the streets of Los Angeles.

He had no faith that prayer would be answered.

His lap felt wet. He looked down and saw that he'd peed himself after all.

CHAPTER TWO

Twenty-five years ago

Drew sat terrified in the small waiting room.

His mother sat beside him, but her presence wasn't going to provide any comfort. After all, it was her fault he was here in this psychiatrist's office. He sure as hell hadn't signed himself up.

The tiny room made him feel trapped. No art hung on the walls. The hard plastic chairs scraped against the tile floor when they moved. The air reeked of artificial lemon trying to mask the smell of disinfectant. Drew imagined the place had been designed to clean easily after one of the nut jobs waiting here went bonkers.

And some of those nut jobs sat around him. Across from him a middle-aged man in a golf shirt couldn't sit still for more than sixty seconds. Then some sort of nervous tic would manifest itself in his arms or legs. To Drew's right, a woman with bright blue hair chewed gum in a slow, open-mouthed manner. One of her arms was covered by a tattoo of Betty Boop beheading a teddy bear with a machete.

These patients were all at least twice as old, and twice as screwed-up, as thirteen-year-old Drew. Drew wondered if he would end up being as whacked as these two losers by the time he reached their age.

The door of the office opened and a pretty young woman in a bright green dress stuck her head into the waiting room.

"Drew?" she said.

Drew and his mother stood up and walked to the door. The woman held up a hand in Drew's mother's direction.

"Mrs. Price, just Drew this time, as we discussed on the phone."

Drew's mother opened her mouth to object. Then she clamped her jaw shut and nodded instead. Drew had the feeling that she was ready to do whatever she was asked to do to get her broken son fixed. This was already the second shrink she'd taken him to.

The woman ushered Drew down the hallway. As the door to the waiting room closed behind him, his sensation of being trapped grew stronger.

The woman took him to an office that was much more hospitable than the waiting room. It hosted a walnut desk and several chairs that would have looked right at home in a living room in front of a TV. The room had no window but there was a door on the right-hand side.

The psychiatrist sat at the desk. He looked the same as the last useless shrink Drew had seen, with short silver hair, glasses with dark plastic rims, and a button-down shirt open at the collar. He wondered if the two had gone to the same medical school and graduated together.

This was going to be another waste of his time. He dropped down into one of the chairs and slumped back.

Unlike the last shrink, this one did not get up, shake his hand, and sit in the opposite chair. He stayed firmly planted behind his desk.

"Drew, I'm Dr. Hakes. You met with Dr. Owens and he referred you to me. How do you feel that session with him went?"

Drew almost said 'fine' just to hurry this process along, get through all the standard questions, run out his fifty-minute clock, and go home. Then he thought, the hell with it. He decided to tell the truth, and see if he could leave now.

"It was a total waste of time," Drew said. "He listened like he didn't believe me, told me nothing useful, and sent me home. All he did was pass me on to you. That totally proves even *he* knew the whole session was bogus."

"He sent you to me because I've treated people who've had the same experiences that you've had."

"No one's had the experiences I've had."

"You'd be surprised. Tell me yours."

Again, Drew decided just to blurt it all out. He'd see the look of disbelief on the doctor's face, get up, and get out of here.

"I've seen monsters."

The doctor's expression didn't change. "Where do you see them?"

"Usually at the mall, sometimes at the bus station."

"Does anyone else see them?"

"If everyone else saw them, I wouldn't be here with you, would I? No one gives them a second glance when they pass by one. I guess only I see them."

"What do they look like to you?"

Drew had seen them often, but could never get used to their terrifying appearance. He shuddered as he recalled the last one he'd seen, two days ago.

"There're like a person, only thinner. So thin you'd think they couldn't stand up. Their skin is black and flaky, like it had been burned real bad. They have wide heads with curling horns like a ram on each side. Their eyes are bright red."

The doctor nodded and scribbled something on a notepad.

"Do you think these monsters see you?" he said.

"They see everything, check out every person as they pass by. But I stay cool, act like I don't know what they actually are. I don't think they know that I can see them the way they really look."

This was where the other shrink started asking questions about how seeing the monsters made him feel (scared, duh) or what his parents were like (great except for recently thinking he was crazy).

This doctor had a different question.

"What do they smell like?"

"Huh?"

"Did these monsters have a certain smell?"

"Uh, yeah. Kind of like hot tar, with a little rotten egg smell in the mix."

"How many fingers did the monsters have on each hand?"

Drew again was surprised by how specific the question was. "Three."

"But they still had thumbs?"

"Yeah." Unless this guy was a mind reader, it was pretty coincidental that he was asking about the details no one else had, and that he seemed to know the answers he expected to hear. "How do you—"

"Drew, you need to know that I believe you. I don't believe that you *think* you saw monsters, but I believe that you *did* see monsters."

The doctor wasn't just blowing smoke up Drew's ass. The look on his face said he was being serious.

"And because I do believe you," the doctor said, "I'm going to have someone talk to you who has specific expertise in this kind of matter."

"Now I'm going to see a third shrink?" Drew said.

"A third person, but not a third psychiatrist."

The doctor got up and went to the side door. He opened it and on the other side was a similar office with the same furniture layout. The shades were drawn, the lights on low.

"C'mon in," a voice said from the other room.

Dr. Hakes stepped aside and gestured for Drew to enter. Drew walked through the door to see a man standing beside the couch.

Despite the dusky light, Drew could see that this man was no psychiatrist. At least he sure didn't look like one. Six feet tall with dark black skin, he wore a tight red t-shirt that stretched over muscles honed by hours of training. His black jeans tapered down to cover a pair of worn cowboy boots. High cheekbones and a trim goatee accentuated his narrow face. His shaved head glistened.

Drew crossed the room and eased himself down into one of the chairs. The man sat down in the chair opposite him. Drew sat up straighter.

"Hey, Drew," he said. He smiled and his teeth practically glowed within his silky black goatee. "My name's Lincoln."

"You're no psychiatrist."

"Not even close. But you don't need one. You haven't seen these monsters as you call them until recently, right?"

"For a few months. I waited a long time to tell anyone because, well, look what happens when you tell people you see invisible creatures out of a horror movie."

Lincoln pulled out his phone and called up a picture. He showed it to Drew. "Your monsters look like this?"

The picture was of a painting of a monster just like the ones he'd seen. Horrific as the picture was, Drew couldn't help but smile.

"Yes! Exactly like that! You've seen them?"

"Not, not me. But hundreds of other people have over thousands of years," Lincoln said. He put his phone in his lap. "It's an awful gift to join their ranks."

"No kidding."

"You don't know the half of it." Lincoln leaned forward. "You aren't seeing monsters, Drew. You're seeing people possessed by demons."

"Like angels-and-demons demons?"

"If you want to believe that story. The tale is that the archangel Lucifer led a rebellion in Heaven. No one wins a battle with God. Lucifer and his rebel angels were cast out into a place God specifically created for them, Hell."

"I saw a movie like that once."

"And that story might just be someone's way of explaining the inexplicable. What I know is true is that these demons live in another plane of existence. Sometimes they escape to here and possess people. And here is way nicer. Hell is basically in a roiling sea of burning oil and tar."

"Which is why the demon's skin is black and charred?"

"Exactly. And these demons you see aren't invisible to everyone else. The rest of us see the person the demon possessed."

"I'm the only one seeing the real deal?"

"You and others with your gift. In fact, if you're close enough to one, you've noticed that you can smell it. Some nasty combination of sulfur and burned meat. If you hear one scream in pain or anger, it might not sound human at all."

"And what do they want?"

"They're stealing the essence of what makes humans different from other animals, what a lot of people call a soul. The energy of the soul keeps the demon alive on Earth. After the soul is digested, the demon has to take another soul. Otherwise, it slips back into Hell."

All of this explanation was making Drew's head hurt. "I don't understand all this."

"And you aren't going to. Not for a while. There's a lot to learn. What you need to know is this isn't your imagination. The demons you're seeing are real. And they're dangerous. Whatever you do, don't acknowledge that you can see them as they really are. For now, we'll keep that to ourselves until you can learn more about protecting yourself."

"How will I do that?"

"First, you're going to leave this office and as far as your mother knows, you're cured. You don't ever mention seeing demons again. The doctor is going to call your mother in first, explain that his hypnosis therapy cured you."

"She'll like that."

"Then he'll recommend redirected rehabilitation, basically learning some technical skills to get your mind working in new directions. He's going to recommend me, a man with a good track record in the Big Brothers program. You and I are going to start meeting each week between the end of school and your mother getting home from work."

Drew's friends list was pretty short, and after-school sports wasn't a thing for him, so he was going to have no problem working Lincoln into his schedule.

"We'll start tomorrow," Lincoln said. "Don't be late. You've got a lot to learn."

CHAPTER THREE

Present day

Drew Price hated Halloween. Unfortunately, his wife, Anna, loved it.

The holiday, and he thought it anything but that, was still weeks away. But the decorating had begun at their little San Fernando ranch house, leading the way among all the other similar homes packed onto their street. Two giant plastic jack-o'-lanterns vied for space on the small porch and a huge spider clung to the front door, right over the peephole. The spider had big googly eyes and a fanged smile.

Halloween decorations represented something scary, while not being scary. Drew never understood what kind of person makes light of things so dark. He thought that the whole event was idiotic. But it made Anna happy, so he just rolled with it.

Drew paused at the front door. Coming home from work, he was still in his Los Angeles County Sheriff's deputy uniform. He took his pistol from his holster, dropped the magazine, and cleared the weapon. He returned the ejected bullet to the magazine, re-holstered the pistol, and put the magazine in his pocket. The whole thing would go into the gun safe almost immediately, but with his seven-year-old son, Kenny, running around the house, he took every precaution. He'd heard too many accidental shooting stories to want to be part of one.

He stepped inside to the yapping of Brutus, his sarcastically named black dachshund. The little dog came charging to the door, tiny toenails scratching against the floor tiles. He jumped up and down at Drew's feet, which for a dog that size translated to more like a bunny's hop. Drew picked him up and gave him a big scratch behind the ears. Brutus thumped his tail against Drew's chest.

The pooch was getting on in years. Gray hair speckled his muzzle and Drew suspected his hearing wasn't still all there. He'd adopted the little shelter rescue before he'd met Anna. The old dog was still surprisingly spunky.

He was relieved to see that the inside of the house hadn't endured the All Hallows' Eve transformation yet. In the living room, a blue couch and loveseat faced a coffee table. A frantic anime cartoon blared from the TV on the wall to an empty room. Pots banged in the kitchen at the end of the hall. Drew hung his car keys on the wall hook and went to the kitchen.

He stepped in and saw Anna standing over the stove, stirring a pot of spaghetti. She'd tied her black hair back in a ponytail and it reached halfway to her waist. At a slim five and a half feet tall, she was a good six inches shorter than Drew, but he'd always thought them to be a perfect fit. The rising steam from the pot sparkled in the stove's overhead light and gave her creamy skin an angelic glow.

He put Brutus down, walked up behind her, and wrapped an arm around her waist. "Cooking again?" he kidded her. "I'm impressed."

Her brow knitted. She didn't look at him. "Cheap pasta, expensive takeout. Do the math."

He knew he'd screwed up. Money had been tight since they'd been forced to take out a loan to repair the roof at the same time her hours at work had been cut back.

"Sorry, that was a stupid comment. Home-cooked is always better. I might have some off-duty work lined up to help out."

It was common for LASD deputies to pick up temporary private security work. He'd snagged some gigs through other deputies' connections the last few months. Every bit helped.

"And your dog did that," she said.

She pointed the steaming spoon at the kitchen table where an expensive green running shoe lay like a battlefield casualty on one of the placemats. The upper had been shredded and the shoelace chewed off to the first set of eyelets. This was one of the ways Brutus still, unfortunately, displayed his spunk. It was why they kept their shoes in the closet with the door closed. He guessed that mentioning that right now would be a bad idea.

He looked down at Brutus. Brutus looked away in guilt.

"I'm so sorry," Drew said.

"You know how hard it is for me to find comfortable shoes," she said.

Now Drew felt even worse. His wife suffered from rheumatoid arthritis, an insidious disease that made her immune system attack her own joints. Short-term pain was often excruciating, long-term damage inevitable. When the disease acted up, she referred to it as the Red Dragon. He knew exactly how long it had taken her to find those good-fitting shoes.

"I'll start searching for a new pair," Drew said. "LA is a big city, I'm sure I'll find one."

She didn't answer and experience told him that this was the time to back off for a few minutes. It definitely wasn't the time to bring up that the spider on the door blocked the peephole. He headed back down the hall to Kenny's bedroom. Brutus followed.

Just before he entered Kenny's room, a small demon leapt out into the hallway with a roar. Drew froze and his heart skipped a beat.

It was actually Kenny, wearing a mask that had far too close a resemblance to Drew's childhood demon visions than he'd like. The mask was long, ending in a pointed chin, with two horns atop the head and a pointed nose. The skin was painted in varying shades of red and black.

He hadn't encountered a demon since his sessions with Lincoln decades ago. He'd tried to push the whole experience, the knowledge of his so-called gift of demon sight, as far from his consciousness as possible. He was finally at the point where he could go weeks without remembering the world of demons really existed, until something like his son's costume reminded him.

The sight of the mask sent a hurricane of emotions roaring inside him. Fear, anger, loss. A flurry of horrific memories flashed through his mind, broken free from the place he'd mentally sequestered them.

But what really chilled him to the core was the awful juxtaposition of the mask's monstrous face on his beautiful little son.

"No!" Drew screamed. Without thinking, he pulled the mask from his son's face and threw it down the hall.

That action revealed the tiny face of his son, with round rosy cheeks and a shock of white-blond hair. His blue eyes radiated youthful excitement.

But in the split second it took Kenny to process what his father had just done, all that changed. Fear filled the boy's eyes. His mouth gaped open. His face flushed red.

Kenny screamed. Tears rolled down his face and he bolted back into his bedroom.

Drew was emotionally gut-punched. He couldn't believe what he'd just done.

"What the hell did you do?"

Drew turned to see a furious Anna standing behind him.

There was no way to explain his reaction. He'd never told her anything about that early part of his life, about demons and death and a part of the world he wished he'd never learned about. He'd never told anyone.

"Kenny," Drew said, "he startled me."

"Startled? You're a deputy. How can a four-foot-tall little boy scare you?"

She pushed past him and entered Kenny's room. The boy's crying echoed in the hallway. She shut the door behind her.

He went to the closed door and listened. Inside the room, his wife comforted his weeping son.

"Daddy didn't mean to frighten you," Anna cooed. "You were just so scary in your Halloween costume."

Scary as hell, Drew thought. *Almost literally.*

He'd be able to apologize to them both, but never explain his reaction. In the same way, he'd never explained his disgust for Halloween, the season that made light of a demonic world he knew to be all too true.

At least contact with that world had stopped since Lincoln's death. He didn't have to deal with demons, just his memories of them. He would have twelve months to reinter those recollections in the mental mausoleum he'd created for them before he had to again face this stupid celebration. Tonight, he'd try to make things right with his family.

He went back to the kitchen and checked the pasta. The stove was still on and most of the water was gone from the pot. He turned off the stove. Anything left simmering too long eventually boiled away the water and caught fire.

He didn't like the analogy.

CHAPTER FOUR

1995

Lincoln's house was on the other side of the city from where Drew lived. It would take a cross-city bus ride with his bicycle in the bus's rack, and then a decent amount of pedaling on his bike to get there. But if Lincoln was going to give him more answers about these demons he'd been seeing, the trip would be worth it.

Drew stopped his bike in front of the address Lincoln had given him. Whatever it was he'd expected a demon hunter's house to look like, this wasn't it. The simple suburban ranch house didn't stand out from any of the others in the subdivision, except maybe the shrubs were a bit overgrown. He parked his bike by the garage door. From the other side came the thump of a bassline from a hard rock song Drew only vaguely recognized. He headed for the front porch.

The garage door began a slow, grinding, upward roll behind him. He whirled around. The opening door revealed a garage filled with boxes and walls lined with hanging tools. Electric guitars blared from two speakers on the wall. In the center was an old gold Chevelle, a big two-door model from the days when Apollo missions still landed on the moon. The car had no glass or a trunk lid. The hood was halfway up.

Lincoln stood in the shadows at the back of the garage. He wore oil-stained coveralls.

"There you are." He turned down the music. "That should keep the next-door geezer McCloskey from yelling at me about the rock and roll. C'mon in this way."

Drew parked his bike in the driveway. It wasn't like the old car was going to be leaving the garage anytime soon. He stepped into the garage and the door rolled down behind him.

"This is Gabriella," Lincoln said.

"Your car has a name?"

"All cars have a name. Sadly, few people ask the car what it is."

Drew began to worry that this Lincoln guy might be crazy. His belief that demons walked the Earth should have been a bigger clue.

"How old is this antique?" Drew said.

"*She* isn't as old as I am, so she'll never be an antique. Keep that straight. This is the first car I ever owned. I learned all about auto maintenance working on her. And so can you."

"I thought you were going to teach me about demons."

"You'll learn both. If I sent you home without learning about something other than demons, what are you going to tell your mother we talked about all afternoon?"

He had a point there.

Lincoln walked up to the nose of the car. A huge workbench covered the back wall of the garage with tool chests underneath it. Sets of screwdrivers and wrenches hung on the wall. Lincoln heaved the car's hood the rest of the way up and hung a work light on the exposed latch. He snapped it on and the engine bay lit up in a soft fluorescent glow. Lincoln motioned Drew to come over.

"Here's your first lesson. Say a car doesn't start. How do you diagnose it?"

"Send it to a mechanic."

"Except that you're going to be the mechanic, if you pay attention. An engine works because gasoline explodes in a cylinder, which pushes pistons up and down, which turns a crankshaft, which eventually turns the wheels."

Lincoln spun the nut off the top of the air cleaner and removed the lid. Inside, a brass-colored device with open chambers in the middle sat in the center of the air cleaner base, bolted to the motor at the bottom.

"That's a carburetor. Air goes into the venturi in the middle. It mixes a bit of gasoline into the air and sends it to the cylinders."

He traced a thick wire along the side of the engine to a spark plug screwed into the motor.

"That's a spark plug. At just the right moment, electricity arcs across the gap in the plug, ignites the gas/air mixture, and the pistons move."

Drew had to admit he'd never even considered what made an engine run. "Cool."

"So, first step to diagnosing an engine that won't start is to see if it has air, gas, and a spark. Then you go find whatever's missing. Now, repeat that back. What's an engine need to run?"

"Air, gas, spark."

"Bingo. That's the lesson you learned to take home."

Lincoln pulled two stools out from under the workbench. He sat on one. The workbench light cast half his face in shadow. He slid the other stool over closer to Drew, who sat on it.

"Human beings also need three things to work properly," Lincoln said. "A mind, a body, and a soul."

"I've taken biology. There's no soul inside us."

"None you can see," Lincoln said, "but I can tell you what one weighs. On April tenth, 1901, in Massachusetts, Dr. Duncan MacDougall conducted an experiment on six dying patients. Each was placed on a specially made scale just prior to his death. The instant life ceased, the weight reading dropped, as if something had been lifted from the body. Everything was taken into account, from the air in the lungs to bodily fluids. It still couldn't be explained. That consistent amount was twenty-one grams."

"That's bizarre."

"People weren't convinced, so Dr. MacDougall conducted the same experiment on fifteen dogs. The dogs died and there was no weight change. MacDougall concluded that only humans had souls."

"Why would we need a soul?"

"It provides what some call the divine spark. It allows us to know right from wrong, gives us empathy and compassion. The religious believe that we were made in God's image, but the soul gives us God's spirit. Others just think it's a useful bit of biological evolution."

"So we die if we lose our soul?"

"Sadly, no. An engine can run without a spark. A badly tuned car can keep running, very roughly, after you turn it off. It's called compression ignition. Running that way damages the engine over time.

"Letting a human being live without a soul does the same thing. Without the divine spark, the person loses the sense of morality and the ability to see his actions hurt others. He starts a fast downhill slide into evil. You've seen people who commit crimes with zero remorse, haven't you?"

Drew nodded.

"Soulless. And proof of this came from someone trying to disprove Dr. MacDougall's research. In 1982 Dr. Lyle Mueller replicated MacDougall's experiment with a dozen men at the moment of their death. He saw no change in body weight in any patient."

"That sounds like he disproved Dr. MacDougall."

"Except that all his subjects were criminals executed by the state of Texas. He monitored them as they received a lethal injection. He proved MacDougall *right*, because like the dogs that MacDougall had experimented on, these murderers had no souls."

"So how can someone lose their soul?"

"Demons. That's why people like us have to stop them by sending them back to Hell."

CHAPTER FIVE

Present day

In 1995, Drew had been certain he would do two things when he grew up: join the LAPD and hunt demons.

In the end he'd done neither. He never had another encounter with a demon after he started learning from Lincoln, and the idea of tangling with one lost all its appeal after Lincoln's death. So he'd taken everything related to demon hunting and packed it away. And while he'd still had a desire to be in law enforcement, nightly news reports of what street cops encountered had made the idea a nonstarter with Anna.

They had compromised with Drew joining the Los Angeles Sheriff's Department. But he wasn't out busting up drug rings and chasing street racers. He worked in vehicle inspections. People came in with registration problems or for inspections after getting cited by the LASD for safety violations. The demon–hunting skills Lincoln had taught him might have ended up being worthless, but the automotive skills Drew learned had definitely come in handy.

Drew occupied one of several deputy's desks in the small office in downtown Van Nuys. The office usually had a steady stream of surly customers. None were there voluntarily, and all were coming in after an unhappy interaction with LASD. There were days when he wondered if street patrol would have been more rewarding.

It was just after nine a.m. when Drew's phone rang. The caller ID read *CSP-CORCORAN.*

The state prison in Corcoran housed over three thousand inmates, most of whom were problem inmates or security risks. Charles Manson had cheated the executioner and died there of old age. Drew braced himself for a misdirected number. There were thousands of phones in the LASD and putting someone through to the wrong one was the automated answering system's specialty. He picked up the receiver.

"Deputy Price," he said.

"Deputy?" the female voice on the other end said. "Hmm. This is Drew Price, correct?"

"Yes, how can I help you?"

"This is Officer Marjorie Gonzales from Corcoran. One of our inmates is in the infirmary and asked to call you, but he's really not strong enough to get to a phone. Out of what is probably misguided compassion, I'm doing it for him."

"Who's the inmate?"

"Bobby Lee Simmons."

Drew's blood ran cold at the name. Robert Lee Simmons, an Aryan Brotherhood asshole named for the Confederate general, was on death row, convicted of two murders. One of which was Lincoln's.

"And what does that piece of human filth want?"

"He said he wants to talk with you in person. Doesn't want it recorded on the prison phone lines. He said he has answers to the questions you had."

Years ago, Drew had questioned the prisoner about Lincoln's murder and the man had refused to answer, using the bluntest of terms.

"Why's he in the infirmary? A well-deserved shivving, I hope."

"No, stage four lung cancer, and the doctors say he's close to the end. I can tell you he sure looks like he is. He seems legit, wants to get something off his chest. If I thought it was a scam or he wasn't serious, I wouldn't have called you."

Corcoran was a solid two-and-a-half-hour drive without traffic. A convict asking to make a deathbed statement was something his supervisor would free him up to listen to.

"I can be there in three hours," Drew said.

"Because you're on the job, I can get you into the infirmary to talk with him. When you check in at the gate, tell the guard that's where you're going. Have him call me to meet you."

"Okay. Thanks for the call."

"I hope he gives you something worth the trip."

So did Drew.

A year after Lincoln's death, the police had hit a dead end investigating his murder. No witnesses, no DNA, no motive. And the savagery of the attack fit no current MO except for maybe a pack of wild hyenas. Then out of nowhere, Bobby Lee raised his hand and confessed to the murder.

He had already been in jail at the time, awaiting trial for murdering a Black man in Riverside who had 'looked at him the wrong way' according to Bobby Lee. His public defender was assembling a defense despite an overwhelming amount of evidence, Bobby Lee's white nationalist ties, and his inflammatory public statements. Bobby Lee still claimed he only threatened, not killed, the man in Riverside, but out of the blue at his arraignment in open court, he pleaded guilty for Lincoln's murder. His public defender quit.

Bobby Lee's murder conviction for Lincoln was a foregone conclusion. At trial the jury had found him guilty of the Riverside killing after thirty minutes of deliberation. Sentencing for the first murder was life in prison, for the second, death.

Bobby Lee's unsolicited confession had never sat well with Drew. It made no sense to confess to a crime he wasn't even suspected of. That was why Drew had gone to talk to him all those years ago. Maybe the man had been coerced, and Lincoln's true killer was still on the loose, unpunished.

As with most other inmates on California's death row, it looked like disease was going to cross the finish line ahead of lethal injection in the race to kill Bobby Lee. Drew hoped he'd get to the prisoner before either of them did.

CHAPTER SIX

1995

Drew lay under Gabriella the Chevelle on a mechanic's creeper, balancing the big steel box of a gas tank on his chest. About a foot away from his face yawned the empty space between the frame rails where the tank would mount. The metal straps that would hold it in place hung from the bottom of the car, one on either side of him.

"You see where the tank's going to go?" Lincoln said.

"You bet."

"Okay, you lift it up there and hold it while I pull each strap across it and bolt them in place."

The tank was about a foot thick and three feet long. It was wide enough that the sides hung out over Drew's bony chest on both sides. Even empty, it was heavy, and it was going to be awkward to lift and hold. But he wasn't going to admit that to Lincoln the demon hunter and look like a wimpy little kid.

"Ready," Drew said.

Lincoln grabbed the end of one of the straps. "Lift."

Drew put the flat of his palms against the cold steel and bench-pressed the tank upward. He shifted it right and left until it fit into the space between the rails with a hollow thunk.

"Perfect," Lincoln said. "Hold that."

He pulled the left strap tight and Drew heard a bolt slide into place to secure the strap. Then came the click and whiz of a ratchet tightening a nut to the bolt.

"Gas is the energy that runs the car," Lincoln said. "Without it, nothing moves. The car is as good as dead. You need a nice clean tank or you'll contaminate the gas."

Drew appreciated the automotive lessons but preferred to not be struggling to hold up heavy parts while he listened to them.

The ratchet noise stopped. Half the tank was secure. Drew's triceps quivered from stress. The other side of the tank slipped lower.

"You have to keep it up there," Lincoln said.

Drew took a deep breath and pushed up. The tank banged back into place. Lincoln pulled the second strap tight. A bolt clicked into place. The ratchet spun.

"So how does a demon pick who it forces itself into?" Drew said.

"Possession isn't done by force. Like all initial demon/human interactions, it's voluntary."

"Voluntary? How does that work?"

"There's a ritual people can perform. It's complex and includes incantations, burning a lot of exotic ingredients, and specific tattoos with what are normally poisons added to the ink. That ritual does two things. First, it weakens the barrier between our world and the one demons live in. Second, it prepares the host body to withstand having a demon's energy inside it."

"Why would someone ask to be possessed?"

"They've been lied to. They think they and the demon will coexist, that the demon will grant them special powers. Some of that does happen. The possessed body gains the demon's incredible strength, rapid healing power, and heightened senses. But touching the consciousness of something so evil is more than the human mind can stand. The host's soul is consumed and their consciousness shatters. The demon takes full control."

"And then the thing goes on a rampage?"

"The demon assumes that victim's life, at least for a short time. Acting like someone else isn't in a demon's nature, though. A demon's got too little respect for humans to play at being one with a job and a family, so it soon abandons that role to live a demonic lifestyle."

"All the people around the possessed have to notice that."

"How many unexplained missing person reports do you think the police deal with each year? How many stories do you hear about people who seem to have overnight personality changes, get a divorce, or move across country?"

"Those are all from demon possessions?" Drew said.

"Hardly. But there's enough non-demon events that the demon-inspired ones get lost in the flow. All the demon needs to do is maintain enough trappings of a human life to keep from arousing suspicions."

"Like taking a shower?" Drew said with a smile.

"Seriously, yes. And changing clothes, and a dozen other things we do every day. What they don't do is sleep or eat. At least they don't eat food, they eat souls. That's what puts gas in their tank."

"So how often do they need to eat a soul?"

"I don't know." Lincoln slid a screwdriver into Drew's hand. "There's two rubber fuel lines down there. Attach them to the sending unit on the tank with the hose clamps on the ends. Fat line goes to the fat fitting, skinny line goes to the skinny fitting, to save you from asking a dumb question."

Drew smiled and rolled to his left where the fuel lines dangled down. "How come I get all the jobs under the car like this?"

"Because you're smaller and I don't have to jack her up so high."

"Good, I thought it was because they weren't any fun to do."

Drew seated one line on a sender tube and began to tighten the clamp. "Demons feed off more than one soul at a time?"

"No, that's why they're always on the hunt, ready to make some poor sucker a deal."

"Make them a deal?" Drew said as he worked.

"They don't snatch a soul, they accept it. If you don't give permission, your soul is safe."

"I can't imagine anyone giving a demon permission to take their soul."

"First, remember that the victim doesn't see the demon inside like you do. They see the body of the person the demon possessed, so their guard is down. Second, the demon can sense when a person is at one of those crossroads of weakness. Maybe a family tragedy has struck, a failure in professional life, blinding fury, consuming greed, uncontrollable lust. A weakened person is primed to take a shortcut. The demon offers it."

"It says 'Trade you a soul to be a rock star' and then rolls out a contract?"

"No, not like the movies. It's subtle. More like 'I can get you a recording contract. All you need to do is hand over your soul.' The demon offers, the victim agrees, usually does some bad deed as a sign of good faith, and the demon takes the soul."

"By what magic does the demon get the guy a recording contract?"

"No magic," Lincoln said. "When a victim agrees to let the demon inside to steal his soul, the demon leaves behind a bit of its essence in the void of the victim's missing soul. That essence creates a doorway to the victim's consciousness. If the demon applies a drop of its blood to the soulless, the demon can compel that person to grant a next victim's wish."

"The soulless ends up like a store owner who gets a favor from the Mafia, only to find out he's on the hook for life paying that favor back."

"Exactly. A soulless cop would let someone under arrest go free, a producer would sign a contract with a singer, a director would give an actor a plum role."

"That helps explain why there are so many famous people with no talent," Drew said.

"In the same way you see demons the way they really look, you can see who's sold their soul. You just haven't noticed yet. To you, the soulless do not cast a shadow."

Drew had to admit he'd never noticed that, but he'd never been looking for it either. "How does that work?"

"I can't tell you the science behind it, if there is any. But everyone else sees the shadow of the soulless, while people with your gift don't. It only works when you see the person face-to-face. In pictures or live video or film, they appear to cast a shadow just like everyone else."

Drew finished tightening the fuel lines and pulled out from under the car. He looked at Lincoln.

"Identifying the soulless might be a neat party trick," Drew said, "but what good does it do me?"

"While the soulless are sociopaths, the best learn how to mimic all the empathy and emotions that being soulless stripped away. But you can still identify them, you know they can't be trusted because they could be compelled by a demon at any time."

"Now I'll be on the lookout."

"You'll be surprised who's revealed. I'll show you tomorrow."

CHAPTER SEVEN

1995

Having two days in a row with Lincoln was exciting for Drew. Learning about the world of demons should have been terrifying, but instead Drew had found it comforting. There was tremendous relief in knowing the things he'd seen hadn't meant he was crazy. And knowing that Lincoln was out there sending these things back to Hell felt very good.

Drew spent the day at school ignoring everything in class and wishing the numbers on the digital classroom clocks would roll forward faster. When the bell for the end of the day rang and he raced out the door, he felt like the cork shot from a bottle of champagne.

In a change of pace, when Drew arrived at Lincoln's garage later, Lincoln wasn't wearing coveralls. His mentor met Drew outside the garage and sent him to the front seat of his faded, ten-year-old pickup truck.

"What's with this?" Drew said.

"Field trip."

A half hour later Lincoln pulled into the parking lot of Blessed Sacrament Catholic Church. The towering old red-brick building sat on Sunset Boulevard in Hollywood. The cornerstone read 1928. Drew guessed this had been a much better neighborhood back then. Now the church stood beside the low-rent businesses on Sunset like a dowdy old matron surrounded by insolent teens.

"You adding religion to my education?" Drew said.

"Hardly. I'm just using the location. A friend of mine is the custodian and lent me a key."

Lincoln led Drew into the church sanctuary through a side door. The church was deserted. Drew followed Lincoln straight back to the choir loft in the rear. They scaled the steps and took up a position at the windows that faced Sunset. Lincoln cranked one open for a better view.

Sunset Boulevard ran east-west here, straight as an arrow in perfect alignment with the afternoon sun. The sidewalks were filled with Angelenos condemned to live or work here, and tourists who mistakenly believed that Hollywood was a glamorous enough location that it was worth visiting. The pervasive seediness, the costumed fake superheroes posing for pictures at a price, and the shuffling homeless soon set the tourists straight.

"Now, just watch the people," Lincoln said.

Drew indulged him and watched the crowd pass by. He noted a lot of bizarre hair and incomprehensible tattoos.

A few minutes later, Lincoln spoke again. "Now look at them the way only you can see them. Focus on the shadows."

Drew redirected his gaze to the sidewalk. The waning sun sent shadows stretching out along the cracked concrete. He soon spotted a woman in a leather vest and biker boots who didn't cast one. His heart skipped a beat.

"Hey, that woman there doesn't have a soul!"

"Relax. Just keep watching."

Over the next thirty minutes, he noted about ten other people without shadows. Some were old, some just into their twenties, half men, half women.

"Damn, there's a lot of them."

"This is Los Angeles. Every place isn't this bad."

Lincoln took a seat on a choir bench. Drew sat down near him.

"The world seems to have bad places," Lincoln began. "Chicago has always been shady, a nexus for gangland bloodshed during prohibition. Las Vegas has always been a hub of gambling and prostitution, and another magnet for organized crime. Even the average person can feel the oozing evil. New Orleans was a center of the slave trade. I walked down those streets alone one night, and the city had a vibe that made my skin crawl.

"Los Angeles, from the start, has had corrupt police, graft-loving politicians, megalomaniacal businessmen. The movie industry started in many different places, but where did an industry perfectly suited to exploit stars and potential stars take strong root? Right here. Tinseltown grew on a reputation of hedonism, abandonment, and treachery.

"Places like these seem to never get cleaned up, no matter who's elected. These locations are weak spots in the fabric of our world, places where the reality inhabited by demons is separated from the reality we live in by the thinnest of veils. These are places where demons are easiest to summon by potential hosts, and where they have the easiest hunting for the next soul after the possession."

"What does all that have to do with me?" Drew asked.

"You won't have to travel the world hunting demons. Your backyard's full of them. I don't know if more keep escaping to LA, or if a bunch of them escaped with one leader long ago. But there's a lot of them here, and they have a never-emptying buffet of people ready to sell their souls for stardom."

"I haven't seen a demon since I started meeting with you," Drew said.

"That's because I took care of the ones you'd been seeing at the mall and the bus station."

That made Drew feel more comfortable. He'd been avoiding those places for a while, afraid of what he might encounter.

"There were soulless out there," he said. "But I didn't see a demon pass by here."

"When the prey density is as good as it is in LA, they don't need to randomly hunt in the streets. They know the clubs and the hangouts where the desperate congregate. There, people are like fish in a barrel."

"If you can't see them, how do you find a demon?"

"Through one of those soulless people out there. They can tell me where and when they made their deal, or at least where and when their luck changed if they look at it that way. Demons tend to keep hunting in the same location. I start my search there, looking for the person who made them the offer."

"And when you find one?"

"We'll save that education for another day."

CHAPTER EIGHT

1995

It was an unnaturally warm day for Los Angeles, and sweat dripped down Drew's face as he worked in Lincoln's garage to the beat of a band he'd learned was called Cream. He hung over Gabriella's engine bay and tightened up the last of the three bolts. A new black metal reservoir hung by the fan at the front of the engine. It had a cap at the top to add and check the level of the fluid and a large pulley on the front.

"And what's this thing?" he asked.

Lincoln sat on a stool between the car and the workbench, out of the glare of the trouble light illuminating the engine compartment. "That's a power steering pump. It creates hydraulic pressure that boosts the force of turning the wheel. Power steering is why you can steer a car with one finger."

"This big car didn't come with power steering?"

"It did. But a friend talked me into tearing it out and putting in manual steering. Convinced me that it would make the car lighter and faster, and the reduced drag on the engine running the pump would leave me more horsepower. For me back then, it was all about speed."

"Was your friend right?"

"No, he was full of crap. The only thing I noticed was that it was hard as hell to keep the car on the road. Steering her was like working out with weights."

"Now you're putting it back in?"

"Age demands that driving take less effort. Now bolt up those pressure lines, and don't overtighten them."

Drew seated the lines in the fittings in the pump and began to slowly tighten them with a wrench.

"No," Lincoln said, "tighten this fitting up first."

Lincoln stuck his arm under the trouble light hanging under the hood and pointed at one fitting.

Drew noticed Lincoln cast no shadow across the engine. Drew stepped back in shock.

He told himself he couldn't have seen what he'd just seen. It must have been a trick of the light, or Lincoln's shadow landed in shadow. But his heart still raced. He gripped the wrench like a club.

"Your shadow…" Drew said.

Lincoln pulled his arm back and grimaced. "Well, you were going to notice eventually."

"No," Drew said, "you couldn't have traded your soul. That's just some trick you know how to do."

"Just like someone talked me into ripping out this power steering, a demon talked me into ripping out my soul."

"You're a sociopath?" Drew's grip on the wrench in his hand tightened.

Lincoln stood up and went to the wall of the garage. He flipped on a switch and two banks of fluorescent lights in the ceiling flickered to life. Drew checked and indeed, Lincoln cast no shadow. He'd never noticed it before.

"I'm a controlled sociopath," Lincoln said. "Not at first, but I am now. You don't have to worry."

"What did you trade the demon for?" Drew asked.

"I wanted to be a NASCAR star."

"I don't remember ever seeing you race in NASCAR."

"Because I never did. I was on the local dirt track circuit in the South. Eighteen years old and bulletproof, certain as hell I could make it to the big show. I'd won a few races, but lost a bunch more. See, in small town, short track dirt racing, money is a bigger determining factor than skill. And I didn't have the money to keep a competitive car running for months on end. I only won when the better cars crapped out and skill could win the day.

"One day, I'm racing Enduro/Pure Stock class at a track in Cottonwood, Alabama, called Dothan Motor Speedway. The season's been tough and I'm so broke I can't pay attention. There's this racist white-trash jackass named Sonny Wright running a near-new car financed with his father's money. I've been eating this guy's exhaust for weeks in the circuit. And he wasn't subtle about telling folks how he'd left what he called a 'tar baby' in the dust each night.

"It was time to put it all on the line. I clean out my bank account to get a new set of injectors and upgrade my tires. I finally have the mechanical edge I need to let my superior driving skills make the difference.

"I take the car out for its qualifying lap and just as I finish, the transmission temperature skyrockets. I roll into the pits with a blown rear seal and who knows how much internal transmission damage from the heat.

"That's it for me. I don't have the money to fix it, and I sure don't have the time. I'm not even sure I have the gas to haul the car home. All I can see is years of work and every dime I ever made going up in the smoke of my overheated transmission. Now I was going to limp home and have everyone who told me I'd never make it give me that 'I told you so' look. In my mind I scream out how unfair this all is as I kick a spare tire around the pits.

"Then a stranger walks over to me. Suave-looking guy, six feet tall and fit as hell. His golf shirt has a major oil company logo on it and his cowboy boots easily cost north of six hundred dollars.

"Now, I'm wary. The world has come a long way about race since I was a kid, but I'm in lower Alabama in the country, and the white upper crust coming to talk to me usually is because I'm blocking their way or they think I'm the help. But he comes over with a big smile, says his name is Quentin, and shakes my hand.

"This guy looks completely normal, but when I shake his hand, I get a chill that freezes me to the core. Ever have a pitch-black thunderhead roll across the sky and stop over your head? That's the feeling I have standing next to him. That should be enough to make me run.

"But it doesn't.

"He says he's got a proposition for me. He brags about his powerful connections, that's all, powerful connections, and he'd like to use those connections to help me out. He's been watching me race, talks in detail about the ones over the last two weeks. He can see that I've got what it takes to make it big, if I could get a ride that could finish a race without breaking down.

"Well, he says everything I want to hear, exactly when I need to hear it. I'm ready to say hell yeah, go do it, but a lifetime of kicks in the teeth has me just a bit suspicious. So I have to ask, what's the catch?

"He says he'll take something I don't need, something I won't miss as long as I live. He wants my soul.

"Suddenly I know why the guy creeped me out so much. He's crazy. I mean, at that point I don't believe that a soul is real, and if it was, he couldn't take it anyway. But maybe he can do the things he promised. People can be crazy about one thing and still be damn good at another. So I tell him he can have my soul, just get me a win and a NASCAR ride.

"I offer my hand to him to seal the deal and he just smiles. He says the deal is signed with a show of good faith on my part. I ask him what and he points to Sonny Wright's ride on the other side of the pits. Out of his pocket, he pulls a small white envelope and pops it open. It's filled with some very nasty metal shavings.

"'Put that in his engine,' he says.

"Now, I know exactly what these will do to an engine. Mixed in the oil, they'd either shred the filter and send the rest of the slivers circulating around the engine to scar the internals for life. Or they'd be trapped so thick by the filter that the engine would starve for oil and blow up mid-race.

"There's about a half dozen ways screwing with another racer's ride is wrong. But Quentin is offering me something I'd never get otherwise, and Sonny Wright is a racist dickhead. So it doesn't take me two seconds to agree.

"The guy hands me the shavings. The pits are empty. I dash over to Wright's car and dump the whole thing into his valve cover.

"Strangest thing was, I didn't *feel* any guilt. That would be normal because Wright was such a jerk. But I loved anything mechanical, and to consciously destroy such a glorious engine, no matter who owned it, would make me feel bad. But it didn't. No second thoughts, no sense of shame. Just something I did. Like breathing.

"I get back to my car and the guy is gone. I start thinking that the whole thing has been a setup by Wright and he had some secret camera tape me trying to ruin his engine. I'm sure that instead of making my life better, I just made it infinitely worse.

"Two men in coveralls so new they practically squeak walk into the pits pushing a big crate on a dolly. They see the number on my car and stop and ask if I'm Lincoln. Then they tell me they've been sent by this transmission manufacturer to install this brand-new tranny in my car. I tell them it's a mistake, but they show me the paperwork and my name is on it and it's marked paid in full.

"It hits me that the Quentin guy might not have been crazy after all. New transmissions don't just materialize like this. I let them put it in."

"And did you win the race the next day?" Drew asked.

"Wright blew his engine about lap three. I led the pack the rest of the time. After that I kept on winning. Every race, something seemed to break my way and I crossed first under the checkered flag.

"So the season ends and I'm doing great. Tons of points, tons of money, and even women at the tracks are throwing themselves at me. Life is good and I'm finally getting what I'm due.

"Then life gets amazing. A rep from a major NASCAR racing team comes by after the last race of the year and offers me a contract for more money than I thought possible. I tell him to hand me a pen.

"As I'm getting ready to sign, he tells me that the team had narrowed it down to two drivers, me and a guy in the SoCal circuit. The other driver had a family, which counted against him because of all the travel in NASCAR, but since he'd kicked ass driving Sprint cars, they kept him in the running. The team owner couldn't decide, but then had the decision made for him when that driver died in a crash during a qualifying run.

"I kind of froze, with the pen in my hand over the contract. If Quentin had been behind all the things that fell in line for me, then he had been behind this as well. This wasn't someone blowing a tire and dropping out on the last lap. This was a dead man leaving a widow and kids behind.

"Now, what made me hesitate wasn't that I felt bad for the driver or his family. What got me was that I *didn't* feel bad. I remembered that six months before, I would have been moved to tears by such a sad story. Now it was just a fact, like how many bales of cotton grew in Mississippi last year. Quentin had really taken my soul after all, and now I was fundamentally broken."

"So you didn't sign?"

"I couldn't do it. I still didn't *feel* like it was the wrong thing to do, but I *knew* it was the wrong thing to do.

"The next day, for the first time since I made the deal, this demon masquerading as Quentin shows up at my house. It asks me why I didn't sign. I tell it, and then I say that by me not getting NASCAR, that ends our contract, and I want my soul returned. It laughs, and man, it is one bone-chilling laugh. It says the contract stays. Me not accepting what it delivered is my problem, not the demon's. My soul is gone and it's not coming back.

"Then the demon tells me it owns me. It cuts its finger with a pocketknife and puts a drop of blood on my forehead. The stuff burns like battery acid. Then Quentin orders me to bang my head against the wall.

"I start to tell it to screw itself, then the next thing I know, I'm banging my head against the wall. Hard. Blood's pouring down my face, my ears are ringing. I can't stop.

"Quentin finally tells me to stop. I do and I drop to the floor. It tells me to get used to being a lapdog, and walks out the door. I'd lived my life on my terms, taking no shit from anyone. The whole experience was humiliating, and terrifying."

"What did you do?"

"I got the hell out of the South and changed my name. I didn't need Quentin finding me and making me its puppet. Eventually I found out ways to ward where I lived against demon senses. I'll show you all that later.

"Next I got another driving job. Driving trucks. It was dull as hell but it paid the bills. And later I decided that the right thing to do would be to stop demons from ruining the lives of others. I wasn't motivated by righteous compassion. I couldn't feel that. But I knew that if I still had a soul, that's what I'd be feeling. And I'm ashamed to say that revenge was a pretty big motivator. You can still crave *that* without a soul. That path I chose led me to sitting here with you today."

"So maybe fighting demons will earn you a second chance."

"That can't happen. Redemption requires remorse. I don't feel that. I'm just working on some kind of ethical memory. My soul is gone, consumed by that demon Quentin. I'm doing this because I know that when I die, I end. Whatever afterlife was possible is impossible for me now if having a soul has anything to do with it. To keep that reality from being too depressing, I'm giving myself purpose now, by stopping demons."

"Do you, well, *feel* like you don't have a soul?"

"There's definitely something different, like there's something missing, but I couldn't tell you what it was if I didn't already know it. And for a soulless person, time seems to pass by faster and the body ages quicker. It's as if being soulless puts the metabolism out of balance. My doctor keeps telling me the things he finds usually happen to much older men. Nothing fatal yet, but my marathon-running days are behind me."

"I'm sorry."

Lincoln gave Gabriella's front bumper a push with his foot. "I didn't tell you to get your sympathy. I wanted you to know another reason to send those demons back to Hell."

CHAPTER NINE

1996

Drew was a day late for his usual visit with Lincoln. But that was Lincoln's idea, not his. Lincoln had left him a message the day before to move the session. The after-school schedule for a shy introvert was pretty open all week, so Drew had no problem moving it. He'd tried calling Lincoln back to confirm the change, but hadn't gotten an answer.

He'd been having his scheduled 'therapy' with Lincoln for over a year now and it had been terrifying and comforting. Terrifying to learn the truth about what happens when the supernatural world bleeds over into his. Comforting to know that he had a mentor he could trust to guide him through those dangers.

He stopped his bicycle at the edge of Lincoln's driveway. Lincoln's truck sat in front of the closed garage door. That was odd. The door was usually at least partway open to get a little air flowing. Drew dismounted, walked the bike up, and leaned it against the corner of the house.

No noise came from inside the garage. No clank of tools, no curt random expletive, no thunder of archaic rock music. A shiver went up Drew's spine. He stepped over to the entry keypad and tapped in the code. The door began a slow, creaking, upward roll.

Before the edge was even knee-high, the smell of sulfur drifted out of the opening. Drew's heart rate spiked. He ducked around the corner of the garage. His mind began to race. Was a demon in there? Was Lincoln in there? What if Lincoln was hurt? What if the demon was waiting to ambush him?

His whole body quivered with fear. His first instinct was to jump back on his bike and race away as fast as he could pedal. But he couldn't do that to Lincoln if he needed help. Drew decided that he had to go in.

But he wasn't going in defenseless. He looked around the yard for any kind of a weapon. A rusting shovel leaned against the wall. He shed his backpack and dropped it to the ground. He grabbed the spade and held it up over his shoulder like a batter waiting for a pitch. Part of him knew that as a demon defense, a shovel was damn near useless, but another part of him was glad to at least look threatening. Or as threatening as a teenaged kid could.

The garage door had stopped in the full up position. Drew took a deep breath and crept around the corner of the building. He paused facing the open doorway.

The place was a wreck. Tools and parts lay scattered on the floor. The right rear tire of the Chevelle was shredded and flat. Up the driver's side of the car, three deep gouges scarred the paint all the way down to the metal.

Demons had three claws.

He looked up on the ceiling. Lincoln had painted what he'd explained was a demon trap on the ceiling. The star-in-a circle diagram could capture any trespassing demons. But now it had a big section scraped out of it and the Sheetrock beneath it was gashed, rendering it powerless. A demon couldn't have done that. It would have been trapped as soon as it stepped into the garage. Someone had come in and set Lincoln up. Someone human.

Drew crept through the garage to the open door to the house. As he got closer, another smell joined the sulfur scent. Copper. And then decay. Like rotten fruit and roadkill mixed together. Drew's hands started to shake as dread filled his gut.

He entered the house. A laundry room acted as a connector to the kitchen and the rest of the house beyond. Drops of dried blood stained the white porcelain floor tiles. He passed by the washer and dryer. At the doorway to the kitchen, he stopped. The shovel fell from his hands and clanged onto the floor.

The kitchen table and chairs had been reduced to a pile of kindling and splinters. Huge holes gaped in the walls. A web of cracks glazed the middle of the three kitchen windows. The ceiling fan hung suspended by three wires.

Lincoln lay on the wreckage in pieces. His body crossed the canted edge of the shattered tabletop, his back arched at an angle no person could survive. From the knees down, his legs were missing. His arms had been pulled from their sockets. The fight had broken his jaw and left his head horribly misshapen. A sick, solid gray color painted his face. Dried blood made a thick puddle that nearly covered the kitchen floor. His right arm leaned against the refrigerator, still gripping an old, pockmarked dagger.

Lincoln had shown him that dagger once before and explained that it had the power to return demons to Hell. If he'd been wielding it, that confirmed Lincoln had been fending off a demon.

Drew's eyes watered and his gorge rose. He clamped shut his mouth, covered it with both hands, and ran outside. He'd barely made it to the grass when he dropped to his knees and vomited all over the ground. Two more throat-searing attempts after that proved that he had nothing left to give. He leaned back away from the acidic smell. Sweat ran down his temples.

He took deep breaths and tried to get control of himself. A demon had definitely killed Lincoln. Nothing else was strong enough to tear the human body apart like that. The blood was dry, so it had been a while ago, maybe right after Lincoln called yesterday to move their meeting.

Now what? he thought.

Drew couldn't call the police, not without getting wrapped up in their investigation. He could explain what had happened, but if he told them, they wouldn't believe it. They'd see his history of psychological treatment, and then guess who'd become their prime suspect? He'd have to make someone else call the police.

Drew swore to himself that if it took the rest of his life, he was going to slay the demon that did this. He needed to take the tools to do that with him, before everything here became evidence at a crime scene.

He went back into the kitchen. He averted his eyes from Lincoln's face, but there was no way to avoid seeing the gore, especially with what he had to do. He tiptoed around the lake of dried blood to Lincoln's severed right arm.

The hand still held the dagger. The demon must have really gotten the jump on Lincoln. Lincoln would have been counting on the demon trap to hold the creature at bay, and had to have been shocked when it didn't.

Drew reached down and tried to take the dagger from Lincoln's hand. Rigor mortis had set in and his fingers were locked around the blade. It was as if Lincoln wasn't letting go until he had another crack at the demon. Drew rested a knee on the wrist and with both hands pulled the thumb and fingers apart. The hand made a snapping noise, like someone cracking open cooked crab. The dagger lay dull and inert in the shriveled palm, an unimpressive damaged blade mounted in a ram's horn handle.

Drew hesitated before taking the blade. He felt like an old-time soldier in combat about to pick up the fallen national flag, knowing now he now had to carry it forward. Owning the dagger came with a similar responsibility, the commitment to use it not just in defense, but in offense. In grasping that ram's horn handle, he wasn't grabbing an object. He was accepting a call to duty. He took a deep breath and picked up the dagger.

He stood and looked at the horrific scene of Lincoln's murder. He felt like he should do something. Say a prayer. Deliver a eulogy, cover him with a sheet. Hell, he ought to bury him in the backyard.

But he couldn't do any of that. He had to cover up any demonic connections, get the hell out of there, and leave law enforcement to be befuddled by this mess. Only his mother knew that he met with Lincoln, and it needed to stay that way.

He went back to the garage. The drawer in the tool chest where Lincoln kept his demon-hunting tools hung open. Underneath it by the Chevelle's front tire lay the dark wooden box Lincoln had stored the demon dagger in. He looked into the drawer and took a quick inventory. The only thing missing was the box on the floor. He imagined Lincoln barely had time to get the dagger out while under assault by the demon. Drew placed the dagger inside the box and closed the lid. The gold inlaid pentagram on the lid glittered as it moved under the light. Drew secured the hasp.

He retrieved his backpack from the side of the house and returned to the open toolbox drawer. He stuffed the contents into his backpack. Then he put the wooden box in last. He had to force the zipper around to close the overstuffed pack.

Realizing how much time he'd just spent in the open garage of a murder scene, Drew jumped up and shouldered his pack. He went to the stereo and punched up some heavy metal music at maximum volume. That ought to get old Mr. McCloskey over here bitching about the noise. He'd discover all this and he'd call the cops.

Drew dashed for his bike. He hopped on and sped out of the driveway. He felt like he had enough energy to skip the bus and ride all the way home. He pedaled faster than he ever had before, trying to distance himself physically and emotionally from the horrific scene of his mutilated mentor.

But the image had been burned into his memory. He knew he couldn't run away from it, couldn't paper over it with some other recollection. With every pump of the pedals, he added more commitment to the resolution that had been born the second he saw Lincoln's corpse.

He was going to find that demon and send it back to Hell.

CHAPTER TEN

Present day

One of the prison guards walked Drew to the Correctional Treatment Center inside the fenced perimeter of CSP-Corcoran. Huge guard towers looked down on the collection of grim, utilitarian buildings. This prison held inmates at a variety of levels of confinement based on their risk level, but all of them came to this building when they got sick. Security was even tighter than he'd seen in the LA County jails.

Officer Gonzales met him at the Correctional Treatment Center door. She was short and stout, and looked more so saddled with the vest and gear of a corrections officer. Her dark hair was pulled back in a tight bun. She gave Drew's LASD uniform a once-over. He'd already checked his firearm and a number of other items at the reception area. She apparently didn't find anything else on him an inmate could turn into a weapon and gave a satisfied nod.

"Bobby Lee's in here," she said.

It had been years since Drew had spoken to the unrepentant racist. Then, Bobby Lee had impressed him as a mountain of a man, with a shaved head and the kind of moustache that finished at his chin like a set of fangs. Swastikas, iron crosses, and skulls made up most of the crude tattoos on his arms and neck. Drew wasn't small by any measure, but he was certain this guy could pound him into mush. He had been relieved that a thick piece of glass had separated them in the visiting room.

Drew had scheduled an interview back then because he knew Bobby Lee was lying. A demon had murdered Lincoln. Even Bobby Lee didn't have the strength to rip a man limb from limb. But somehow

Bobby Lee had known enough unreleased details of the crime to convince the police he'd done it, and after a year of investigating, they were happy to close the book using a despised human being like him. Drew wanted to know why Bobby Lee had taken the fall.

At that first meeting, his hopes had soared when Bobby Lee entered the visitation room. He seemed to cast no shadow, though the lighting in the room made it hard to tell. But the interview had been a disaster. The racist had been a seething mass of anger from the minute they met. Bobby Lee denied lying, peppered his replies with racial slurs about Lincoln, and beat on the dividing glass so hard that guards had to drag him away. Drew hadn't heard from him since then.

Even behind prison walls, hospitals smelled the same, a combination of antiseptic and the clean scent of cotton bandages and fresh linen. The windows that lined the upper quarter of the walls let in a lot of light despite the wire mesh embedded in the glass. All the medical equipment looked as good as he'd seen in any hospital.

Officer Gonzales walked Drew to the last bed in the infirmary. "Bobby Lee Simmons."

Drew barely recognized the man. The robust tower of terror he'd last seen in the visitation room had shriveled down to a frail old man. Drooping, parchment-like skin hung on his bones. Gray, messy hair covered his formerly shaved head. At some point he'd made the stupid decision to tattoo WHITE POWER in gothic letters across his forehead. The ink was now fuzzy and faded, and deep creases in his skin folded over the lettering. His eyes had been a deep, piercing blue, but now they were dishwater gray. Both hands were cuffed to the rails on the sides of the bed.

"Deputy Drew Price," Bobby Lee said as he sat up in bed. "You made it before I crossed the finish line."

"I'll leave you two to talk," Gonzales said. She bent closer to Drew's ear. "He's cuffed and dying, but don't think that means he's safe. You know the drill."

Even though Drew did vehicle inspections and not corrections work in the jail, he did indeed know that any inmate could turn dangerous in a flash. He sat in a chair a few feet from Bobby Lee's bed.

"I look like shit, don't I?" Bobby Lee said. "No asshole in this prison could whup me, but cancer sure did."

Small talk with murderers wasn't Drew's thing, and given how useless his last discussion with Bobby Lee had been, Drew didn't want to drag this out for nothing.

"What did you want to tell me?"

"Last time you was here, you was wanting to know about Lincoln, said he was like your mentor. I acted like a real prick."

Drew stopped himself from saying that acting that way had been the story of Bobby Lee's life.

"I had my reasons," Bobby Lee continued, "and I'm about out of time to explain them."

Drew just waited for him to get on with it.

"You were right. I didn't kill Lincoln. Wasn't nowhere near the place ever. I ain't saying that to clear my name or nothing. I'm telling you for revenge."

Drew's interest began to grow.

"You was right about another thing. I done made a deal to confess. You brought that up and I went berserk so the guards would drag me away, keep anyone from thinking I told you about it. Keeping it secret was part of the deal."

"A deal with...?"

"A devil, a demon, whatever that thing was."

The sound of the word 'demon' sent Drew's heart racing. In his brief meeting with Bobby Lee years ago, Drew hadn't brought up demons or soul trades or anything supernatural. He gripped the arms of his chair to steady himself.

"Don't look at me like you don't know what I'm talking about," Bobby Lee said. "All those strange questions you had them years back? That's what you was asking about without asking about it. I ain't stupid. This was a goddamn demon, human on the outside, but not on the inside."

Drew guessed his interrogation of Bobby Lee hadn't been as guarded as he'd thought it had been. "I believe you. I've seen demons, in their true form."

"The thing visited me in jail," Bobby Lee said, "while I was waiting trial for the other murder. Asked me what it would take to make me confess to a second murder since I was already going down for one. Told it I wanted high rank in the Aryan Nation and an organ donor for my brother, who needed a kidney. All I had to do was secretly trade my soul. I figured that was no loss."

While half of Bobby Lee's demand was altruistic, Drew noted that the white supremacist part of the request came first.

"And what made you believe this person was possessed by a demon?"

"The damn thing told me. As proof, first off, the dude was standing in front of my cell door in the middle of the night. The damn governor couldn't walk through all the jail security and stand there unescorted. Then it grabs the bars of my cell, and bends the sons of bitches. Then it straightens them back out. That was proof enough that it was something other than human to me."

Drew could see that Bobby Lee was telling the truth. He checked the wall behind the bed. The bed cast a clear shadow. The sitting figure of Bobby Lee did not.

"So the demon told me what to say to convince the cops I done it. And were they ever happy to hear it. Sure enough, the next day after that, the leader of the Aryan Nation calls me over in the exercise yard, sits me down, tells me what a standup guy I am for ridding the world of two animals, and puts me right next to him in the hierarchy."

That certainly squared with what a demon could deliver. Who would have been more likely to have made a deal and be subject to demonic leverage than a white supremacist?

"And your brother?" Drew asked.

"Two days later, there was a donor. A motorcycle accident. Rider got T-boned."

Drew wondered what the guy who ran the motorcyclist over had gotten in his deal.

"So why are you telling me all this now?"

"'Cause a year after the surgery, my brother died anyhow. Weakened immune system. Some kind of bullshit excuse like that. All the demon had said it guaranteed was a surgery, but I assumed the operation would make him whole, you know? Then last year, I got my diagnosis, cancer they can't do nothing to cure. Well, the demon might have done its parts of the deal, but having both of us dead anyhow feels like I got cheated. And at this point, the son of a bitch can't make my life any worse, so someone ought to know the truth."

"And why tell me instead of the whole world?" Drew said. "And why like this?"

"Who's gonna believe me, recanting on my deathbed? And talking about making deals with demons? Anyone here heard that and I'd spend my last day on a psych ward tranquilized to the gills. I'm telling you so you can get even. Find that thing and kill it."

"What makes you think I can kill it?"

"Why the hell would you have been trying to track it down all those years ago if you couldn't?"

"Where can I find this demon?"

"Possesses the body of Dominic Carrera. Big Mexican with a dragon tattooed on his chest. Beady little black eyes. Wears huge jade rings."

Drew didn't need the detailed description. He'd see Carrera in his true, demonic form. The demon would be unmistakable.

"I hear that now most of the demon's deals are done at Whitney Memorial Hospital," Bobby Lee said. "Shit neighborhood, desperate relatives. It trades for a soul and then, a miracle! Some big shot doctor swoops in doing free surgeries."

Drew knew the area around Whitney Memorial. Prime hunting ground for sure. The fact there were shadowless doctors in debt to a demon made Drew sick to his stomach.

"I'll see what I can do," Drew said. "This will put some points in your column in the end."

"Too late for that shit for me. Soul's already gone. I'm a killer and I'm glad I did it. I just want to go out knowing you killed that son of a bitch. Extra credit for you if you make it slow and painful. That double-crossing asshole."

Drew got up and took one last look at the dying husk that had once been a scourge to the people of his city. An unrepentant, racist murderer would die in prison. No one was going to mourn that loss. He walked over to the door where Gonzales waited.

"Did he have anything useful to tell you?" she asked.

"The cancer must have eaten his brain," Drew said. "He told me demons stole his soul."

"Sorry I called you, then. I thought, you know, deathbed conversion, that kind of thing."

"Some people don't get saved."

★   ★   ★

The drive back to the office turned into a slow roll as traffic clotted south of Santa Clarita. That gave Drew plenty of time to think.

He had a lead on the demon that had killed Lincoln. If he'd had that information the day after the murder, he'd have charged after the demon without a second thought. That would have been more due to teenaged recklessness than any kind of actual heroism.

But now he was an older, wiser adult, one with a wife and son. Demon hunting was damn dangerous. Lincoln's murder was proof of that.

But Lincoln's murder needed to be avenged. The person the system had brought to justice hadn't done it. The thing that had murdered him still walked free in LA. Worse, the demon was still making deals and eating souls. Every day that thing spent out of Hell, it set more psychopaths like Bobby Lee free in Drew's city.

He'd joined the LASD to help people, to make a difference in the community. Many times he had thought that he wasn't really doing much of that in vehicle inspections. Ridding the world of the demon masquerading as Carrera would be doing just that. And Drew was probably the only person in the city who knew how to do it.

He'd dig out the tools for the job when he got home, and then see if he could find Carrera tonight.

CHAPTER ELEVEN

1995

"Let's go look at my other car," Lincoln said.

That was an odd request. In all the time Drew had been coming for...whatever this was with Lincoln, they'd never looked at any car but Gabriella the Chevelle. Drew followed Lincoln out the open garage to the pickup truck. Lincoln had already released the hood as it sat ajar and slightly higher than the fenders. Lincoln raised it.

"So, what do you think of that engine bay?" he said.

It seemed like every cubic inch of space under the hood had been crammed with something. Wires, vacuum hoses, an air cleaner. Four different accessories behind the radiator run by a single large serpentine belt. Under all that somewhere was an engine, Drew guessed. By contrast, the Chevelle had so much extra space under the hood that Drew could practically climb inside the engine bay to get at certain bolts.

"It looks full compared to the Chevelle," Drew said.

"Sure, it's a much newer car. There are a lot of electronic and emission controls that hadn't been invented back in 1970."

"It also has an air conditioner, and those *were* invented back in 1970."

"Who needs it?" Lincoln said. "Gabriella has two-fifty air. Roll down two windows and drive at least fifty miles an hour."

"New cars are better. They come with power windows, heated seats, windshield wipers with more than two speeds."

"A lot of conveniences that come with a cost." Lincoln slammed the hood back down and led Drew back to the Chevelle. "The first is literally price. You could drive a new basic car off the lot for under three grand back then, add extras if you wanted them. Now all the extras aren't extras, they're standard."

"Because everyone wants cars with air-conditioning," Drew said.

Lincoln gave him a sideways look. "The second cost is complexity. All those conveniences are going to break sometime. So there's more things to fix, and those things cost more to repair."

"But it's more fun to drive."

"More comfortable to drive, definitely not more fun."

Lincoln leaned back against the workbench and wiped his hands with a rag.

"You're going to face that same kind of trade-off with your life," he said. "You've got the gift of demon sight. Unless you're a total jerk, that comes with a responsibility to keep humanity safe from them. If you're like Gabriella here, running with just the solid basics, it's easier. Not many extra things in life to look after and worry about. But if you're like a new car, with a life full of things, you've got more to worry about. Every one of those worries is a potential distraction from sending demons back to Hell. Get distracted at the wrong moment, and you'll end up dead."

"Lucky me, growing up poor without a lot of stuff."

"I'm not just talking about things, Drew. I'm talking about people. The more of them you have close to you, the more people depending on you, the more distractions you'll have."

"That sounds lonely."

"It's for their own good. Every one of those people is a potential weak point a demon can exploit. And they will, trust me. A demon will kill your family before it kills you, to maximize your agony."

Drew wasn't a social butterfly, but he did have friends. "You're saying I need to become some kind of monk or something?"

"Hardly. But you need to think hard about having a family."

Drew rolled his eyes. "I'm in middle school. No problem there."

"But there will be, later. You need to always remember that when you let a girl get close to you, you're going to put her at risk. And you'll be making that decision for her, because unless your first date conversation includes demon hunting, she'll have no idea what she's getting into."

"That's why you live alone?"

"I learned this lesson the hard way. Trying to keep you from having to do the same."

Anything like that was so far away that Drew wasn't going to worry about it. He couldn't imagine even discussing all the messed-up demon world stuff with anyone, let alone a girl he wanted to impress.

There were plenty of times he wished he'd never learned about the hidden portion of the world where demons walked among us. There was no way he'd never make anyone else part of it.

CHAPTER TWELVE

Present day

Drew cleared away some dishes while Anna made Kenny finish his dinner. He rinsed a few plates in the sink, then leaned back and watched her offer the promise of ice cream to coax him into chomping the last few green beans.

These were the moments he really cherished. Normal family time. Having the demon sight had made him feel like he wasn't part of his own family, and that made his family time even more special, a unique experience. That made it all the more difficult to lie to them both.

Anna thought he was picking up some easy security work tonight at a retirement community, covering for a friend in the department like he often did. But not tonight. The security he'd be doing would be in the parking lot of Whitney Memorial and the perpetrator he'd be watching for would be a demon.

There was no way to explain what he was going to do without sounding batshit crazy. And if Anna did believe him, she certainly wouldn't say, "Oh, sure. Go hunt a murderous supernatural force all night. I'll make you breakfast in the morning." Lying about it was the fastest and easiest way around this relationship minefield.

Kenny finished dinner and Anna trundled him off for a bath before dessert and bed. She'd told Drew that this schedule let her nurture the hope that Kenny might forget about dessert and on rare occasions she'd been rewarded. Once they'd closed the bathroom door behind them, Drew went out the front door.

Drew had learned a lot from Lincoln. One of the ways he emulated him was to keep the tools of the demon-hunting trade outside the house. After Kenny had been born, making the family home free from any taint of the supernatural became even more important. The idea of having the dark items he'd taken from Lincoln's garage anywhere near his son made him sick.

The small garden shed in Drew's backyard looked the same as any of the ones in his neighbors' yards. He'd convinced Anna they'd use it to hold all the outdoor tools they would need now that they'd upgraded their life to a house with a yard. He'd bought the heavy-duty plastic kit at a home improvement store and put it up himself, including the circular landscaping of pine needles around the base.

But just under that thin veneer of needles lay a base of concrete bricks with a demon trap painted on top. Anything supernatural that broke in to steal the items Lincoln had left him wasn't getting out.

He stepped up to the shed door and dialed the combination into a big lock on the hasp. There were everyday thieves to keep at bay as well. He pulled the lock free and opened the door. With the flick of a switch, a battery-powered light he'd mounted to the ceiling blinked on.

Any thief expecting riches would be disappointed. A rusting lawnmower sat in the middle of the shed. Battered garden tools leaned against the walls. A pair of garden gloves covered the handles of a set of clippers, looking like they were waving Drew hello. Big black trash bags covered the walls, hiding the warding symbols painted underneath them. He pulled a yard sale-sourced plastic tackle box from the corner of the shed.

Inside were all the things Lincoln had used in his demon-hunting mission. Lincoln had told him that if anything ever happened to him, Drew was to take all of this with him to keep taking the fight to the demons. He'd stuffed them all into his backpack that awful day.

After he and Anna married, the old tackle box became an inconspicuous place to store them. When Anna had asked about the box one day, he'd told her he used to go fishing with a childhood mentor, Lincoln, and he still kept it as a memento. The first of many demon-related lies and omissions he would subject her to. He hadn't opened the tackle box since the day he'd filled it.

After Lincoln's death, Drew had been more than ready to send the next demon he saw back to Hell. But the reality of being fourteen years old sank in. He really didn't know how to find a demon, didn't even have a way of hunting down the one that had slaughtered Lincoln. Even if he could, was he going to hop a bus to do it? He realized the idea of being a teenaged demon hunter was ridiculous.

The decision whether to don the demon-hunting mantle ultimately had been made for him. He never saw another demon, perhaps a testament to his mentor's hunting prowess. As years went by, the pressure to rid the world of the supernatural relented. Like smallpox and the Black Death, perhaps demons were a thing of the past.

Just after he'd joined the LASD and had his dead-end first meeting with Bobby Lee, he'd even given up on finding the demon who killed Lincoln. And though he felt guilty about it, his reaction to giving up had been a sense of relief. Facing down demons hadn't been his calling. Lincoln and Fate had thrust the job upon him. He was fine leaving that task to someone else, if it even still needed to be done at all.

But yesterday's interview with Bobby Lee had changed all that. Drew finally had a solid lead on the demon who turned Bobby Lee into a patsy for Lincoln's murder. And Drew wasn't a kid anymore.

Seeing the unrepentant killer wasted away to nothing by cancer reminded Drew that time passed faster than one realized. It also brought back his memories of Lincoln fresh and clear, especially the memory of finding his corpse. Revenge on the demon who did it went from simmering on the back of the stove straight to the front burner at full boil.

Drew turned out the light in the shed and relocked the door behind him. He went to his car and put the tackle box in the trunk.

For now, he'd head back inside and do his fatherly duties like nothing special was about to unfold. He might grab a quick nap, then he'd need to be out of the house before midnight.

He had a demon to kill.

CHAPTER THIRTEEN

1995

Lincoln lay under the Chevelle on a mechanic's creeper with Drew beside him on another one. He pointed to a ball-shaped tie rod in the front suspension.

"That needs to be replaced," Lincoln said. "We need a pickle fork."

"What's a pickle fork?"

Lincoln rolled out from under the car and Drew followed him. Lincoln led him to the center tool chest along the garage wall. He opened a middle drawer and pulled out what looked like a thick fork with only two tapered tines. The handle of the fork was a stout piece of round metal.

"You place this pointy end between a tie rod and whatever's attached. Hammer on this other end. The fork tines wedge under the tie rod. As it moves forward, it separates the two pieces."

"Clever."

"Sure beats trying to pull them apart. But the pickle fork is a one-trick pony. It's only good for this one, infrequent task."

"Use the right tool for the right job, you always say."

"And I'm going to introduce you to some of the right tools for the job of killing demons," he said. "Like a pickle fork, it's all they're good for, and you've got to keep them someplace safe until you need them."

"Don't you use an exorcism or something like that?"

"That's just in the movies, or some bogus thing some religious people believe in. A demon would kill you before you got out the first Latin phrase."

Lincoln went to the bottom right drawer in the far cabinet. He took out a wooden box the size of a shoe box. He brought it back and set it on the workbench between them.

The box's dark brown wood had a very odd pattern to the grain. Into the top, a pentagram had been inlaid in gold, with strange symbols added at each of the five points. Polished gold hinges attached the lid. A matching hasp kept it closed.

"That box took a lot of work to make," Drew said.

"More work than you know. The wood is manchineel, possibly the most toxic plant on the planet. The tree weeps a poison so fatal that drops of it may cause death. I know a man temporarily blinded by the slightest brush of a leaf against his face."

Drew stepped back. "Seriously?"

"Completely. But this wood was baked and treated to remove the toxins centuries ago. But you can be sure that people died doing it. It would be impossible not to." He pointed to the carving in the lid. "This pentagram is a demon trap. Copy it precisely on the ground and once activated, any demon that steps in can't ever step out, unless the diagram is broken."

"How is the trap activated?"

Lincoln opened the box. A red velvet lid covered the interior. A piece of white parchment with handwritten instructions on it was glued to the inside of the lid.

"Follow these instructions," Lincoln said. "You'll mix a bunch of ingredients, say the incantation written here, then light the mixture on fire in a silver bowl placed in the center of the pentagram. After that, the trap is set. Getting the demon into it is a whole different problem."

Lincoln removed the velvet cover and exposed a dagger. The blade looked incredibly old, pitted and tarnished. Deep nicks marred the dull edges. The handle looked like it was made from an animal horn.

"This is the demon dagger," Lincoln said.

"That looks like it would break if you stabbed anyone with it," Drew said.

"It probably would," Lincoln said, "unless the thing you stabbed was a demon. It'll slice through them like a hot knife through butter."

Drew hovered his hand over the box. "Can I...."

"Go ahead."

Drew picked up the knife. Whatever magical experience he expected did not happen. The bone handle felt cold and heavy. He ran a finger along the blade. The metal seemed weak, reminded him of rust-damaged steel you could snap in half.

"Underwhelmed?" Lincoln said.

"Just a bit."

Lincoln pulled a glass vial from the drawer. Caps screwed to both ends kept it sealed. Inside was a black claw, several inches long. It looked like a bear's claw Drew had once seen in a museum, but wider.

"This is the claw of a demon," Lincoln said.

"How did you get that?"

"A story for another time. Hold up the dagger."

Drew raised the dagger and Lincoln eased the vial closer to the dagger's blade. He touched the glass to the metal.

The handle became uncomfortably hot. The blade took on a bright yellow glow as the surface hardened and the chips and imperfections filled in and disappeared. The power of the blade seemed to creep up Drew's arm the longer it glowed. The sensation began to unnerve him.

Lincoln moved the vial away from the dagger. The dagger's glow died and the handle cooled. Lincoln set the vial down on the workbench.

"The dagger only comes alive when someone is holding it in the presence of a demon. The handle gets so hot it's hard to hold with your bare hand, but you've got to for the blade to work. Then the dagger transforms into something powerful.

"Demons heal damn near instantly. Shoot one and it will react, but it will barely slow down. But slash or stab a demon with this dagger, and you'll wound it the same way a normal knife hurts a human. Worse really, because the dagger keeps torturing the demon even after you pull it out, like it oozed acid or something. Keep it plunged in the demon, and the bastard is left in debilitating pain.

"And that's important because there's only one way to kill it. Any wound, even from this blade, may incapacitate it, but will quickly heal. Even severed limbs grow back. Being possessed screws up the host's internal organs, turns the blood black. You need to cut out what passes for its heart, a fist-sized, black, oily organ where the bottom of a human sternum would be. Once someone slices open a demon with this thing, he doesn't need demon sight to see what's really inside."

"Who made this dagger and how?" Drew asked.

"The truth? Who knows. The myth? This was the knife Abraham put to the throat of Isaac when an angel demanded he sacrifice his son. The mythos is that artifacts that have been in the presence of the power of God retain enough power to sever the demon's grasp on Earth and return them to Hell. Of course, that might all be crap and some black magic spell makes the dagger work. Might be the power of positive thinking for all I know. I don't care why it works. The important thing is that it works."

"How do you know?"

Lincoln took a seat on one of the stools by the workbench. Drew settled on the other.

"It wasn't long after my epiphany of no empathy that I decided to get even," Lincoln began. "I figured that if the escaped demons aren't playing fair, humans needed to level the playing field. Step one was to find out all I could about how demons and their deals work. There are way more sources on that than you'd think, and almost all of them are crap. I sifted through the good and bad. Through a chain of black marketeers, I located that dagger for sale. It cost me almost a year's wages, but I figured if it worked, it would be a bargain.

"Turns out, demons are lazy. They're usually convinced that no one is onto their game, so they keep hunting for souls in the same places. Also makes it easier for the demon to build a network of previous victims who can be possessed to grant the wishes of new victims. I assumed Quentin would be no different.

"So when I wasn't driving my truck, I was following the small-town-South dirt track circuit. When I was driving, I scheduled loads that sometimes lost money, but put me near an active raceway on race day.

"Then I went to the tracks. I dressed in crap clothes I normally wouldn't be caught dead in. I mean serious local hayseed specials. That, and the fact that it had been years since I'd raced, meant that no one recognized me.

"I know the bars where the racers hang out, and one night while I'm in one of them, I overhear a conversation one driver is having with a friend, about a guy named Quentin who wants to help him make it big. Gale Holt was the driver's name. I'd seen him race and honestly, you could have put him out there in a million-dollar car and he still wouldn't have won. He hadn't made the deal yet, so I follow him, knowing that demon Quentin won't drop the sales pitch once it's started.

"Holt is staying in this fleabag motel. One of those one-story places where the rooms all open to a sidewalk and the broken neon signs still advertise TV and air-conditioning like they were rare amenities. I set up shop with a thermos of coffee and the blade in that box. Just before midnight, a glossy black SUV pulls up and out steps Quentin."

"Demons travel by car?"

"Once they're on Earth, they have no supernatural power except for being able to separate you from your soul. They can't teleport or do any other magic tricks.

"Anyhow, I head in to intercept. I meet the demon in front of the door to Holt's room. The last time we'd spoken was when it told me my contract was ironclad, my soul long gone. Quentin looks ticked off that I'm there. It tells me to beat it before I say something that will get me hurt.

"Right then, Holt opens his door to see what the commotion is about. That distracts Quentin. I jump at the opportunity. I shove Quentin through the door. Holt goes flying backward and Quentin lands on the floor facedown.

"Now a warning to you if you ever get in this situation. Where a demon is different from a human is that they're strong as a bull. Their body looks human, but it's really that charred-out demon that you demon-sighted people can see. And that creature is goddamn strong.

"Quentin rolls over and looks up at me in total fury. The pupils of its eyes turn red as its anger makes just a bit of the illusion drop. It tells me it's going to tear me apart.

"As far as Holt can tell, some crazy man just attacked his meal ticket right there in his hotel room. He jumps up ready to go in on Quentin's side. I can't win if this goes two-on-one and there's no way I'm going to get Holt to see the truth of the situation and stand down.

"I draw the dagger. It transforms into a gleaming, robust blade. And I jump onto Quentin to pin it to the ground. The demon rabs under my chin with one hand. It's like being stuck in a vise. I can hear my jaw crunch as it squeezes. And that hand? It felt hot, literally hot as Hell. It was like brimstone still smoldered under that charred demon skin.

"I know I'll be dead in a split second if I don't do something. I slash its arm with my dagger. Its skin rips open but doesn't reveal red muscle and white bone. Everything under the skin is black, like over-roasted meat. Flecks of glowing red crawl through it like a swarm of fleas.

"Quentin howls in pain and shock. The demon releases me and I drop on it, one hand hard against its chest.

"Holt shrieks out, 'What the hell is he?' Apparently, he can see what's inside Quentin's wound just as well as I can. That means I don't have to worry about him jumping into the fight. I raise the dagger and drive it down into Quentin's chest.

"The demon's eyes roll up in its head. Its body goes into convulsions. Those red glowing fleas seem to rise up and swarm the underside of its skin. This blade is clearly the real deal. I remember what I have to do to kill it. I pull out the knife, then drive it down just under the sternum. I cut a circle in the demon's chest and tear away the patch of skin.

"Inside beats this glossy black, kidney-shaped organ. Black veins pulse all along the outside. The prize.

"Ripping open that gaping wound brings Quentin back to reality.

It makes a fist and pile drives me in the chest. I feel ribs break and I fly off it and into the wall. The knife sails off to who knows where. Quentin roars and stands to face me. The demon heart in it pounds like someone beating a drum. Chopping a hole in the demon hasn't slowed him down much.

"Holt finally reacts. Whether he was trying to help me or just heading for the door I can't say. But he runs toward Quentin. Quentin notices and half turns in Holt's direction. With no effort, it catches Holt's forehead in one hand. With a flick of the wrist, the demon snaps Holt's neck into a right angle. Holt crumples to the floor.

"I spring straight for Quentin. It turns back to me a moment too late. I plunge my right hand into the hole in its chest. The demon heart is searing hot. Touching it sends horrific visions of roiling seas of lava through my mind. I can hear the wailing of millions of the damned in infinite, immortal pain. I want to break away.

"Instead I grab and pull. The heart rips out of Quentin's chest. There is just enough time for shock to cross its face as it sees what's been torn from it. Then the demon drops to the ground.

"The human form fades away. Its true demon body takes its place. The heart in my hand beats one more time and goes still. I drop it and it hits the floor with a splat. Black blood oozes from it.

"Then the body and the heart turn red, then disintegrate. The flecks and ashes sift down in a slow spiral and disappear. Quentin was gone, presumably returned to Hell. That was the first demon I killed."

Drew looked down at the old blade in his hand with renewed awe.

"If this is an artifact of God," he said, "you'd think he'd send us down a lot more of them."

"Wherever this came from, and however it works, I can tell you there aren't many other demon killers around. This is something that's got to be closely guarded. In the hands of someone who doesn't know what it is, it'd be useless. If it falls into the hands of a demon or one of its soulless followers, we'll never see it again."

Lincoln took back the dagger and set it inside the box. He closed the lid.

"There are other stories of killing other demons I'll share with you later. It'll take a long time for me to train you to hunt down demons. But whether you go out looking for a fight, or whether the fight comes looking for you, this is the only weapon that's going to put the balance of power in your favor."

He put the box back into the drawer in the tool chest.

"You're going to keep hunting demons your whole life, aren't you?" Drew said.

"Don't see any way to stop now. I've kind of taken it on as my responsibility. But if you don't want to, I won't think any less of you. It's an awful job. No one is going to force you to use your gift for the good of others. Keep quiet about this ability, and no one will even know that you have it."

"I think I'd feel guilty if I didn't do it, and more people ended up without souls."

"I think you're right."

"I don't see a paycheck in it, though," Drew said.

"There should be, but there isn't. There's no paycheck in me teaching you about the demonic either, but I'm doing it anyway. You'll need to get a real job. Demon hunting is the world's most dangerous hobby."

"I want to go with you on the next hunt. I can use what you've taught me, learn more faster, help you kill these things."

Lincoln's face grew dark. He picked up a screwdriver from the workbench and pointed it at Gabriella.

"Now, that car behind you? You know when I first decided I wanted one like that? I was about your age. I was riding my bike on my hometown's main drag when a red one with white racing stripes roared by me. It was love at first sight. If I'd bought one then, what do you think would have happened?"

"You'd have been arrested for driving without a license."

"There are times I ought to dope-slap you. Seriously, I wasn't ready to do what we're doing now. I didn't have the money, the time, the experience to do a car like this justice. I'm sure that at the time

I thought I did. But I didn't. Took me years before I bought Gabriella."

He tapped Drew on the chest with the screwdriver.

"You might think you're ready to tangle with demons before you're even old enough to vote, but I'm here to tell you that you aren't. Those things have been around since the dawn of time. They're strong, smart, and experienced. I can make a mistake restoring this car and have to buy a new part. You make a mistake hunting a demon, and you're dead, and your gift dies with you."

"I get it."

"So we're going to hone the skills you'll need. You'll research and learn everything you can about how demons act, how they think, what their weaknesses are. The day will come when you'll need to face down your first demon alone, and you'd damn well better be ready for it."

CHAPTER FOURTEEN

Present day

A full moon shone down on the parking lot of Whitney Memorial. The entrance sign to the emergency room glowed red over the double door entrance. Dying palms on either side of the doors had failed in their attempt at landscape beautification.

Drew sat in the front seat of his car about midway back in the parking lot. Two things worked in his favor tonight. The full moon brought out the crazies, and it was after midnight. No one here at this time was dropping by for elective surgery. A demon couldn't walk through the ER without tripping over people desperate to make deals.

A search through the LASD-accessible databases had told him a lot about Dominic Carrera. A history of arrests in the LA area for minor crimes. No convictions. What a surprise. Spread a little demonic influence in the right places and suddenly you catch some lucky breaks. Drew made a mental note to start checking judges for shadows.

Drew had looked up the address on Carrera's driver's license and it turned out to be bogus, a warehouse building downtown off East Compton. That revelation had dashed his hopes for finding Carrera where it lived, so this location was his best bet for tracking the demon down.

But tonight's surveillance was still a long shot. Assuming that Bobby Lee was right that this was where Dominic trolled for souls, did the demon go there every night? How long did a soul keep a demon alive before it needed another one anyway? Even Lincoln hadn't known the answers to some questions.

Several hours of waiting proved he was right about one thing: this place was busy. A steady stream of ambulances and worn-out private vehicles stopped to unload new patients. A real parade of tragedies.

As the clock blinked past two a.m., it became a struggle for Drew to stay awake. Twice he drifted off to sleep for a second, only to yank himself back to reality before he completely slipped away. He considered going for coffee, but had no idea what was open in this neighborhood, and had a feeling that as soon as he left, Carrera would wander by and snatch up some unfortunate's soul.

Then he saw the demon. A surge of adrenaline jolted him wide awake in an instant.

Carrera walked out through the Emergency Room doors. Drew hadn't seen a demon in a long time, but it wasn't something he'd ever forget. Toothpick-thin arms and legs, a misshapen, oblong head with a pointed nose and ears. Every inch of skin looked like scorched, barbequed chicken.

The sight of the demon brought a flood of memories and emotions surging back over Drew. He re-experienced all the fears that made his boyhood miserable. The dread of seeing these inexplicable ghouls. The trepidation that he might be going insane. The nights of terrifying dreams that always followed every sighting. The powerless, hopeless sensation of a boy up against something he did not understand, except that it was evil and dangerous. His sweating palms felt slick against the car's steering wheel, and he wiped them on his pants.

Carrera had its arm around the shoulder of a distraught-looking Black man who still wore what looked like a janitorial uniform from some big corporation. What catastrophe had forced this poor man to rush from work straight to the hospital? And what awful deal was he about to make with Carrera?

The two parted ways on the sidewalk. Drew's first instinct was to follow the janitor, warn him to stay as far away from Carrera and its twisted offers as possible. But if he did, he'd lose Carrera and the opportunity to take the king off this chessboard. If Drew took Carrera out, the janitor would have no one to make a deal with. He had to hope that the janitor hadn't already done something stupid. Drew started his car.

Carrera went to the corner of the parking lot and got into an expensive black BMW, one of the *M* versions with all the speed upgrades. Drew's theory about the kind of people who drove those cars was validated. The headlights flared to life and the car accelerated out of the lot with a chirp of its tires.

Drew noted the license plate out of habit and followed the car. Relatively empty streets made tailing the BMW at a distance easy, even with Carrera speeding. The on-ramp to North 405 came up and Carrera zoomed up it. Drew punched it and followed.

Unlike every other city in America, Los Angeles highways were never free of traffic. Even at this tragically early hour of the morning, plenty of cars dotted the six lanes of the 405. Drew always wondered where the hell all these people had to go in the middle of the night.

Carrera had no plan to blend into traffic. As soon as the car cleared the merge lane, the BMW opened up and put all those expensive engine enhancements to work. Drew floored it to follow. If this chase had to go on very long, his compact car would be no match for the Bavarian rocket sled. He hoped the rest of the traffic would slow Carrera down to a speed he could manage.

Carrera treated the other vehicles like an obstacle course to be run. The BMW darted between cars, executed wide, multi-lane sweeps across the road, and wedged itself between two semis, earning a furious blast from one truck's horn. This demon certainly was willing to exploit its indestructibility.

Drew did his best to follow. His engine screamed as the tach hit the redline under hard accelerations. His tires squealed as he changed lanes far too quickly. He could practically hear Lincoln scolding him for trying to make this daily beater run like a race car.

Every time the BMW's taillights seemed about to vanish into the distance, some combination of cars would force Carrera to slow down. The BMW's brake lights would flare red, and Drew would regain a little of the lost ground, only to have the gap widen again as soon as the BMW nosed into open road.

Up ahead, a trio of trucks blocked the three right lanes. Cars slid to the left to pass and made a rolling blockage even Carrera wasn't going to be able to zip through. Drew raised a fist in victory. Just the stroke of luck he needed.

An explosion of flashing red lights lit up Drew's rear window. A California Highway Patrol cruiser filled his rearview mirror. The cop blipped his siren.

"Son of a bitch!" Drew said.

He eased off the accelerator and drifted over to the right shoulder. Carrera's taillights disappeared around a curve in the highway. Drew came to a stop, put the car in park, and pulled out his LASD badge. He rolled down the window as the CHP officer approached the car.

"I was speeding," Drew said. "I'm sorry."

"Speeding?" the CHP said. "Add bouncing around the highway like a pinball."

Drew offer him his badge. "I'm on the job."

The cop looked at the ID, then pointed his flashlight in Drew's face. Convinced the two matched, he pointed the flashlight down.

"Don't tell me. LASD has stooped to using this vehicle as an unmarked car and you were in hot pursuit."

Drew ignored the jibe. "No, I was heading home from a security gig at Whitney Memorial. I was anxious to get as much sleep as I could before I have to get up for my shift tomorrow."

Drew's experience had taught him that the more truth there was tucked inside a lie, the more credible it seemed. This cop could see that the 405 was the most direct route between downtown and Drew's house in San Leandro. Cops worked off-duty security at all the major hospitals. All the pieces fit. This fabrication was going to work.

"Where's your uniform?"

Shit! He'd have been working security in uniform. How was he going to explain....

"In the trunk in a plastic bag. Homeless guy in the ER puked on my pants. Another reason I was rushing. The last thing I need is for that smell to latch on to my trunk."

The cop turned his flashlight to Drew's trunk. Drew's heart sank. What a stupid story to use. What if he asked to see in the trunk, and then opened up Drew's tackle box of demon fighting tools? How would he explain all that?

The CHP handed Drew back his badge.

"I hear you there," the CHP said. "I had a patrol car that we never got the smell out of. Okay in the winter, but in a hot summer sun, whoa. Get home. Just do it at something closer to the speed limit."

"Roger that. I owe you one."

"Stay safe."

The CHP walked back to his car. Drew collapsed back against his seat in relief. Then he realized that Carrera had gotten away to parts unknown. Why couldn't this conscientious cop have nailed the racing BMW instead of his beater? The CHP probably knew he couldn't catch the BMW.

And now neither could Drew. The cop pulled out into traffic and drove off. Drew waited for the lane to clear, pulled out, and headed home.

Demon hunting was going to take a lot more time than he'd imagined.

CHAPTER FIFTEEN

Late the next day, Drew's supervisor stopped at Drew's desk on the way to the door. By now he was the only other deputy in the office.

"I'm already impressed by your work ethic," she said, "if that's what you're staying late to accomplish."

"No, I have to finish that online training class and I'm right at the end of it. Be done in a few minutes."

"You'd better be. My overtime budget is already shot to hell. And while we're chatting, have you thought about using some of your accrued vacation we talked about?"

Drew hadn't taken much time off in the last year. Anna's reduced hours meant money for vacations had been nonexistent.

"I need to talk it over with my wife," he said.

"Convince her to take a break," she said. "All work and no play makes Drew a stressed deputy."

A vacation won't fix the kind of stress I'm experiencing, Drew thought.

She left Drew alone in the silent office. Drew closed out the training class and called up the DMV database. He'd lost Carrera on the 405 last night. The address on Carrera's license was bogus, but maybe the registration on the car wasn't.

He tried to remember the plate number. He could only come up with the first four letters and numbers. Leave it to a demon to not get an easy-to-remember personalized plate. He plugged those into the database with a filter for black BMWs.

Two cars came up, but only one of them was in the Los Angeles area. He pulled up the details. Drew whispered a frustrated curse.

It wasn't registered to Carrera. It was registered to Katherine Vinson at an address near Topanga Canyon. He called up her driver's license information and her address matched the same address, but the license had expired. Her date of birth put her in her eighties.

She sure as hell wasn't driving her car last night. Drew switched databases to see if it had been stolen. There was no report of that. He searched Katherine Vinson. A missing person report came up. It was thirty years old.

He double-checked her license. It had expired soon after that. Now how did a missing person buy a new BMW and keep the registration current?

He called up the missing person report. Katherine's employer had called in for a welfare check after she had missed work for five days. Police went to the Topanga Canyon house and found nothing out of order. Without any indication of foul play, the case was left open but inactive. Next of kin was notified, her son from an earlier marriage.

Dominic Carrera.

All of this had occurred before Lincoln's death and Bobby Lee's coerced confession. Drew put the puzzle together.

A demon possesses Dominic Carrera. It goes to his mother's house and kills her, stashing the body where no one ever finds it. Maybe it eats the corpse, it's a demon, who knows. It plays the innocent when the police notify Carrera his mother is missing. With no other relatives in the picture, all it would take would be a forged power of attorney to live with everything still under Katherine's name. As long as she was never legally declared dead, the demon could do that indefinitely. And the only person who would push to file for a death certificate would be Dominic. A great way to live off the radar with almost no paper trail.

If all this was true, he knew where the demon was holed up. And that place where the demon felt secure would be the perfect place for the element of surprise to work in Drew's favor.

Later tonight, he needed to take a drive to Topanga Canyon.

★   ★   ★

Anna had made sure that the Halloween spirit had been represented in the family's kitchen. A plastic black cat, back arched and yellow eyes glowing, sat near the kitchen sink. As Drew moved each dish from the sink to the dishwasher, he swore the little cat's eyes followed him, goading him into broaching the subject he was sure would get a fight cooking tonight.

When he finally screwed up the courage to break the news to Anna, he kept his eyes on the dishes as he said it, not wanting to see her reaction.

"Santiago called and got me another shift tonight at Leisure Village."

No answer. He could feel the heat from her burning gaze bore into the back of his head.

"Tonight?" she finally said.

"Yeah," he said with as casual an air as he could fake. "It won't run as late as yesterday. I need to leave in about half an hour."

The dishes were all loaded and he had no excuse to not raise his head. He turned to look at her. Her face was red, her eyes narrowed.

"What the hell?" she said. "You already came home late from work today. And that was after getting home at four a.m. this morning, followed by keeping me awake by churning up the bedsheets when you were sleeping."

He barely remembered the dreams he'd had during his brief sleep this morning, but he did remember they were unnerving and full of demons.

"It's easy work," he said. "Santiago needs help covering it. The pay is good. It's a win all the way around."

"Except for us. You being out of the house like this all day and night leaves me taking care of everything. You want to end up one of those cop statistics where his kid doesn't know his father?"

"I think you're overreacting."

"No, I'm *early* reacting. When we got married and I had reservations about you being in the LASD, you told me that you'd be working in vehicle inspections. Nine to five. No high-speed chases, no shootouts. 'A normal job with a badge.' Remember calling it that?"

He had promised her a mundane life. Her friends had fathers in law enforcement. She'd seen how the stress of the job had broken families, how on-the-job injuries had turned strong men into hollow shells. She'd been adamant from the start that she did not want her life going in that direction. Her worries only increased after Kenny had been born. Drew couldn't count the number of times she'd not-so-casually mentioned other safer security-related job opportunities she'd heard about.

"It's been a little busy this week, but it's nothing risky."

"Why would a place hire armed security if it wasn't risky? It's LA. What street corner isn't risky?"

"Babe, I'm not going to put my life on the line at a retirement community. Trust me."

She looked deep into his eyes. He twitched.

"I want to trust you," she said. "But you compartmentalize so many things in your life. There are times I get the feeling that you do that to hide things from me."

She could tell he had secrets. In her wildest dreams she'd never imagine how awful they were. And in her waking life he'd make sure she'd never know.

"There's nothing to hide," he said. "Just doing something extra to make ends meet, maybe lay the groundwork for connections to get a cushy gig when I retire from LASD. I'll make up the time this weekend. The three of us will spend the day doing something fun. There's that law enforcement discount at Ducky World this month. Let's go."

Kenny had been begging to go to the Ducky World amusement park for months, a desire no doubt spurred by watching reruns of Dingbat Duck cartoons every afternoon. Every television commercial break trumpeted the park's great rides and the opportunity to meet Dingbat Duck in person for a picture and an autograph.

Anna paused as she mulled the peace offering. "Okay. And no extra shifts next week anywhere."

"Deal."

Anna went off to get Kenny ready for bed. Drew poured soap into the dishwasher and shut the door. He'd just made some promises he needed to uphold. He hoped demon Dominic Carrera didn't keep him from making them happen.

CHAPTER SIXTEEN

There were still a few places near Los Angeles that weren't paved in concrete and separated into perfect rectangles by sidewalked streets. Topanga Canyon was one such place.

The area north-west of the city had been spared the cancer of urban sprawl by steep canyon walls and narrow, snaking roads. Decades ago, it had been a refuge for hippies, but now the affluent had arrived and built or rebuilt homes on the few level tracts available. What that created on Old Topanga Canyon Road was a winding two-lane through forested hillsides, with a smattering of homes along the road. Some were humble ranches; others were gated compounds.

Drew drove cautiously up the road. Streetlighting was almost nonexistent and that gave him an enhanced appreciation for how limited car headlights really were in piercing the darkness. Luckily, there were no other vehicles out on this road. Improved Highway 27 had shunted most traffic to the east and turned this area into a backwater.

He watched his navigation app tell him he was getting closer. If the address on the BMW's registration turned out to be one of the high-security mini-mansions, he wasn't sure how he was going to be able to get in and see what was going on.

He slowed as he approached the address. An older ranch house rose a few dozen yards from the road down a tree-lined dirt driveway. It hadn't been gentrified since Katherine had bought it. That was good news. A black car was parked beside the house, but there wasn't enough light to make out if it was the BMW. There was only one way he was going to find out.

Driving his personal car down the driveway wouldn't be the least bit stealthy, and surprise was one of the few things he had in his favor, He pulled ahead to a spot with a wider shoulder, stopped, and shut off the car.

Nervous energy made the tips of his fingers tingle. There was a good chance that he was going to confront a demon at the end of that driveway. Sending demons back to Hell might have been a specialty of Lincoln's, but it was something novel for Drew. He had to do it, though. More people did not need to lose their souls to this abomination. And Lincoln's death had to be avenged.

He got out of the car and shifted his gun belt back to hang more comfortably. He wasn't going to repeat last night's mistake. Tonight he wore his LASD uniform. Best to exude an aura of authority if anyone caught him wandering around where he didn't need to be.

He went to the trunk. He popped it open, then opened the tackle box within. The manchineel box sat on top. He would never look at it without remembering the story Lincoln had told him about how deadly the wood of the box had once been. He wondered if that was part of the reason this dagger had the power to do its job.

Inside the box, the dagger lay tucked into its sheath. He hadn't seen it in a long time and the sight of it kind of took his breath away. He pulled it from the sheath and inspected it under the trunk light. Dull, gray, and pockmarked, it was as unimpressive as he remembered it. He assumed it still worked. It didn't have batteries or anything.

With his free hand he dug around in the toolbox until he found the glass vial with the demon claw in it. He picked it up and held it near the demon dagger. The dagger handle grew hot in his grip. The blade assumed a golden glow and became sharper and stronger. Drew's hand tingled.

The dagger was ready for a fight. He hoped that he was.

Drew put the demon claw back, then closed the trunk lid. He tucked the sheath into his belt just behind his pistol holster. With cautious steps, he walked along the side of the road in the dark until he got to the driveway. No cars had passed by.

He began a slow advance on the sandy trail to the house. Light shone from the front windows. There were no signs advertising a security system. Of course, why would a demon need one? Drew stayed in the shadows and approached the car parked by the house.

Sure enough, it was the BMW he'd tried to follow on the 405. Katherine's car was at Katherine's address, but without any Katherine. Carrera was probably inside, but was anyone else? And if people were, did they know it was a demon, or were they fooled into thinking it was as human as they were?

Drew was starting to understand that he hadn't thought through this plan as well as he should have. He'd need to be much better prepared before he confronted Carrera. For tonight, he'd settle for figuring out if Carrera lived in the house alone.

Drew crept around the tail of the car and toward the house. A small porch ran in front of the front windows and the main door. He tiptoed by the porch with a plan to listen from all sides of the house to see who might be inside.

The front door opened. A voice boomed out through the screen door. "Who the hell is out there?"

The porch light popped on and the beam lit the porch and the front yard well past where Drew stood. He felt like an escaping prisoner. He blinked in the bright light and realized he was screwed.

His first instinct was to run. Then he remembered he was in uniform.

"Sheriff's Department," he said. "Responding to a call about a disturbance."

The screen door opened. Carrera stepped out into the light, one hundred per cent hideous demon. Drew had never been just a few feet from one before. The smell of sulfur and burned flesh nearly overwhelmed him. Close up, the creature's face was more revolting than ever. Charred flesh parted to reveal red, glowing skin in a few places. Lips had been burned away and revealed a lower jaw filled with teeth like a shark. Twin red eyes burned like embers from the recesses of its eye sockets. Drew swore he could feel heat coming from them.

"Do you hear any disturbance?" Carrera asked.

Drew got a grip on his fear. Carrera didn't know Drew saw through its human disguise. He was just a deputy. He needed to act like one.

"Is Ms. Vinson at home?" Drew said.

That caught Carrera off guard. Drew guessed that no one had asked for Katherine Vinson in decades.

"No, she took a trip to the mountains this week. A getaway from the LA air."

Drew stepped to the edge of the porch. Being this close to the demon ignited a primal fear that made the hair on the back of his neck stand up. He wondered how the hell Lincoln had ever done it more than once. His hands began to shake. He tucked his thumbs into his gun belt to steady them. The palm of one hand covered the handle of the demon dagger.

"The call was for a woman screaming," he said. "Anyone else in there with you?"

"No, just enjoying a quiet night alone."

Protocol on this kind of call was to do a check of the house. If he didn't ask to, that would seem suspicious, even to a civilian, but especially to someone with as many run-ins with the law as Carrera had racked up.

Drew was getting sucked into this like soap suds heading down a drain.

"Mind if I came in and check?" he forced himself to say.

Maybe Carrera will refuse, Drew thought. *Then I'll say I'm going to check with a supervisor, and then I'll just leave.*

Carrera smiled, which on a demon looked horrifically sinister. It stepped aside from the front door.

"Help yourself," it said.

Shit.

Drew walked through the front door. Carrera followed him and stopped inside the threshold, blocking the doorway, Drew felt like a mouse that had just stepped into a trap.

"There aren't any houses near mine," Carrera said. "Who was it that called in the complaint?"

"They don't tell me that information. Just to respond and check it out."

Drew looked around the living room. A heavy coat of dust covered everything, the way it would in an abandoned house. From the analog sound system, to the boxy television set, to the disco-era style of the furniture, nothing here had changed in decades. This demon might make an appearance of living here, but no actual living got done.

"And another thing, Deputy," Carrera said. "Where's your cruiser?"

Now this was going seriously sideways. "Parked at the end of the driveway."

"Because you needed a little exercise?"

The sarcastic tone said Carrera knew Drew was in way over his head. Carrera took a step closer and inhaled. The air made a rattling noise in its pointed nose.

"Do you know what I smell?" Carrera said. "Fear. The splendid scent of incapacitating, bone-chilling fear. Should a well-armed deputy feel that way standing in front of an unarmed man?"

Sweat began to run down from Drew's armpits. His bladder felt two sizes too small.

Carrara reached out one long, clawed finger. Charred skin hung down like strips of old wallpaper. The demon leaned forward to touch Drew's shoulder. Drew jumped back.

"I think," Carrera said, "that you can see beneath my pretty mask."

Faster than Drew thought possible, the demon stepped forward and sent a hand crashing into Drew's protective vest. It could stop bullets, but the creature's claws punched right through it and scratched Drew's chest. The demon gripped the front of the vest, tore it off Drew, and cast it aside. The rear section dropped to the floor.

Drew nearly tripped over it as he backpedaled and ended up against the living room wall. Training kicked in and he reached for his gun. Carrera laughed.

"Please do."

Bullets would be useless. The sound of gunfire would be loud enough to get the few area neighbors to call LASD for real. More backup just meant more victims for Carrera. Drew reached behind his back and pulled out the demon dagger.

Carrera looked at the unimpressive, dull knife. "Now I'm really scared."

It charged at Drew. As the demon closed in, the dagger blazed to life. The handle heated up, the blade glowed and sharpened. Power surged through Drew's hand and wrist.

But unlike when he'd set the dagger beside the demon claw, that power surge did not stop at his wrist. It coursed up his arm, across his chest, and down the other arm. His body felt electrified.

Carrera's hand shot out and clamped around Drew's neck. It squeezed, but Drew's neck muscles had turned tough as steel. Claws punctured his skin, but his windpipe did not crush. The demon looked confused.

Drew slashed the demon's arm with the dagger. The blade sliced through flesh down to the bone. Viscous black liquid spurted from the wound. Glowing red dots swarmed within the gash, like ants around a crushed anthill. The demon cried out, more in shock than pain, and released Drew.

Drew lunged for Carrera. The demon sidestepped the blade and backhanded Drew with its uninjured arm. Drew sailed across the room and crashed into a lamp on a table. The lamp shattered and Drew hit the wall hard.

Any other time, that kind of impact would have broken multiple bones. But all he felt was bruised. This dagger was delivering strength and a level of physical protection. To Carrera's shock, and his own, Drew jumped to his feet. He charged the demon again.

Drew swung the dagger in a wide arc. Carrera blocked the attack with its good arm, then managed a weak swipe at Drew's chest with its injured arm. That was enough to rip open Drew's shirt and carve three deep scratches in his torso. Each gouge felt like a trail of burning gasoline had been left behind in the wound. Drew screamed.

He spun away from the demon's raised arm and sent the dagger on a backhanded sweep across the demon's midsection. The blade cut deep and clean. Obsidian-colored fluid burst from the wound, followed by organs Drew could not identify. The demon clutched its gut with its bad arm and delivered a left hook to Drew's head with the other.

The force drove Drew's head straight back in a motion that should have surely snapped his neck. But his rock-hard muscles kept his head attached to his spine. The impact still threw him back and onto a couch.

The demon leapt into the air and dove onto Drew for the kill.

Drew raised the dagger and as the demon fell upon him, he thrust the blade up and under the creature's pointy chin. Carrera gagged and more black blood ran from its mouth and the new wound. Drew heaved the demon aside without letting go of the handle. He was taking no chances.

Carrera collapsed on the floor. The demon's hand fell away from the wound in its gut. Drew straddled it across the chest, pulled the dagger from Carrera's chin, and laid the blade against its neck.

"Who the fuck are you?" the demon sputtered as blood filled its mouth.

"The guy getting revenge for you killing Lincoln Jordan."

The demon looked confused, then laughed. The laugh sent the demon into a choking fit.

"You think..." it spit out something black and solid, "...that I killed Lincoln? Boy, you are in so far over your head."

Drew was done with the creature's lies. He raised the dagger and drove it into the demon's forehead. Carrera shuddered like it was being electrocuted. Then it went limp and lay still.

The demon's stomach-churning smell, so close, was unbearable. Drew pulled the dagger from the demon's head. Lincoln had told him the only way to return it to Hell was to cut out the heart. He sliced open the creature's abdomen.

A black ooze covered everything inside the abdominal cavity. Within it danced little red flecks, like a swarm of fleas. In the center of the abdomen beat an oblong organ with several arteries attached to it. That looked like a heart to him. The contractions continued, slow and weak. Damned if it wasn't going to bring this demon back to life.

The glowing dagger's blade cut through surrounding tissue with the ease of a laser scalpel. Drew bit back his revulsion, reached in, and pulled out the slick, beating heart. He threw it across the room. It hit the wall with a splat and slid to the floor, leaving a slick black trail on the wall in its wake.

The demon's body began to glow red. Drew jumped up and back. The heart and all traces of the demon's blood also began to glow. Each item's details grew indistinct, then it all turned to red ash. It snowed down through the floor and disappeared.

Drew staggered backward and leaned against the wall. The dagger returned to its inert, unimpressive state. All the energy it had pumped into Drew's body evaporated. He felt completely exhausted and slid down to the floor. He noticed that the demon blood that had coated him had also vanished.

But the wounds from the demon's attack had not. Three slashes crossed his chest. Not deep enough for stitches, but they hurt like hell. Demon claw punctures on his neck felt like a set of bee stings and he was certain that his body would be bruised for a long, painful time.

Drew's elation did not last long. He was sitting in the middle of a crime scene. Sort of. Was sending a demon back to Hell a crime? Whether it was or not, this place was a wreck. And when someone came to check on it, an investigation would reveal that Carrera and Katherine Vinson were both gone, and that she'd been gone for years. There would be a mountain of questions detectives would never get the true answers to. One thing he didn't want was to be involved in the investigation.

He rose from the floor and returned the knife to its sheath. He scooped up the two halves of his protective vest, and then double-checked the rest of his equipment to make sure he hadn't lost anything during the fight. Some of his trace DNA was probably around the place, but there was no way he could scrub all that. He considered lighting the place on fire, but the hazard to the rest of the canyon doing that was too great.

Instead, he opened up all the doors and windows. Access to the open air would make the place messier and start any DNA degrading. Plenty of wild animals crawled around the canyon. With any luck at all, they'd move right in and trash the place. Even better, maybe kids would find the open house and that would turn it into a disaster area. He was going to have to trust that at least one of those things happened before any law enforcement got called to check the place out.

He left the house and limped back up the driveway. He stopped worrying about the loose ends he'd just left behind, and started worrying about how he was going to keep all of this from Anna.

CHAPTER SEVENTEEN

2014

Drew's new house in San Leandro was either a complete disaster or had great potential.

He got out of his car and gave the ratty-looking front yard a sideways glance. With some effort, he could imagine green grass and bright blooming azaleas instead of brown dirt and dead boxwoods. A weekend of effort could turn the sagging porch into a rocking chair getaway. All the roof needed was a fresh layer of shingles. Drew decided that the house was awash in great potential.

It had to be. Kenny was almost a year old, and their one-bedroom apartment had been bursting at the seams. More space wasn't a luxury; it was a necessity. He and Anna had sunk every spare cent into a down payment for the little ranch, and the mortgage payment was only borderline manageable, even with his new job at the Sheriff's Department.

The undiscovered territory of new home ownership still made him nervous. He told himself that they had only been moved in a week, and that once they got settled into a routine, everything would work itself out.

He entered through the front door to find Anna standing in the living room, looking pissed off. He cycled through everything he'd done over the last twelve hours to see if he might be the cause. He came up with nothing.

"Hey, what's going on?"

She gave a box at her feet a kick. "You want to tell me what all this is?"

He gave the old box a closer look. It wasn't one of the ones they'd packed for the move. Then he recognized it and a rock of dread formed in his stomach.

This was the box he'd packed with all the demon books. He hadn't opened it in over a decade, long before he'd met Anna. But the yellowed tape was split, and the box was opened now.

After Lincoln had died, Drew had felt like he still knew next to nothing about these demons his supposed gift let him see. He'd started a collection of books on demonology, a few new, but many older, some ancient and brittle. He'd hidden them under his bed as a teenager, then packed them into this box when he'd moved out of his mother's house. The net result of all his research? The authors were contradictory and confusing, and while the older books better matched the things Lincoln had explained to him, there was a good chance that none of the authors actually knew anything.

"I guess you looked at the books in there," he said.

"Would I be this freaked out if I hadn't?"

"I can explain them."

He could. This would be the perfect chance to sit down and share the only part of his past he hadn't shared with her. Or anyone. He could tell her about his demon vision, about how it nearly made him crazy, about how Lincoln had saved him, and then died at the hands of one. He could sum it up by saying that it was all behind him now, and as far as he was concerned, those books could all go straight in the trash. The idea that he could unburden himself of this secret filled him with a sense of liberation.

But he really had put it all behind him, had never seen a demon again. All his terrifying thoughts, all his paralyzing fears, all that horror had been packed away and sealed shut as sure as that box had been. Once he let all of that out, he feared it would never get put away again, and Anna would never again look at him like he was normal. Even if she thought he was stable now, she'd forever remember he'd once been seeing demons like a crazy person.

"That was all part of a teenaged phase," he said.

"A phase?"

"Like the way kids get obsessed about dinosaurs or rock stars or whatever."

"You think dinosaurs and demonic possession are on a par?"

"No, no. Look, there was this run of horror movies my friends and I watched, then there were these ghost-hunting shows on TV. I got all into the supernatural and paranormal stuff. I had this collection of books I picked up at thrift stores and used book sellers. When I moved out of the house, I packed up everything I owned. Some boxes never got unpacked, especially stuff I collected as a kid. That box was one of them."

"I love Halloween," Anna said, "but that's all goofing around. Some of these books look like practical guides to summoning demons."

"Seriously? You believe in that kind of stuff?"

"No, but now I'm afraid that you do."

"Not in the least," Drew said. "You didn't find a Ouija board or a summoning bowl in there, right?"

Anna's anger seemed to have burned itself out. She sat down on the couch.

"Nothing like that," she said. "But finding all those books was shock enough."

"As it should be. I'm sorry I forgot about them. They should have been thrown away years ago. I'll do it right now."

"Sorry I got so mad." Anna's eyes drooped with sadness. "Everything is just different since Kenny was born. Things I never worried about before, I worry about now. He's so small and defenseless. I'm anxious about anything that might threaten him."

Drew moved to the couch and sat beside her. He put an arm around her and held her close. She rested her head on his shoulder.

"I feel exactly the same way," he said. "Kenny's the most amazing thing that's ever happened to me. I'll never let anything bad cross our threshold. He's going to grow up safe and happy."

Anna kissed his cheek and stood up. "Okay, well, I was too pissed off at you to make dinner, so I'm going to order pizza. Go check on your son."

"Ten-four."

Anna left for the kitchen. He started to think about all the events that had happened twenty-plus years ago. He had ziplocked all those memories away and tossed them in a mental deep freezer. But now Anna was right. He had to take seriously any threat to his family. He had forgotten about those old books. But he hadn't forgotten about the demon dagger and the other artifacts he'd inherited from Lincoln. They were still hidden away, packed inside an old tackle box packed inside some other box.

After Kenny had been born, he'd had a doctor inoculate his son against microscopic diseases that Drew had never even heard of. Shouldn't he do something to protect his son from supernatural evil he'd actually experienced? Better safe than slaughtered.

The new house needed to be warded. The proper sigils were in Lincoln's notebook. He'd start hanging pictures tonight so he could hide the symbols on the wall behind them. The demon dagger needed to be someplace where he could access it if needed, but where no one would run across it accidentally. He'd mentioned putting a garden shed in the backyard. Maybe it could serve a secret purpose as well.

He'd have to start on this tomorrow. Now that the idea of being vulnerable to demons had occurred to him, he was practically panicked about getting a line of defense in place.

And the best part was, he would never have to tell Anna. He could take all these clandestine precautions, demons would never cross their path, and his secret could stay that way forever.

CHAPTER EIGHTEEN

Present day

When Drew approached his house, his watch said it was after midnight. The plan was to trash his savaged uniform and crash on the couch without waking anyone up. If he could shower and dress in the morning before Anna awoke, he could avoid having to discuss his injuries or what had happened tonight. By the end of the day tomorrow, he'd look less beat-up, she'd forget she'd been ticked off about his extra work, and everything would be fine.

But as he pulled into the driveway he found that the front porch light was on, as were lights in the living room. That was not a good sign. Anna never stayed up when he worked late shifts. Kenny was always her priority and she had to be up before he was every morning.

Drew eased himself out of the car. He'd already returned the demon dagger to the manchineel box in the trunk. He was too tired to put it back in the shed tonight and he didn't want to explain what he was doing out there to Anna if she was awake. Returning the dagger to its safe spot could wait until morning. He went to the front door. Before he could put his key in the lock, the door opened.

He looked up into Anna's eyes. She was furious.

Then she saw the condition of his uniform, the scratches across his chest. Her anger turned to shock.

"What happened to you?"

He started to concoct a story. "There was a fight outside the retirement village gate. A road rage thing. I went to—"

"Stop." Anna turned around and walked over to the couch.

Drew stepped in and closed the door. Anna did not sit down. She just looked at him.

"There were two guys," he continued, "and—"

"Stop lying. Now. You weren't at any retirement community. Not today, not yesterday. I called their security office. They never heard of you."

Drew gave up. His body ached, he was physically exhausted, and mentally spent. With holes shot in his story, he didn't have it in him to fashion another lie. He collapsed into an easy chair and stared at his shoes. His own blood speckled the toes.

"My first thought," Anna said, "was that you were cheating on me. Some slut offered it up to pass her car inspection, maybe some woman with a uniform fetish. Who knows, men are stupid that way."

That she could think he'd cheat on her really hurt. He'd never even considered it.

"Then you come home beat to hell. So, you're either screwing Catwoman or it's some other illegal shit. What do you and your sheriff buddies have going on? I've heard rumors about rogue deputies. Is it drugs? Extortion?"

"Anna, it's nothing like that."

"Really? But it's something that tears you up like you've been attacked by pit bulls? What the hell have you gotten into?"

There was no getting around this, no string of lies that would create a story credible enough to cut through her justified feelings of anger and betrayal. But if he tried to tell her the truth, she'd never let him get through a second sentence after the first one contained the word *demon*.

"Come outside and let me show you something."

Drew stood up. Anna backed away.

"Hell, no. The way you look, I don't trust that I'll make it back in the house alive."

Drew sighed. He reached for his gun. Anna shrieked. Drew froze, then raised his free hand to her, palm up in submission.

"Relax. I would never hurt you."

He slowly pulled his gun from the holster with two fingers. He flipped it up in the air, caught it by the barrel, and then offered it to Anna, handgrip first.

"Proof of good faith," he said.

Anna grabbed it and switched off the safety. She kept the barrel pointed at Drew. He'd taken her to the range several times and knew she could hit a target much farther away than this. And she knew that he knew it. Some of her nervousness bled off.

He led her outside to the trunk of the car. She followed a few feet back, pistol at the ready.

"I'm not doing anything illegal," he said. "Just unbelievable."

He popped the trunk, reached inside, and opened the tackle box. Anna watched from a distance over the gun's barrel.

"It's hard to believe," Drew said, "but demons walk the Earth. Tonight, I killed one."

"For Christ's sake. That's your story?"

"I knew you wouldn't believe it. I wouldn't either if you told it to me. So, I need to show you something."

He reached into the tackle box and took out the glass tube with the demon claw in it. He held it under the trunk light so she could see it.

"This is a demon's claw."

He handed her the tube. She gave it a close examination.

"Have you ever seen anything like that?" he said. "Can you even think of another creature that has a claw like that?"

"Well, no. But it could be a fake."

"That I carry around just in case I need a prop for a bogus demon-hunting story?"

She didn't say anything.

"There's only one way to send them back to Hell," he said, "with a special dagger. I'm taking out that dagger. Don't shoot me."

In slow motion, he opened the manchineel box and then took the dagger from its sheath. In the weak light of the trunk lamp, the blade looked even more gray and deteriorated than usual.

"Drew," she said, "that won't cut butter."

"Hold out the claw."

She extended the tube with the claw in it toward Drew. Drew raised the dagger to the vial. The handle warmed against his palm. The blade took on a yellow glow as the tip extended to a point. The light from the blade cast their faces in gold. Anna's jaw dropped and she lowered the pistol to her side.

"How does that...."

"I couldn't begin to explain it," Drew said. He slipped the tube from her grasp and put it back in the tackle box. The dagger dimmed and then went dark. "But I can explain a lot of other things. Let's go inside."

★　　★　　★

An hour of explanations later, Anna sat across from Drew at the kitchen table. She had a blank look on her face. Drew had told it all to her. From his first sighting of demons, through the education Lincoln gave him, all the way to sending Lincoln's killer back to Hell tonight. It was a lot to absorb.

"You're the only person I've ever shared all this with," he said.

"Because it would get you committed."

"All the times you felt like I was holding something back, or keeping a secret, that was it."

"And when we first moved," she said, "and I found those demon books...."

Drew hung his head. He was so hoping she'd forgotten about that.

"You were already lying to me about it," she said. Her cheeks began to flush. "Not just skipping telling me, but outright lying! Damn it. Couldn't those demon things decide to hunt us?"

Drew got up and went over to a large painting on the wall. He lifted it off the hanger and exposed a red symbol painted on the wall that looked like a combination of an Egyptian ankh and two oblong ovals.

"This is a sigil," he explained. "It masks the house from demonic senses, kind of turns it into a blank space. Even if a demon walked by the house and saw it, it couldn't sense what's inside."

"How many of those are in the house?"

"At least one on each wall."

Anna's anger swelled again. "And that demon graffiti has been there how long?"

"I protected the house as soon as we hung the pictures."

"And now I remember you making us do that early, and how weird it seemed."

She stood and paced the room. She favored her left leg with each step and Drew realized her rheumatoid arthritis, her Red Dragon, was tormenting her tonight. His guilt multiplied as he realized he was adding emotional anguish to her physical misery.

"I don't want to live like this," she said. "I don't want to raise my son like this. I don't want you out hunting demons."

"I won't be," Drew said. "It was a terrifying, brutal thing I did tonight. I came in contact with an evil darkness I never want to touch again. And I can promise that I won't. I don't need to. I sent the demon who killed Lincoln back to Hell."

"No more demon chasing?"

"Lincoln's avenged, and I'm out. Until now, I hadn't seen a demon since Lincoln had died. I'm not planning on seeing one again."

"I don't want you putting Kenny in danger."

"Believe me, he won't be. I'll make sure that you two are always safe."

CHAPTER NINETEEN

Since escaping from Hell two weeks ago, Nicobar had been busy.

Its breakout had been courtesy of a drug-addled woman in her thirties. She thought allowing herself to become possessed by a demon would give her the power to access an unlimited supply of heroin. She'd been wrong. She thought possession would be a partnership. Nicobar saw it as a hostile takeover.

Nicobar had been waiting decades to return to Earth, and beggars couldn't be choosers, but this woman was one sad excuse for a vessel. The archdemon would never pass unnoticed with a shock of purple hair, scabby arms, and perpetually bleary eyes, even in Los Angeles. Gnossian, last of the demons Nicobar had in the area, had given the woman the ritual and ingredients to summon Nicobar for possession. Nicobar would ensure that Gnossian paid some penance for selecting such a train wreck as its vessel.

After the possession, Nicobar consumed a few souls among the homeless to recharge its batteries, and then set out for a makeover. One bodega robbery financed a decent haircut, a suitable outfit with long sleeves, and a hotel room to scour the dirt and vermin off this body. By the time the archdemon emerged, it looked like a soccer mom who'd just dropped her kids off at school. One carjacked Toyota later, the disguise was complete.

An archdemon reigned supreme in Hell, which made the limitations one had to endure on Earth frustrating. Possessing a corporeal form meant limitations in so many things. The need for physical transportation, a slowing of its usually fleet mental processes, the loss of instant obedience by lesser beings.

But Nicobar would not have escaped if the benefits had not

outweighed those inconveniences. First were the sensations. Smells, taste, the feel of a breeze across one's skin, all these things were invigorating. Compared to eternally rising and falling into a sea of molten rock and boiling oil, the sensations were doubly refreshing.

Then there was the passage of time. In the everlasting fires of Hell, the concept did not exist. Everything happened in the now, a now without beginning or end, a now that would never change. But on Earth, seconds passed, then minutes, then hours. Before the archdemon knew it, days had flown by. Time added immediacy, gave existence a horizon, gave every action an edge.

Most of all, Nicobar relished the freedom. Sure, in Hell the archdemon could do with the other demons as it wished. But there were only so many degradations one could exact in Hell's uniform environment. Here on Earth, the variations were infinite, the victims varied, the outcomes less than guaranteed. And the level of destruction a demon could do, both physical and, the more enjoyable, mental was breathtaking. Evil could be unleashed, hatred indulged, sadistic needs satiated.

The last time Nicobar was here, it had roamed the city for over a century and freed a squad of demons from Hell to possess the gullible. The archdemon's network had spanned Southern California. Souls had been consumed and mayhem sparked. A day did not pass without a news headline it could take credit for.

Then came Lincoln Jordan.

The pathetic little meat sack had taken it upon himself to send Nicobar's demonic minions back to Hell, as if he had any right to Nicobar's property. Several had vanished before Nicobar realized someone was daring to hunt its hunters. The worst of it was that this pathetic insect wasn't some pious do-gooder like the priests practicing their worthless exorcisms. This man was soulless. He'd made a deal and now wasn't only going back on it, he was killing the dealers. Nicobar took the insolent affront personally, and had decided to settle the score the same way.

Nicobar visited the site of each demon slaying. Sending a demon back to Hell caused a rip in the fabric between the dimensions, and in that rip remained a trace of the aura of what caused it. A demon dagger had sent its servants back to Hell. The weapon could be fatal to its less-powerful underlings, but to an archdemon it was as dangerous as a toothpick. The archdemon was confident it had nothing to fear from Lincoln.

So it sent one of its soulless to damage the demon traps and scrape the sigils from Lincoln's home while the man was out. Nicobar arrived to slay the demon slayer confident of its invulnerability.

Nicobar's first surprise when it invaded Lincoln's home had been that the bastard wasn't alone. But his partner, Greg, was little more than an inconvenience, another human to crush. The second surprise had been alarming. The two had unearthed the Lance of Vladimir. That thing hadn't seen the light of day in centuries. Nicobar had considered it a myth.

The revelation of its existence had been painful. The lance sent it back to Hell. The archdemon's only consolation had been killing Lincoln first. Now that Nicobar was back, it had a score to settle with Greg, the surviving demon hunter.

Nicobar spent a day cruising the city to see how much had changed in the decades it had been gone. As one who thrived on chaos, it was glad to see that the city had gotten worse in almost every way. Then it fed to build up its strength. Small-time criminals were the easiest prey. Most required a demonstration since Nicobar's soccer-mom vessel wasn't very intimidating. But after that, they all sold out cheap, some for nothing more than a car. Soon Nicobar again had regained all the power of an archdemon.

Now it was time to find Gnossian, which was possessing the vessel named Dominic Carrera. The demon should have been present at Nicobar's summoning ritual but wasn't. There'd be more penance to do for that transgression as well.

Nicobar drove to the address in Topanga Canyon where Gnossian had lived before. It was as good a place as any to start the search. When it arrived, the front door to the ranch house stood wide open.

As an archdemon, Nicobar could sense the aura of another demon from miles away, the way a mother cat can find its kittens, but without any of the maternal attachment. To Nicobar, finding a demon was more like collecting lost property. This place was ripe with Gnossian's aura.

Nicobar stepped through the doorway. The living room was in shambles. Leaves and pine needles littered the floor. Torn seat covers screamed out wads of cotton stuffing. Lamps lay on the floor, shades crushed like battered skulls. An empty bookshelf had vomited its contents across the room and left a pile of volumes with torn covers and shattered spines.

This disaster scene could easily be attributed to vandalism. Empty syringes near the window seemed to reinforce that theory. But Nicobar sensed something that human investigators would not.

The floor at its feet still carried the aftereffects of a forced passage, a tear between this world and Hell. Pushing a demon back through to Hell left behind traces of that destination, a scent of sulfur, the sharp feel of burned metals, the screaming agony of a demon's physical pain and psychic anguish as they are reborn incorporeal into the eternal torments below. The forced repatriation had been recent, but before most of the rest of the damage here had occurred.

Nicobar laid its fingers upon the wall and traced them across the surface as it walked around the area where its demon had dissipated downward. The walls fairly hummed with the residue of a demon dagger. Only a demon dagger could have dispatched Gnossian, and in a struggle, the blade's power left an unseen mark upon the things around it, the way a flame can singe cloth it does not touch.

Nicobar stopped cold.

It recognized the signature of that dagger. Nicobar itself had been cut by that very blade. That was the same one Lincoln had wielded in his losing fight all those years ago.

Nicobar's elation about its earthly freedom morphed to concern. The dagger had not been lost, or consigned to a museum or attic as an unidentified antique like so many had been. It had been retrieved from the scene of Nicobar's downfall, and was still in the hands of someone who knew how to use it. If there was still a demon hunter active in Los Angeles, that put Nicobar's plan of returning more of its Hell-ensconced minions to Earth at risk.

Lincoln had not been alone that day of his death. Nicobar deduced that the other who'd been there, the one who'd actually pierced Nicobar with the Lance of Vladimir, would have kept both blades. Now he still used it, or had taught someone else how to.

Nicobar now had two imperatives before setting in motion its plan to re-demonize Los Angeles. The first remained killing the pathetic worm of a human who'd sent it back to Hell all those years ago. Then Nicobar would avenge the attack on Gnossian. Maybe accomplishing the first would also complete the second. Or maybe Nicobar would get the chance to spread the gratification of its revenge among a wider group of victims.

The archdemon strode out the front door and began the hunt.

CHAPTER TWENTY

The pain in Bobby Lee's gut felt like something was chewing on him from the inside. The truth of the matter was, that was exactly what was happening. This goddamn cancer was going to remind him every minute of every one of his last days alive that it was here to kill him.

Supposedly his IV was laced with morphine, but it sure as hell didn't feel like it was. He thought one of the nurses was probably pocketing the drug and giving him sugar water instead. That's just the kind of shit they did to prisoners all the time, treating them all worse than animals.

The medical ward never went dark, even now in the middle of the night. If he'd been able to sleep, the nonstop lighting would have really pissed him off. But since he couldn't sleep, at least the light seemed to keep the waking nightmares from surprising him out of the shadows.

And, man, had he been having nightmares.

Maybe it was the lack of sleep, maybe it was from the anti-cancer cocktail in his veins screwing with his head, but he'd seen a lot of people on this deserted ward tonight. A lot of dead people.

Eddie Nelson had been the first ghost to show up, looking furious with the rope burns from his lynching still red and bleeding around his neck. Bobby Lee and some buddies had administered some Aryan justice to him decades ago. Eddie held a bloody noose in one hand. He raised it up and slid the knot down while grinning at Bobby Lee. Just as Bobby Lee was about to cry out, Eddie vanished.

The second was Haley Durham, a dirty blond skank the Brotherhood had used to sell meth. She opted to keep too much product for personal use and ended up chained to concrete blocks and dropped in a lake.

She appeared, still dressed in the soaking-wet shorts and crop top she'd been wearing when she'd drowned. Algae tinged her gray skin green. Her bloodshot eyes wept brown water and she filled the room with the stink of rotting fish.

She walked up and stood at the foot of Bobby Lee's bed. She opened her mouth like she was going to say something, but instead leaned over and vomited about a gallon of murky lake water all over the bottom half of Bobby Lee's bed. Decayed fish and dead weeds floated in the water. Bobby Lee had screamed and the whole scene just disappeared, Haley, lake water, and all.

Those two were just the first. What had followed was a damn parade of the dead.

He knew it wasn't his fault there were so many corpses in his past. People couldn't see how all his life he'd been screwed over by minorities. They always got the good job, always got all the breaks. He'd just naturally ended up in situations where revenge had to be exacted, examples made. He'd killed some people, helped get a bunch of others killed. Sometimes even brothers turned race traitors had earned the honor.

Well, all those people had come by to pay their last respects, so to speak, or to show they were waiting for him. Bobby Lee couldn't tell which. None of them said anything. Most just walked up to his bed, stood there staring, and then vanished like smoke from a campfire.

Bobby Lee dozed off to awaken to a strange woman standing by his bed. He might not remember everyone he'd had a hand in killing, but this woman definitely wasn't one of them. But she wasn't dressed like someone who worked in the prison, or like an inmate. Her brown hair was parted in the center, cut short above the collar of the blue long-sleeved polo shirt she wore with a pair of tan khakis. With her fair skin and brown eyes, she looked like someone out of an ad for dish soap.

The woman smiled and Bobby Lee's blood ran cold. The grin was positively malevolent. The edges of her eyes curved up in a way that Bobby Lee had only seen in snakes. Bobby Lee had stood beside some evil mothers. That kind of person exuded a darkness that inspired fear.

This bitch had them all beat. She made the hairs on Bobby Lee's arms stand on end.

"Who the hell are you?" he said with as much bravado as his crumbling body could muster.

"Someone who can make your so-called life miserable."

"Too fucking late, cancer beat you to it."

"A friend of mine was killed, Gnossian. You knew him as Dominic Carrera."

Bobby Lee would have shit his pants if he hadn't been on a liquid diet.

"I, I don't know who that is."

The woman stepped closer. Bobby Lee swore he could smell rotten eggs and something like burned skin and fur. His heart beat faster than it had in months.

"Sure you do. He's the one who got you to take the fall for me in the Lincoln Jordan killing." The woman tapped Bobby Lee on the chest. "Took a little something from here to make all your dreams come true."

Bobby Lee hadn't had physical contact with a woman in years. Despite being so overdue, this woman's touch sent a spike of ice into Bobby Lee's chest. Then that spike turned a small space inside him into a frosty rock. Bobby Lee's hands shook so hard they rattled his handcuffs against the sides of his bed.

"You're like him," Bobby Lee said. "You're a demon."

"No. I'm worse than him. Compared to me, he's a cherub. You betrayed Gnossian, broke the deal. Who did you tell?"

"Fuck you. If I don't talk you gonna kill me? Shit, girl, I'm already dead. You gonna torture me? Worse than the black swallowing me from the inside is? Good luck."

"So, the white-trash loser wants to do it the hard way? No problem."

The demon reached out with one hand and yanked the IV needle from Bobby Lee's arm. He jerked at the sharp pain. Blood ran from the site down his sallow skin.

The demon pricked its finger with the IV needle. Blood oozed out, but the blood looked black and greasy. Then it put the bleeding fingertip on Bobby Lee's forehead.

Bobby Lee felt like he'd been touched with a blowtorch. He opened his mouth to scream.

"Quiet," the demon commanded.

Bobby Lee's scream came out as a dry wheeze. A dread deeper than the deepest well filled his body and he found he couldn't move.

"Now," it said, "tell me who you betrayed my demon to."

The story spilled out of Bobby like water from a broken dam. From his first meeting with Deputy Drew Price to the last one where he'd told him about Carrera.

The demon took its finger from Bobby Lee's forehead. The relief of the demon's departure was the best sensation Bobby Lee had experienced in decades.

"Now, you could have answered my question so that I'd skip all that," the demon said, "but I probably would have done it anyway. I mean, why should I trust your word, right?"

Bobby Lee was supremely exhausted and his head hurt like a dirt bike had been doing laps in it. He just wanted this damn thing to go away.

"Being uncooperative and disloyal has to be punished though," the demon said.

It reached one hand behind Bobby Lee's neck and pinched his spine. Vertebrae crunched.

"Good news and bad news," the demon said. "I always lead with the bad. The nerves I just crushed have left you paralyzed."

Bobby Lee knew that wasn't true. He didn't feel paralyzed. He went to raise his hand to prove it. It didn't move. He tried a leg, nothing. Being paralyzed was the nightmare of all nightmares for him. He screamed in fear, but nothing came out.

"Yes," the demon said, "even the vocal cords. But I said there was good news. You still get to feel all that pain of the cancer eating you alive."

The hopelessness and horror of what lay ahead pushed Bobby Lee's mind to the point of breaking. The demon gave Bobby Lee a pinch on the cheek.

"Don't say Nicobar never gave you anything."

The demon stepped out of Bobby Lee's line of sight. All he could see was the wall across from his bed. No picture, no window, no clock. Just faded paint with a hairline crack that ran down one side. This would be his world view for the rest of his miserable life.

Haley Durham reappeared at the foot of his bed, dripping water and bits of algae onto the floor. Her gray face showed no emotion as she crawled up onto Bobby Lee's bed. She straddled him at the waist and leaned forward. The stink of the lake covered him like a blanket. She vomited a torrent of fetid lake water onto his face. His mouth opened in an involuntary, silent scream and filled with the rank, viscous water.

The true horror was knowing this wasn't going to kill him.

★   ★   ★

Nicobar returned to the door of the hospital ward. The soulless guard Nicobar had commanded to escort it to the ward waited dutifully in the hallway. The guard walked Nicobar back out and then returned to wipe clean all the surveillance video. The archdemon returned to its car.

This Deputy Drew Price who'd questioned Bobby Lee told him he'd been some kind of pupil of Lincoln's. Apparently pupil enough to retrieve the demon dagger from the scene of Lincoln's death and know how to use it against demons.

The deputy had admitted to Bobby Lee that he had the demon sight. That would make getting close to him without him noticing very tricky.

An example had to be made and revenge exacted. Humans couldn't be allowed to think killing demons could go unpunished. And this Deputy Drew Price was going to have a unique punishment. Not death, but an existence that would make him long for death's sweet release.

CHAPTER TWENTY-ONE

The sun crested the eastern hills and sent brilliant morning sunlight down on the playground. A light rain the night before had turned the grass a bright shade of ultra-green and smoothed out all the golden sand around the slide and jungle gym. Veterans Memorial Park was a few blocks from Anna's house and the playground was Kenny's favorite. When he was first born, she used to walk him down in a stroller and do laps around the park. When he'd gotten older, she'd chased him around the slide and pushed him on the swings.

But the Red Dragon had put an end to that kind of workout a while back. She'd called rheumatoid arthritis the Dragon since she'd been diagnosed as a child. On its worst days, RA felt like a creature breathing fire into her joints.

And it was all because her body hated itself. Her immune system thought her joints were some kind of infection, and massed the troops to attack them. The cause of the disease was unknown, as was a cure. There were treatments, but they were all less than one hundred per cent effective at providing relief while being one hundred per cent effective at delivering side effects, at least in her case. The long-term prognosis was crippling joint damage. Each year her circle of accomplishable activities shrank a bit more. Hurray.

Today the Red Dragon had been roaring from the moment she'd awakened. She'd managed to appease it a bit, but as usual, no chemical St. George existed to slay it.

This morning she'd driven Kenny down and parked at the playground. She sat on a bench and watched as he entertained himself digging in the sand with a plastic shovel. Behind him kids played on the jungle gym under the watchful gaze of hovering parents.

She looked to the right of the playground and noted something that had changed in the park since Kenny had been born. Way more homeless people. A woman dozed on the ground in the shade of a tree a dozen yards away. She was probably in her twenties, though her lifestyle had aged her appearance well past that. Her skinny body spoke of long-term drug addiction and the sun had bronzed her face to the unhealthy color of a leather purse. Anna wondered how she was managing on the street in just a t-shirt, cut-off shorts, and flip-flops. She realized she probably didn't want to know.

But that woman wasn't scary like some of the incoherent men Anna often saw in the park. She would keep an eye on the woman, but she wasn't afraid for Kenny's safety as he sat before her in the sand. The pack of other mothers didn't pay the woman much mind either. Sometimes the homeless became almost invisible.

Her phone rang. It was her sister Cassandra, biologically two years younger but the case could be made for being far younger measured by general maturity. She lived with her boyfriend in a room they rented over an organic grocery store. Anna reluctantly picked up.

"Hey, Cass."

"Annabelle!" Cassandra always called her that even though it wasn't her given name. "I have something awesomely good for you."

Anna sighed. She knew what was coming.

"I read online about this RA treatment using yucca root, ginseng, and flax oil."

Cassandra had a never-ending parade of dubiously sourced natural remedies for everything, including rheumatoid arthritis. All of them worked about as well as her all-natural homemade deodorant, which is to say not at all.

"Great," Anna said. She'd learned the fastest way to derail this train. "Send me a link to it."

"Totally. It's like on the way. So, how's everything else?"

"Kenny's great, currently building a sand fort by the playground slide."

"And Drew?" Cassandra said.

Cassandra had never liked anyone in authority, and Drew being a sheriff's deputy put him squarely in that category. As a result, Cassandra always lent a sympathetic ear when Anna had Drew problems. And Anna sure had some now.

"Things are a little rough." Anna wasn't about to give Cassandra all the details about the demon books. "Some things from his past came up that he never shared before. Pissed me off that he didn't think they were important enough to tell me."

"That's how men are, all locked up in their masculine boxes. No one really gets in, none of their secrets get out. Don't tell me. He was in a gang. Cops tend to have violent pasts. That's why they want to be oppressors."

Her sister sometimes had a bizarre take on the world. Now Anna was regretting mentioning Drew at all.

"No, nothing so big. It got blown up because he's been working too much. We've blocked out some family time to go to Ducky World this Saturday. Kenny wants a picture with Dingbat Duck."

"So cool. Ducky World is like the most awesome place ever."

Cassandra and her boyfriend were Ducky World passholders, which Anna considered another symptom of their arrested developments.

"We should totally meet you there," Cassandra added.

The last thing Family Saturday needed was to inject Cassandra into the mix. Her dislike for Drew was matched by his loathing for her and her anarchistic tendencies. If the plan was to relax and have fun, that would not happen with Anna's sister around.

"I beat Drew up about making family time," Anna said. "Probably best to keep it that way."

"Got it. Need to give Big D some time to chill."

Anna was done with this entire interaction.

"Kenny's chasing some insect," she said. "I have to go, Cass. Talk to you later."

She hung up and shoved her phone deep into her purse. She sat up and felt the Red Dragon exhale in her hip joints. She levered herself up off the bench. Time to get moving again.

"C'mon, Kenny," she said. "Mommy has to stretch her legs."

*　　*　　*

Nicobar watched Sheri, the homeless girl under the tree, from across the park.

The girl's eyes snapped open and ended her feigned sleep. Sheri watched as Anna took Kenny by the hand and walked away from the playground and the scrum of other mothers with their kids. Once Anna was out of sight, Sheri got to her feet. She walked over to a place behind the restrooms where bushes shielded her from the park's security cameras. She tucked herself in next to the wall.

Nicobar had compelled the soulless girl to shadow the woman and her boy when they left their house and then eavesdrop on them in the park. It wondered how the hell she had quit when it hadn't compelled her to. The archdemon approached the restroom building, ready to tear the stupid girl apart.

"Why did you stop following her?" Nicobar said.

"Because I found out what you asked me to get."

Nicobar listened while Sheri relayed that Anna had said the family was going to Ducky World for pictures with Dingbat Duck on Saturday.

Nicobar smiled. "Surprisingly well done."

"That's it?" Sheri said.

Nicobar wiped the dried demon blood from the woman's forehead. "That's it."

She scratched at the track marks on her arm. "So, can you get me a little something? A reward, like?"

The useless bitch had agreed to serve demons at their command when she'd surrendered her soul years ago. To expect anything more than what she'd originally agreed to infuriated Nicobar.

"How about this?" Nicobar said.

It shot out one arm and slammed the girl back-first into the wall. Ribs cracked. Her face went red and her eyes bugged out. She gagged and grabbed Nicobar's wrist with both hands.

Even if she hadn't been a drug-wasted wreck, she wouldn't have been able to break Nicobar's iron grip. The archdemon pressed hard against the girl's chest. Bones crunched and organs tore until Nicobar's hand touched the wall through two layers of the girl's skin. Her body went limp and Nicobar dropped the corpse to the ground.

It had gotten exactly the information it needed. Nicobar could dispatch this demon murderer Drew as easily as this street slut it had just killed. But it was in the mood to deliver a more prolonged torture to the human who thought he could pass judgement on a demon. It wouldn't take Drew's life. Nicobar planned to take everything else, and let him keep his life once it had become a living hell.

But to get that started, the archdemon needed to get Kenny alone for a few minutes.

And now it knew exactly where it was going to make that happen.

CHAPTER TWENTY-TWO

1995

Lincoln handed Drew an automotive battery. It felt like it weighed a ton.

"This is heavy," Drew said.

"All full of energy. Twelve volts and eight hundred cranking amps. Powerful enough to get the big engine in Gabriella to turn over." He pointed to the empty battery tray in the nose of the car. "Put it in there. Don't drop the damn thing."

Drew lugged the battery from the workbench to the car. He heaved it up over the grill, and set it down in the tray. Lincoln handed him a ratchet.

"Tighten the clamp on the bottom. Then put the red cable on the plus post, and the black cable on the minus post."

Drew went to work securing the battery.

"The battery provides that spark we talked about to get the engine running," Lincoln said. "Then the alternator recharges the battery so you can start the car again. But a battery doesn't last forever. Maybe four years if you're lucky."

Drew finished securing the clamp and went to work on the red cable.

"Souls are like that after a demon takes one," Lincoln said. "Well, more like a battery without an alternator to recharge it. The demon keeps drawing power from it until the soul has nothing left."

"Then the demon needs another soul."

"And a younger soul is like a newer battery. It has more life ahead, more energy. That's why the worst of the demons target kids."

"Kids are too young to understand giving away their souls," Drew said.

"You think this is some sort of fair system? Anyone who gets that he's making a trade, even a child, can lose his soul. He can trade the thing for a damn piece of candy. There's a reason not talking to strangers has been preached so far back they tell you not to do it in Grimm's fairy tales."

"How does the demon know what kid to pick?"

"Usually a child in some despairing situation, like an awful, abusive family. A kid desperate for deliverance. The perfect target for a demon offering a way out. All it has to do is get the kid alone when it's vulnerable."

"So those soulless kids," Drew said, "they're sociopaths from then on?"

"The traits can begin to manifest right away. With no conscience, with no internal voice inside telling right from wrong, the poor kid is screwed. They turn clueless about obeying commonsense directions. They cut or burn themselves just to see what it feels like. Eventually they progress to torturing animals and killing them. It keeps getting worse and they always turn criminal, never seeing that what they're doing is wrong. They almost always become killers, frequently serial killers. Once their souls are gone, they create pain for others for the rest of their lives."

Drew hated to bring up the deal Lincoln had made with a demon, but he had to.

"But you aren't a serial killer," he said.

"Not as far as you know." Lincoln broke into a smile and laughed. "Just kidding. No, I'm no killer. But I had a soul and a conscience for decades. While it doesn't register to me that something bad is wrong to do, I remember that once I would have felt awful doing it. I have enough experience and self-awareness to use the memory of my departed conscience.

"A kid can't do that. They've got no reference for normal. Once their sociopath train starts chugging, it just keeps accelerating until it goes so fast it flies off the track. There's no stopping it."

Drew slipped the black cable over the minus-labeled battery terminal. A tiny spark arced between the post and connector as he seated it. He applied the ratchet and tightened up the connector. He thought about someone his age, or younger, condemned to a life that would end in prison, or worse.

"Can't we, like, put the kid's soul back in?"

"It doesn't work like unbolting a battery, taking it out and then putting it back in. It's more like the demon ripped out the battery and the cables and the tray and then scratched the paint on the way out. A gone soul is gone forever. And when it's taken from an innocent child, that's the worst. The road ahead for that kid will be nothing but misery for him and everyone around him."

CHAPTER TWENTY-THREE

Present day

Saturday morning traffic was blessedly light. Drew drove the family down the interstate using his internal autopilot. Ducky World was several exits down, but Drew's attention was directed much farther away than that.

He'd been reliving the fight he'd had with the Dominic Carrera demon. He'd been running through it over and over again all morning. Move by move, emotion by emotion, breath by breath. He'd never been in much of a fight before, and certainly never in one as violent as the one with the demon.

It stuck with him because it had been disturbing on so many levels. The sheer speed and violence of the fight, the gut-wrenching terror of touching a demon, the undeniably all-consuming power the demon dagger transferred to him. It was as if the whole thing had happened too fast for his mind to clearly process, so he had to re-experience it a hundred times and accept one detail at a time with each review.

A voice in the car caught his attention. He mentally pulled back into the vehicle and listened.

"Drew!" his wife, Anna, yelled from the passenger seat.

"Yes!" he said. "I'm right next to you."

"Well, I wouldn't know. You haven't heard a word I've said."

Drew glanced over to see fury firing her ice-blue eyes. He winced and checked the rearview mirror. In the back seat, Kenny sat plugged into a portable game, oversized earphones masking the sounds of the world. Anna's shout hadn't registered with the boy. Thank god.

"I've been planning out our day in my head," Drew said.

"Seems like your mind is a million miles away," Anna said. "Not ten miles down the road at Ducky World."

Last night, he'd promised to be honest with her from now on. Now would be a good time to start.

"Truthfully, the fight with the..." he checked the review mirror again to make sure his son was lost in his video game world, "... demon was unnerving. I keep thinking about it."

"Well, now's not the time," Anna said. "It won't be much of a family day if you aren't interacting with your family."

She was right. He needed to push the event out of his mind, let his subconscious chew on it for a while. He reached over and held her hand. It felt warm and soft. He was embarrassed to admit he could not remember the last time he'd done that.

He looked into the back seat at Kenny. The boy's brown eyes danced around the tiny video screen. He bobbed his head in time with whatever was playing through the headphones. He was completely in his own back seat world, unaware that in the front seat his mother was trying to convince her husband to act like a father. Drew loved the boy so much that seeing his son always made his heart ache.

"Okay," he said. "Today is about family."

A bit later, he steered the car down the Ducky World exit ramp. It emptied straight into the theme park parking lot. A huge sign spanned the entrance road. Dingbat Duck arose from the center and underneath him huge letters in annoying Comic Sans font proclaimed *DUCKY WORLD*. Smaller print underneath encouraged all to *HAVE A DUCKTASTIC DAY!*

"I don't know if I can do ducktastic," Drew said.

"Suck it up and try," Anna said.

They smiled at each other and Drew had trouble remembering the last time they'd done that, as well.

He slowed the car as he approached the parking lot attendant. He passed a pimply young man some cash and got a ticket in return. He eased the car back in line and crawled into the lot. He handed Anna his phone from its cubby on the center console.

"Here, babe. Turn this off for me."

Anna broke out in a big smile. "Now you're talking!" She tapped and swiped at the screen until it faded into darkness. She tossed it back to him and he buried it in his pants pocket.

"No interruptions," Drew said. "No calls. A few hours off the grid."

"A few hours of normal."

A few hours of fatherhood, he thought.

Drew pulled into an open parking spot. Minivans and SUVs rolled in on either side.

Kenny looked up between the front seats. He shouted to hear himself over his headphones.

"Are we there?"

Anna pulled the phones off his head. "Yes, we are. Put the game away."

"Woo-hoo!" Kenny said.

Kenny's infectious enthusiasm spread to Drew and he grinned.

Anna got out and opened the rear door. She grabbed the family bag from the back seat. Drew swore that it had to be enchanted by some kind of magic. Somewhere in its depths Anna always found whatever was needed during family outings. He realized how few times over the last few months he'd told her she was amazing.

Kenny scrambled out the open door and Anna slammed it behind him.

Drew engaged in a mental debate with himself, then let his fatherly side win. He pulled up the leg of his jeans and checked the pistol in the ankle holster.

The park allowed, even encouraged, off-duty law enforcement to concealed-carry firearms on the property. Their chief of security once said that the only thing that stops a bad guy with a gun was a good guy with a gun, and the chief was in favor of more good guys in the park.

Today, Drew was going to take a break from being part of the thin line between anarchy and civilization. He would leave everything that wasn't about quality family time here in the car. He pulled his weapon out from its holster and tucked it under the seat.

He exited the car and walked around to the back. Families exited SUVs all around him like prisoners escaping detention. The morning sun warmed his skin. The air smelled of sunscreen. Anna stood beside Kenny as he hopped up and down with anticipation.

"Starting to wonder if you were coming," Anna said.

"Decided to go in unarmed. Just a happy camper like everyone else."

Anna hugged him around the waist. "Let's have a perfect day."

"C'mon!" Kenny whined. He grabbed one parent with each hand and dragged them down the row of cars. At the end waited the brightly painted shuttle that would take them to the main entrance. A lead vehicle pulled four open passenger transport cars. The lead vehicle was a giant fiberglass head of Dingbat Duck. Drew guessed, and hoped, that the driver saw through the big duck's eyes to steer.

"Daddy, you know what I want to do first?" Kenny said.

Drew knew the answer, but had to play along. "What, champ?"

"I want to see Dingbat Duck!"

CHAPTER TWENTY-FOUR

A naked corpse lay in the corner of the dim dressing room.

Nicobar slipped the deceased's white shirt over its own. It was too small and as Nicobar buttoned it, a seam on the side tore open. Luckily, the suit coat would hide the damage. A black jacket with tails seemed overly formal, but attracting a crowd was the whole purpose of the day.

The archdemon donned a bow tie, and then bent down to its feet. It pulled a pair of black overshoes on over its own. This time, the fit was perfect.

It sensed prey shuffling by outside the room. Souls by the hundreds milled about so close that their radiated energy made its hunger swell. All it had to do was make the deal, place its mouth by the host's mouth and inhale. The soul's sweet essence would tingle as it flowed past the archdemon's lips, warm it as the soul cascaded down its throat, engorge it as it absorbed and despoiled the soul.

Nicobar selected a white glove from the dressing table and eased it on. It flexed its fingers. No skin showed to betray the wearer. It slid on the other glove.

Nicobar's growing excitement heightened its predatory senses. Even through the wall, it could now differentiate its prey within the swirling masses beyond. The most tender morsels, the souls of the children, beckoned to it. Innocent, undefiled, bursting with life force. Once they became soulless, its victims would sow decades of mayhem. Added icing for Nicobar's cake.

Nicobar covered its head with the molded plastic head the corpse had planned to wear and the costume was complete. The soccer mom vessel Nicobar possessed had a bland anonymity that let the archdemon blend into a crowd. But this costume would let Nicobar bait the crowd in close, clueless that one of Hell's reigning royals was wearing it.

The time had come.

It left the dressing room and crossed the hall to a steel door. It pushed through the door into the large, adjacent room. Though there was a professional photographer and camera in place, cartoon versions of cameras and spotlights also surrounded the faux stage the archdemon now stood upon. A line of families snaked out in a tight *Z* behind the photographer.

The crowd froze. One girl holding a blue balloon spied Nicobar and broke into a smile.

"Mommy!" she screeched. "It's Dingbat Duck!"

CHAPTER TWENTY-FIVE

The building had been designed to look like the straw house that Dingbat Duck lived in, complete with thatched roof and the crooked shutters that, realistically, were too narrow to close across the windows to begin with. A close inspection revealed that the straw was solid concrete with each fake strand hand-painted a slightly different shade. As were most things in Ducky World, the building was a work of art. The sign over the front door read *FOTO HUT: MEET DINGBAT DUCK.*

"It's Dingbat's house!" Kenny said.

"We need to get a picture of Kenny with Dingbat," Anna said.

"If for no other reason than to humiliate him in front of his date on prom night," Drew said. "Let's get it out of the way before the line gets any longer."

The sign by the front door announced the wait time was thirty minutes. The idea of standing in line with that many whiny kids held no appeal to Drew. He glanced across the street to the faux-old-time ice cream parlor. A line of customers stretched out the door.

"Tell you what," Drew said. "You take Kenny in for the photo. I'll get in line for ice cream sundaes and have them waiting for you when you come out."

Anna smiled. "You won't eat it all before we get back?"

"The way the line over there looks, you may be out of there before I even get served."

"No nuts on mine, double cherries."

"You think I don't know that after all these years?" Drew said with a grin.

"I think you *should* know it. But I'm not the kind of girl to take chances on ice cream." She kissed his cheek and turned to Kenny. "Okay, kiddo. Time to meet Dingbat!"

Kenny bolted for the entrance. Anna ran after him.

Drew smiled and wandered over to the end of the ice cream line. A customer who had just been served passed him carrying a banana split the size of a football. Drew's mouth watered.

Anna had been right. This was the perfect place to relax. Everything around him was an artificial construct, an idealized version of something, and the crowd had collectively decided to go with it. They pretended the horse-drawn fire truck on Main Street might really put out fires and that the barbershop quartet on the corner were really four barbers out for a lunch break croon. All had left their worries at the main gate for a day in this trouble-free version of Americana where your water pipes never burst, there were vendors on corners selling roasted turkey legs, and above all, demons didn't stalk the streets. Drew was ready to accept the collective denial.

He joined the back of the ice cream line.

★　★　★

Nicobar went through the motions of being Dingbat Duck. A few broad hand gestures and a waggle of its feathered tail for each kid, then a pose with the kid or the whole family for the picture.

It took a phenomenal amount of self-control not to dive into this walking smorgasbord of young souls. Their energy cried out to be consumed. But the archdemon had to wait for its prize.

And soon the prize arrived. The spawn of its nemesis, the son of Gnossian's murderer, stepped into the room. Nicobar smiled.

But Drew wasn't with the boy, just the wife. Nicobar had so wanted Drew to see it extract the soul out of his son, to be swept up with panic as it tossed aside this ridiculous costume and revealed itself to this one with demon sight.

A less than perfect setting for its plan, but certainly good enough.

One by one, children and families had pictures snapped. Kenny and his mother approached. Finally, their turn arrived. The mother spoke to the photographer. The boy ran up with a big smile on his face.

"Dingbat!" he said.

Nicobar knelt down. It hadn't said a word to any other child, in fact a sign in the dressing room reminded the costumed characters not to. But for Nicobar, the rules did not apply.

"Kenny," it whispered. It pulled a Dingbat Duck toy figure from its pocket. "Want to trade me for this?"

Kenny's eyes lit up. "Oh, yes!" Then his face fell. "I don't have anything to trade."

"Of course you do. Your soul."

Anna was still talking with the photographer. The bulbous mother of a little girl in pigtails joined the conversation.

"What's a soul?" Kenny said.

"You don't even know you have it. You'll never miss it. And without it, you can do anything you want and never feel bad about it."

"Okay!" Kenny said. "Trade!"

Nicobar pressed the Dingbat Duck toy into Kenny's hand. Then it placed its gloved hand on the boy's shoulder and centered the costume head's mouth in front of Kenny's. Unseen by all, a blip of white light zipped from Kenny's lips and passed through the mask.

A rush of energy swept over Nicobar's lips. It sensed the young, confused consciousness of the naive boy. The soul joined the muted chorus of the others within Nicobar, swirls of souls in various stages of consumption. It released the boy's shoulder.

The little girl in pigtails, bored with waiting, sprinted from her mother's side straight for who she saw as Dingbat Duck. Her mother didn't notice. The girl skidded to a stop beside Kenny.

"Dingbat!" she said.

Nicobar decided it was time for this newly soulless boy to start having fun.

"Give her a kick," Nicobar said to Kenny. "She cut in line. She deserves it."

Kenny grinned and kicked her in the shin.

The girl screamed. Anna and the girl's mother's attention cut immediately from the photographer to their children and Dingbat Duck. The two parents swept in.

"He kicked me!" the girl wailed through a torrent of tears.

The girl's mother reacted as if her daughter's leg had been shattered. "Oh my god! What did your monster do to my daughter?"

"Kenny!" Anna said with equal parts fury and embarrassment.

Kenny tried to offer an explanation, showed her the toy in his hand. She didn't listen.

Nicobar stepped back from the boiling melee. The handlers in the area rushed in, separated the arguing women, and ushered them and their children out the door. And while all the employees were distracted, Nicobar slipped out the backstage door.

CHAPTER TWENTY-SIX

Drew balanced three ice cream sundaes in Dingbat Duck bowls on a cardboard takeout tray. The Southern California sun beat down on his head and he wondered how long until these expensive frozen concoctions melted into something his son would end up drinking through a straw. He stepped under the shade of an awning across the street from the Foto Hut.

The building had an exit separate from the entrance, so when a large woman in an orange dress was ejected through the entrance by two employees, it was startling. A crying little girl in pigtails followed her out. The employees pointed down Main Street and the furious-looking mother grabbed her daughter's hand and huffed off.

Another over-entitled guest, Drew thought. *So glad that Anna would never—*

Suddenly Anna and Kenny appeared in the doorway, getting the same bum's rush from two more employees. Anna looked mortified. Kenny looked confused. One employee flipped the wait time sign over to read *CLOSED*. Drew hurried over as the employees retreated back inside.

"What happened?" Drew said.

"I don't know," Anna said. "We were setting up the picture, when Kenny kicked some little girl."

Drew whirled and looked down on his son. "You did what?"

Kenny fumbled with the Dingbat Duck toy in his hands as he looked down at the ground.

"She cut in line," he said. "Dingbat said to do it. He gave me this toy as a trade."

The scent of sulfur wafted out of the entrance to Dingbat's faux house. Then Drew made a heart-stopping observation.

In the midday sun, Kenny cast no shadow.

Drew dropped the tray of sundaes. Ice cream splattered over all of their feet. He knelt down and grabbed Kenny's shoulders. He gave him a little shake.

"Who touched you?" he said.

"No one touched *him*," Anna corrected. "*He* kicked a little girl."

Drew ignored Anna. He shook Kenny again. "Who touched you?"

"Just Dingbat," Kenny said, on the verge of tears.

Drew ran into the building. Irritated tourists stood in the accordioned line inside a darkened waiting area. Drew barreled through the line, manhandling the uncooperative and leaving a wake of irate people behind him. He made it to the edge of the picture stage without someone deciding to punch him out.

A manager in a tie and white shirt had arrived. He looked furious. Several hourly employees surrounded him.

"And then where did Tristan...." He looked at the visitors, who were looking at him. "I mean Dingbat go?"

One employee pointed to a door near the stage. "He just ran off backstage."

That was all Drew needed to know. He sprinted past the group and made for the door.

"Hey," the manager said. "You can't go through there!"

Drew pushed open the door, then slammed it shut behind him. He expected to be backstage behind the building.

Instead, he found himself in a short hallway at the top of a small staircase. Low-grade lighting illuminated concrete risers that led down to a tunnel a few feet below ground. Ducky World used these to get employees and supplies all around the park without breaking the park's illusion of seamless entertainment. The tunnel was wide and tall enough to get a golf cart through with a good driver at the wheel. He scrambled down the stairs.

He realized that he had nothing with him to keep a demon at bay.

No demon knife, no pistol to at least slow one down. He had launched himself in pursuit fueled by panic and despair, not reason. He'd have to improvise when the moment came.

At the bottom of the stairs, the stink of sulfur still lingered in the air. Running footsteps echoed down the right corridor. Drew ran in that direction. The corridor up ahead ended at a T intersection.

He neared the intersection and the sulfur smell grew worse. A scent of over-charred rancid meat kicked in as well. He was closing in on it.

He made it to the end of the corridor. The right tunnel was empty. He checked the left.

Dingbat Duck stood inches away, facing Drew. The goofy, welcoming smile on the plastic head grinned at him. Then the duck's right hand shot out and clamped around Drew's neck. The velvety white glove was soft, but the grip still rock-hard. Drew gagged.

The duck raised Drew off the floor, then slammed him up against the wall. The impact sent his head reeling.

"Did you think you could kill Nicobar's children and never pay?" the duck said in a voice not in the least like Dingbat Duck's.

With its free hand, the demon pulled off the oversized Dingbat Duck costume head. It revealed a demonic head unlike any Drew had seen. It was half again as large, with a blackened pointed nose. Atop its head, twin horns swept out to the sides and then curled inward. Long, charred ears tapered to points at the top and bottom. Its eye sockets appeared infinitely deep and completely black, save for dots in the center that glowed like red-hot coals. It cast aside the costume head.

"I could kill you as retribution," the demon said. "Instead, I'll let you suffer as I consume the soul of your child over the next eight decades. And as a bonus, I left a bit of me in place of his soul, a way to jump-start the fun. So for the rest of your life as you look into his eyes, you get to see the eyes of Nicobar staring back at you."

The demon slammed Drew against the wall again. For a moment he blacked out. When he came to, the Dingbat Duck costume lay in a pile on the floor. The demon walked down the tunnel to a set of stairs at the end. Like the demons he'd encountered before, its blackened arms and legs seemed impossibly thin to support it. But instead of its body being a burned-out husk like the others, this one was robust. Two bony projections sprouted from its shoulder blades.

The opaque skin on its back pulsed and stretched as unidentifiable things writhed beneath it. As the demon mounted the steps, something pressed hard against that skin as if trying to burst out to freedom. It stretched the skin into the shape of a human countenance.

Drew recognized the impression of the face he'd traced with his fingers a thousand times, kissed goodbye every day. His son.

Kenny's eyes went wide and his mouth opened in a silent scream that Drew could still understand.

"DADDY!"

The demon paused and faced Drew. Its mouth split into a sickening smile. It rolled its shoulders and its head did a satisfied little shake. Then the demon disappeared up the stairway.

Drew pulled himself to his feet to continue the chase.

"You!" a deep voice commanded behind him. "Do not move!"

Drew turned to see two park security officers standing in the tunnel. Both had pistols pointed at Drew. He raised his hands.

"I'm with the Sheriff's Department," Drew said.

"Sure you are," the guard said. "Lie facedown on the ground. Now!"

CHAPTER TWENTY-SEVEN

An hour later, Drew sat in a small room, handcuffed to the top of a table. He much preferred being on the other side of this kind of encounter.

There had apparently been a fight over the room's décor between the security people and corporate, because as a counterpoint to the windowless room's utilitarian metal table and chairs, the walls were decorated with pictures of Dingbat Duck and other, lesser characters. It definitely took the edge off the intimidation factor.

The bigger of the two security guards who'd intercepted him in the tunnel stepped into the room, leaving the door open. Sergeant's rank was pinned to his collar and his nametag read *HOLCOMB*. A bushy moustache accentuated his round face. Drew had spent a lot of time around deputies and cops. He could tell that this guy had never been one. LAPD and LA Sheriff deputies looked at each other with derision, but they both rolled their eyes at private security. Sgt. Holcomb tried to look intimidating. Instead, he managed to look constipated.

"Are you going to tell me what you were doing in a restricted area?" Holcomb said.

"Probably not," Drew said. He pointed to the cartoon image of Dingbat Duck on the wall. "I feel too unsettled."

"Yeah, well the room usually has lost kids in it, not adults on their way to prison."

This idiot's complete lack of understanding about law enforcement procedures would have been laughable if Drew hadn't been handcuffed to cheap furniture.

"Look, my son came out of the photo shoot with the duck and said the creep fondled him. I went in to confront the pedo just as he made a break for it. So I followed him. Wouldn't you?"

"We do extensive background checks. We never hire people like that."

But you do hire people possessed by demons, Drew thought.

A skinny security guard with a sunken chest stepped into the doorway. "Sgt. Holcomb?"

Holcomb gave Drew a weak attempt at a withering gaze. "Stay there."

Drew ran the chain between his cuffs back and forth through the bracket in the top of the table. "I think that's covered."

Holcomb stepped over to the other guard, who looked barely out of high school. The kid seemed scared.

"We found Tristan French," the guard said. He lowered his voice to a stage whisper. "Dead in the dressing room for the Foto Hut."

"Holy shit." Holcomb went white and faced Drew. "What did the man you were chasing look like?"

Demon, Drew thought, *above average height, charred extremities, my son screaming from inside him.*

"I didn't see anyone," he said instead. "I turned the corner and there was a costume on the floor. Then you stopped me from catching him."

The sagging look on Holcomb's face telegraphed that the guard knew he was in way over his head. Drew went for the kill.

"You are about to dive into a whirlpool of shit," Drew said. "You let a pedophile killer loose inside your park. The LAPD are going to arrive in force and make what you're doing to me now look like an invitation to tea. You let me go before they get here, and my lawsuit won't include damages for imprisoning me. I'll leave the park before the news crews arrive looking for witnesses to interview."

Holcomb fumbled with the keys on his belt, then found the one for the cuffs. He stepped over and unlocked Drew. Drew stood up and rubbed some feeling back into his wrists.

"You aren't a real deputy sheriff," Holcomb said. "You work at vehicle inspections."

"Maybe someday I'll work my way up to a heroic job like yours."

"Get out of here," Holcomb said. "And you're banned from the park."

"Like my family would ever set foot in here again. My lawyer will be in touch soon."

Holcomb turned to the skinny security guard. "Escort him out of the park."

The skinny guard responded with a 'who me?' look on his face, then took a deep breath and faced Drew. "Let's go."

Drew strode out of the backstage security office. The unfinished back side of the facades along Main Street stretched out in front of him. The guard led Drew to a door labeled *CAST MEMBER ENTRANCE*. They passed through it and into the tourist bustle of the park's main drag.

Outside the shops, the sea of smiling humanity swirled and ebbed. Parents tugged at children to keep them moving. A vendor sold blue balloons with Dingbat Duck's face on the side. A teenager pushed a laughing old man in a wheelchair. Everyone here wandered lighthearted, their cares hundreds of miles away.

In reality, an employee had been murdered just yards away, and a demon had just stolen a soul while disguised as a cartoon icon. Rarely had the world everyone lived in and the secret world Drew knew existed been so close together and so far apart.

"I need to find my family." Drew took out his phone and called his wife. She picked up on the first ring.

"Where are you?" she said.

"On Main Street by the ice cream parlor. Is Kenny all right?"

"He's fine. We're by the park exit."

"On my way."

Drew hung up and headed for the park exit at the end of Main Street. The security guard looked relieved that Drew was leaving quietly.

Drew's heart soared when he caught sight of his family through the crowd. Anna stood with her back against a lamppost, scanning the throng for him. Kenny stood at her side. She had one hand cupped around the back of his neck, as if determined that the second of the two men in her life was not going to disappear in this park today. Kenny still held the Dingbat Duck toy.

Only one member of his family cast a shadow.

Drew's heart sank. His poor son probably didn't even know what had happened to him. Not yet, at least. And neither did Anna.

Drew worked his way through the crowd. He waved at Anna and caught her eye. She smiled in relief, but that expression quickly turned to grim fury. The normal family event she'd planned on hadn't happened after all. And as far as she could tell, it was his fault. He stopped beside her.

"What the hell was that all about?" she said. "We went into the photo house to find you after you rushed in and security men said you were being detained."

"They were a little overzealous. My fault, really. I overreacted."

"You're damn right you did. And over what, by the way?"

There was no way he could tell Anna the truth. There had been plenty of time in the Dingbat Duck holding cell to sort out the lie he was about to deliver.

"A stranger giving Kenny something just set off alarm bells. The deputies working the jails have so many stories of total creeps and child predators. Maybe I'm a little paranoid."

"A little? You think so? You scared us both to death." She noticed the skinny security guard standing behind her husband. "Is he with you?"

"And I got myself banned from the park. So there's that." Drew turned to the security guard. "You can tell your sergeant you escorted me to the gate. There's no trouble here."

The guard nodded with relief and speed-walked back into the park.

Drew bent down to get eye to eye with Kenny. "Are you okay?"

"Yeah. But I didn't get my picture with Dingbat."

Drew glanced at the shadow-free ground behind his son. Kenny had lost something far worse than the chance at a picture.

"We've had more than enough fun for today," Anna said. The controlled wrath in her voice had the ominous quality of a pitch-black thunderhead. "Let's go home."

Drew nodded and followed his wife and son out the exit and into the parking lot. He kept staring at the ground, hoping that somehow his son would sprout a shadow.

The demon that called itself Nicobar had targeted Kenny specifically because he was Drew's son. It knew that Drew had sent the Dominic Carrera demon back to Hell. The demon had referred to Carrera as one of its children, and it certainly looked different from the demons he'd seen, including Carrera. That did not bode well. Lincoln had never mentioned any kind of demonic family father.

Drew was going to need to hunt that demon down and find a way to not only release his son's soul, but to put it back where it belonged. And he needed to do it fast. It was just a matter of time before his shadowless son started down the trail of the psychopath.

CHAPTER TWENTY-EIGHT

Kenny teetered atop the pinnacle in the center of the valley.

He stood in his underwear atop an impossibly high column of stone that was slightly smaller than his feet. It soared at least a thousand feet in the center of a canyon hundreds of yards wide. It looked like pictures he'd seen of the Grand Canyon, but there were no reds and oranges in the lines along the canyon walls. All the layers were different shades of black and gray. They blended into the sky, which was a roiling mass of purplish, turbulent clouds.

Lightning flashed so close that he could feel the electrical charge on his skin, followed instantly by thunder so loud that it shook the column beneath his feet.

Strong winds buffeted him from all sides as icy pellets of hail and arrows of sleet lashed against his skin. To keep from toppling over, he had to lean in one direction, then quickly shift as the wind whipped in from the other side. Each breeze cut through his soaking-wet underwear like an assault of icicles and chilled him to the core.

He didn't understand where he was. He'd been with Dingbat Duck at the Foto Hut and then suddenly he was here.

He also didn't understand *who* he was. He knew he was Kenny Price, who lived at 13602 Searles Street with Brutus and his parents. But he didn't feel like himself. He felt...partial. Like the time he had a fever and he had dreams while he was awake. Everything about how he felt and where he was terrified him.

He thought he'd heard his father, or at least felt that his father had been somewhere just past what he could see. He'd cried out to him to come get him, to make him safe. But then the feeling disappeared, and he was all alone in the center of this canyon.

Then he sensed other presences out in the raging storm.

They came close enough to see, flying by in the driving sleet. People. Or almost people. Phantoms of their former selves, translucent ghosts of men, women, and children. All wore what looked like gauzy nightshirts, stained and ragged. They swirled closer to Kenny, then farther away in a great whorl of tortured spirits. Each of them had a wail that waxed and waned as they came closer and moved farther away.

When they swept past him, he could catch glimpses of their faces. Wan and wasted, decayed and diseased. All of them seemed to be rotting away.

Two giant red eyes blinked into existence over Kenny's head. The spirits scattered like minnows at a heron's approach. A fresh sheet of sleet lashed at Kenny. A smell like skunk and rotten eggs filled the air.

This creature with the red eyes said nothing. It didn't have to. Kenny knew it was the master of this horrific realm, the one who chose what spirit lived and what spirit was consumed. Its malevolence made Kenny quiver.

Whatever this awful place was, Kenny knew that creature was never going to let him leave.

CHAPTER TWENTY-NINE

The ride home from Ducky World was traffic-clogged and silent.

Kenny sat in the back, uncharacteristically quiet, with his handheld game on the seat beside him. Drew's attempts to get him started talking were met with one-word answers. Anna stared out the passenger side window. She radiated anger as she tapped a finger against the armrest. She avoided all eye contact with Drew. He had a feeling eye contact would light the fuse of the emotional bomb ready to go off inside her. She didn't want to explode in front of Kenny, and Drew didn't want her to either.

He finally pulled into their driveway and shut off the car. Anna reached into her purse and pulled out her house keys. She disabled the alarm with the attached fob, then turned and handed the keys to Kenny.

"Go ahead in," she said. "Grab a snack from the pantry. Daddy and I will straighten up the car and be right in."

Normally, the freedom to select the snack of choice from the pantry was cause for celebration. But Kenny accepted the keys with no reaction. He popped open the door, slid out, and shut the door. Once the front door of the house closed behind him, Anna faced Drew.

"You need to leave," she said.

Drew was stunned. "What?"

"Leave the house. That outburst in the park was the last damn straw. Whatever combination of dealing with the criminal element all day and this newly exposed demon hunting has turned you into a person I don't want around my son."

"*Our* son," Drew corrected. "And I think you're exaggerating."

"Am I? You just ran around a theme park like a paranoid lunatic and got banned from the place. Does every father on the block get tossed out of Ducky World on their ass?"

He hadn't been acting paranoid. It wasn't paranoia when there really was a demon attacking his family. Drew was about to employ that line of defense when he saw where that would lead. He'd need to admit what had happened, that a demon had not only stalked and targeted his son, but had consumed the boy's soul. If he thought Anna was angry now, she'd be homicidal after she found that out.

"You're right," he said. "I overreacted. My demon encounter made me jump to the worst-case scenario first."

"Jesus, Drew. First you scare the hell out of Kenny about his Halloween mask. Then I find out all this demonic past and you almost get killed by one. And now you completely lose it in a kids' theme park. By this morning, I couldn't trust what you told me, now I can't trust you to even act rationally in public. You're scaring and scarring our son."

"That's not true."

"Really? Did you see him as he left the car? He's shell-shocked."

Drew's own anger was starting to simmer. "We never know what might be out there. Being sensitive to that isn't overreacting."

"You told me there'd be no more demonic crap going on. Now you're saying there might be more? No. I did not sign up for this."

"What the hell, Anna? That's not fair."

"But it's true. And I'm not going to have all the darkness you're messing with enter my house and envelop my son. Look at how he acted out in the Foto Hut. Kicking that girl when she got too close to him. He didn't learn that kind of violent response from me."

This bullshit line of attack sent his fury to full boil. There was a goddamn demon in the park sucking souls out of kids. And Drew had never shown any anger or aggression in front of Kenny. He saw enough of it on the job to be sensitive to bringing any of it home. But if he threw all that back in her face now, at the decibel level she deserved, it would only reinforce what she just accused him of.

"Fine," he said through gritted teeth.

"Tonight, you sleep on the couch. Tomorrow, take what you need and sleep anywhere else. We need a break from all this craziness."

Drew wasn't going to leave that kind of arrangement open-ended. "For a week. Then we'll make a call on what we'll do. I'm not just going to walk away from the life we've made together and I'm never walking away from Kenny."

Anna looked like she was going to protest. Instead she said, "Fine, come back next Sunday morning and we'll lay things out when I'm calmer and have had some time to do some mental sorting." She paused. "I don't want to walk away from our lives either, but I will not keep living like this."

She got out of the car and headed for the house.

Drew knew his clock had just started. He had until next Sunday to find that demon Nicobar and get his son's soul back. Anything short of that wasn't going to be enough to get Anna's forgiveness.

He was going to have to get started right away. Step one was to get a good look at that demon.

CHAPTER THIRTY

The DVR clock read 2:35 a.m. Drew rolled over on the lumpy couch. If he'd slept at all since turning out the living room lights, it sure as hell didn't feel like it.

When he'd tucked Kenny into bed that night, Drew had told him that he'd be away at work all next week, on a special operation for the LASD. Kenny accepted the revelation without any emotion. Drew could have looked at that as Kenny being old enough to understand that temporary separation was just that, or perhaps the indifference was a result of Drew's frequent moonlighting absences. What he didn't want to credit was some sort of trauma after the Nicobar encounter.

Drew got up and went to the kitchen. He considered surrendering to the idea that this was the start of his day and making coffee. But he didn't want to wake anyone else up banging around in the kitchen. He'd hit a drive-through later, on the way to setting up his temporary housing. He already knew where that would be.

He'd packed a bag after putting his son to bed. During that, Anna hadn't said a word, hadn't even stayed in the same room with him. The theme park was the breaking point, but she'd obviously been harboring resentment for a long time. He was mad at himself for not seeing it. He wanted to apologize to her, but this was not the time. She'd be more receptive to him slashing his own wrists.

His bag sat by the front door. He grabbed it on the way out and locked the door behind him. He told himself over and over that this was not the last time he'd ever walk out of his house. He had trouble believing himself.

He tossed his bag in the back seat of the car, then went to the side of the house. He'd been defenseless in the tunnel at Ducky World. He wasn't taking on a demon empty-handed again.

He went to the toolshed in the backyard. Inside he found the old tackle box. He double-checked that the manchineel box containing the demon dagger was still inside. Then he shut the tackle box, closed up the shed, and took the tackle box to the trunk of his car.

Leaving the tackle box sitting in the open in the trunk seemed a little too risky. He moved the box to the side and pulled up the trunk liner, exposing the plastic spare-tire cover. He spun off the giant wing nut that held it in place and lifted the cover. His spare had dry-rotted itself into uselessness years ago and he'd never replaced it. He put the tackle box inside the wheel well. He realized that now that it was out from the protection of the warded garden shed, a demon might be able to find it. He needed to ward the spare tire carrier, but he didn't have time to do that now. He replaced the cover, the nut, and the trunk liner, then slammed the trunk lid closed.

He took a long look at his house. All the windows were dark, Anna and Kenny likely sound asleep. How many more nights would they have like that before the loss of his soul began to have an effect on Kenny's behavior? How much faster would it happen with Nicobar leaving something in that soul's place? It depressed the crap out of Drew to drive away right now, but he had to. Not only to give Anna the space she asked for, but to give him the freedom to pursue Nicobar wherever and whenever the trail took him.

He got in the car and pulled out of the driveway.

★   ★   ★

The Starlight Motel was one of those small motels that sprang up in the post-war boom seventy years ago. The L-shaped two-story building had twenty rooms with doors facing the parking lot inside the angle. A separate office occupied the open corner of the lot. The faded star-shaped sign for the business perched atop a twenty-foot pole. In its heyday, bands of neon surrounded the star and ran through the

Starlight Motel script in the star's center. Now all that remained were the neon's black mounting holes in the logo's peeling paint.

The one-two punch of the interstate's bypass of this area and higher expectations from travelers had sent the motel down hard for the count, and now it rented rooms by the week to people one paycheck away from being homeless. They also rented rooms to the LASD. Witnesses needed a place to stay under the criminal world's radar, and accommodations didn't fly lower than this place and still remain relatively safe.

Drew went to the office to get a room. Business was done through a window that looked like a third-world bank drive-through. A pimply faced girl sat inside playing a game on her phone. The kid looked up with the dilated, glassy eyes of one completely stoned.

"Dude," she said.

"I need a room."

The kid looked around the lot through the window. "How many hours?"

Apparently, this location did an entirely different kind of late-night business the LASD was not aware of.

"A week," Drew said. He pressed his sheriff's badge against the glass. "The department has a negotiated rate."

The girl practically fell out of her chair. Her phone skittered across the floor. She tried to look coherent as she rushed Drew through the paperwork. She gave him an honest-to-god metal key on a diamond-shaped plastic tag and sent him to room 205. Drew parked his car under that room, grabbed his bag, and climbed the stairs to the balcony walkway that ran in front of the rooms. He walked to his room and slipped the key in the lock.

Some commotion erupted around the parking lot. He glanced over the balcony to see hastily dressing men and scantily clad women tumbling out of their rooms and scattering. Two men who'd look completely at home in one of LASD's jails burst out of a room with a bulging gym bag in one's hands. They jumped in a black Dodge Charger and roared away. They'd left their room door open.

The glazed-out girl at check-in had wasted no time alerting the guests of a criminal persuasion that a member of law enforcement had checked in. He didn't mind. He felt much safer knowing the untrustworthy prostitutes and the gangbangers had left the premises.

He entered his room, threw his bag on the bed, and turned on the lights.

A king-sized bed sat in the middle of the small room. The mattress had two sagging depressions where people had likely been sleeping since before phones had push buttons. An anachronistic television almost as deep as it was tall sat on a stand across the room. A single worn easy chair occupied the corner accompanied by a floor lamp. A door in the far wall led to a bathroom he was in no hurry to investigate. Everything about the place was worn-out, but it did look and smell clean. So, things could be worse.

And this stay wouldn't be for long. He'd try for a few hours' sleep. In the morning he'd call in to work and take a week of the accrued vacation his supervisor kept begging him to use. Then he'd clean up and get started hunting for his son's soul.

CHAPTER THIRTY-ONE

Consciousness announced its impending arrival. Anna pushed it away.

She relished this time of the morning, that blurry line between awake and asleep, aware enough to know she was alive, not aware enough to know the burden of living.

Until she moved, the Red Dragon remained asleep. Unlike strained muscles, which felt better after a night of rest, rheumatoid arthritis made her joints feel worse after any prolonged inactivity. Getting out of bed was usually an excruciating ordeal, and she was in no hurry to get started on it.

She opened one eye. The other half of the bed was empty. She remembered Drew's well-earned banishment to the couch last night. That brought back a rewind and fast-forward of Saturday's miserable events.

Today has to be better than yesterday, she prayed. *Please.*

The red numbers on the bedside clock read 7:04. She couldn't put off rising any longer. Time for the Dragon to raise the curtain on Anna's Theater of Pain.

She initiated a slow, painful roll to face her side of the bed.

She jolted completely awake with wide eyes and a racing pulse. Kenny stood inches from the side of her bed, staring down at her. His eyes looked lifeless.

"Kenny! You startled me. What's wrong?"

"Nothing," he said.

Kenny was never in their bedroom.

"What are you doing, then?"

"Watching you sleep."

Goose bumps erupted all along her arms. It wasn't just that what he said was creepy and out-of-character. He said it in a bizarre monotone as devoid of life as the look in his eyes.

"Go to the kitchen and have your father get you breakfast."

"He's already gone."

"At this hour? Okay, go to the kitchen anyway. I'll be right there."

Kenny's face remained impassive. "Okay, Mom."

He turned and left her bedroom. Anna took a deep breath and sat up. The Dragon belched flames into her hips and knees as she pivoted to the edge of the bed. She tucked her feet into slippers and pain exploded in her toes. She paused and exhaled hard. The idea of lying back down demanded to be taken seriously. But with Drew out of the house already, she couldn't leave Kenny to his own devices, especially with whatever was going on with him this morning. Maybe this was one of those developmental phases. Maybe it would only last a week.

She shrugged on her robe. Brutus came scrambling into the bedroom, eager to investigate the activity. He gave a little yip and then looked around the room. He made a whimpering circuit of the bed, then sat at Anna's feet with a longing expression on his furry little face.

"Drew's not in here," she said. "All you have are me and Kenny for a while."

Brutus cocked his head at her, as if waiting for an answer that better suited his needs.

Anna shuffled past him and headed for the kitchen. Each cringing step was slightly less painful than the one before. Motion didn't tame the Dragon, but it cooled its breath. She rounded the corner and winced at the morning sun streaming through the windows over the sink.

Kenny sat at the kitchen table. He had a bowl of cereal in front of him; an open gallon jug of milk stood watch beside it. A few puddles of milk pooled on the vinyl Halloween-themed tablecloth. He shoved a spoon full of Froot Loops into his mouth.

"Kenny!" Anna said.

This was not how things were done. Kenny knew that either she or his father made him breakfast, both to control what he was eating as well as to avoid the kind of mess he'd made on the kitchen table. But he looked up at her with a confused expression.

"What?"

"You know you don't make your own breakfast."

"Dad was gone and you weren't up yet and I was hungry."

"None of that makes a difference." She marched over and screwed the cap back on the milk jug. "You have to follow the rules for your own good."

"Okay." There was no repentance in his voice, no hint that he understood the concept she was trying to get across to him. It was more like he was acknowledging that he heard her.

He returned to eating his cereal. She put the milk jug back in the refrigerator. As she closed the door, she noticed the note Drew had left under one of the door magnets.

I'll be at the Starlight Motel. See you Sunday.

– D

Drew had shown her that motel once. The department used it for witnesses and such. Five-star accommodations it was not. She was about to feel sorry for Drew when she remembered how his paranoia had gotten the better of him and ruined their day at Ducky World.

Ducky World! That's why Kenny is acting so strangely. His father had a personal security meltdown, got pseudo-arrested, and thrown out of the park. The poor kid had been traumatized. His father had probably ruined Dingbat Duck for Kenny for life.

All Anna's anger over Kenny's odd behavior transformed into sympathy. She grabbed a sponge from the sink and went back to the table. She wiped up the spilled milk. Kenny finished the last of his cereal and dropped his spoon in the bowl. She took his bowl.

"How about we go ride our bikes this morning?" The Dragon would not be pleased with that plan, but Kenny loved to ride his bike. And with his little legs, she could still keep up with him on hers.

Kenny managed a smile. "Yeah, let's go."

"Let's get you in some clothes and sunscreen then."

Kenny jumped down from his chair and rushed to his room. That behavior was a little more normal, a little more animated than earlier. She breathed a sigh of relief. Maybe a normal day would deliver her a normal Kenny again.

Dealing with Drew would be a whole different thing.

CHAPTER THIRTY-TWO

Drew parked in the lot behind the Van Nuys courthouse. The vehicle inspection offices were inside and the whole building would be empty this Sunday afternoon. He left his car, unlocked the door to the vehicle inspection station, and stepped inside.

The silence struck him as bizarre. The office was always bustling with activity, printers humming, keyboards clacking, customers complaining about how the inspection violations weren't fair. But now, empty with the lights still off, the place was a tomb.

He locked the door behind him and kept the lights off. Sure as hell, someone would pull in if it looked like the place was open. He went to his desk in the corner and turned on his computer.

Through legal and some extralegal means, he'd gotten access to the LASD and the LAPD databases during his search for Lincoln's real killer. As long as he did his work from this computer and the IP address showed as one in the Van Nuys courthouse, he'd never raise any suspicions. The LASD database was a boon in identifying the potentially soulless incarcerated, and the LAPD database was great for updates on active and pre-trial cases. That latter database was where he needed to go fishing this morning.

The media had been silent on the Ducky World killing. No surprise there. In a town that lived and died on entertainment production, Dingbat Duck's parent studio and those like it held a lot of influence. It had been that way since the Silent Era and it hadn't changed since. Drew bet that the call for police assistance to the murder scene had gone through the chief of police, not 911. And the chief had sent detectives who knew how to avoid the press.

But everyone had to file reports.

Drew began a search for that report. He found it right away and opened it up.

Tristan French's body was found in the dressing room behind Dingbat Duck's photo opportunity house. His neck had been broken. And not just broken, snapped in two like he'd taken a header off a high dive into an empty pool. He certainly didn't trip in his dressing room.

There was a pretty gruesome crime scene photo. The poor guy looked about twenty. His head was turned almost 180 degrees around. It hung to one side at an unnatural angle and his neck had been twisted so hard that the skin looked like the threading on a screw.

Drew couldn't wait for the medical examiner to try to explain that one.

A smell of sulfur in the air prompted a brief evacuation of the Foto Hut until it was determined that there were no natural gas lines in the area.

The report detailed that the murderer donned the Dingbat Duck costume and interacted with multiple kids before escaping the building through the employee access tunnels. Security found the costume discarded in the tunnels. The tunnels did not have video surveillance.

No mention of a member of the LASD chasing the suspect through the tunnels or of being detained afterward. That was a pleasant surprise. Maybe the private security didn't want the first responder to this incident to have been an off-duty sheriff's deputy. Maybe they didn't want to highlight two intrusions into the backstage area instead of one. Drew didn't care about the reason as much as the result, and the result was his name was nowhere to be found.

With his ass covered, it was time to start the hunt.

Despite having no video surveillance in the tunnels, the park was chock-full of it. The file notes included a link to the theme park security server and a passcode. That would make it easier for multiple investigators to screen the saved videos at once. Drew was willing to masquerade as one of those people.

There was no way the demon could get out of the park without being on a camera somewhere. The demon would look like a normal person to everyone it passed. It would even look like a normal person to Drew on the video feeds. It was going to be a needle in a haystack, but if he was going to find his son's soul, it was better than having no needle and no haystack at all.

He pulled out the folded theme park map he'd gotten when he'd entered the park Saturday. He opened it up and laid it out on his desk. Brightly colored cartoon versions of all the attractions filled the page with the locations and streets clearly labeled. He found Dingbat's Foto Hut. The backstage area behind it was all grayed out. He put the tip of a pen on the location behind the photo shop where he estimated the tunnel entrance would have been.

Once inside, he'd turned right, which meant the tunnel ran parallel to Main Street. It ran ramrod-straight for fifty yards before it hit the stairway the demon had climbed to escape. Drew did a rough estimate on the scale-free map and moved his pen to a spot farther up the street. It was on the other side of a dead-end alley between a t-shirt shop and a faux Fifties soda shop.

Whatever clandestine route the demon Nicobar took to get backstage unobserved, it would take the fastest route to get out. As soon as the dead body was discovered, security would lock down the backstage area and the employee exits. The demon would have tried to get lost in the visitor crowd ASAP and exit through the main gate.

Near his estimated position of the tunnel exit, there was another employee door to Main Street. Drew found the camera angle that included that door. He searched until he found the time stamp that corresponded to when he'd entered the photo house. He let the video play.

The tourist crowd churned up and down the street. Strollers clogged the way, people saddled with bags full of souvenirs slogged toward the park exit. A kid licking an ice cream cone gave the scoop of vanilla an aggressive upward lick and sent it rolling out of the cone and onto the pavement. The slapstick element of the moment was hilarious. The kid's look of despair wasn't funny at all.

At one point an employee from one of the shops approached the doorway. She plugged in a code to a keypad and pulled the door open. She disappeared backstage and the door closed behind her. At least that confirmed that the door worked. Drew would give this view a little more time.

A minute later, the door opened. A middle-aged woman stepped through. She was dressed casually in jeans and a red long-sleeved shirt and carried no purse or bags. Straight, dark hair grazed the collar of her shirt. She gave the crowd a furtive glance, as if checking to see if she'd been noticed.

Drew paused the playback and squinted at the image. Sure, a demon could possess anyone who performed the summoning ritual. But he couldn't imagine this woman performing it. Was a demonic cult part of her romance book circle? Did her country club have a basement room set aside for seances? This woman couldn't be who he was looking for.

He restarted the video. The woman seemed satisfied that she'd arrived unobserved. Then she rolled her shoulders and gave her head an exultant shake as she smiled.

Drew's jaw dropped. He rewound the video a few seconds and watched again. The motion the woman made with her shoulders and head was the exact expression of self-satisfaction he'd seen the demon do earlier in the tunnel.

Was this the demon after all?

He watched her walk down Main Street without reconnecting with family members or looking in any shops. She walked off-screen and he switched to another camera feed. The woman cut through the crowd efficiently, not pushing anyone or bumping them, but at a faster clip than the group was moving. She made a beeline for the main exit.

She passed through the exit gate without acknowledging the wave of the employee there.

Drew switched to the parking lot cameras. Hundreds of cars stretched out across acres of black asphalt. But at this time of day, no one roamed the rows. The families were all inside the park waiting in lines and munching overpriced burgers. The solitary woman stood out as she entered the lot. She looked right and left to see that she was unobserved. Then she sprinted.

Demons had tremendous physical power and could move with remarkable speed. Drew had never seen one sprint any distance before. It was astounding. The demon became a blur as it ran the multi-right-angle pattern between the cars in the lot. He double-checked that he hadn't hit the fast-forward key on the viewer controls. The demon stopped at a green four-door Toyota Corolla. It got in the car and drove off.

Drew reversed the video and paused it with a rear view of the car. He zoomed in, but the license plate turned into a fog of pixels.

Dammit! Now he had to track down a middle-aged woman with a popular compact car. How hard could that be among the ten million people in Los Angeles County?

He realized there was one other bit of footage he'd like to see. He found the camera that covered the exterior of Dingbat Duck's Foto Hut. The angle put the house at the lower left corner. He called up the time frame when the world went to hell for him. It started to play and he hit pause.

There he was, clutching a paper tray full of sundaes, frozen mid-stride walking back from the ice cream shop. A stupid smile filled his face.

"You idiot," he whispered.

He thought of all the times he'd been overprotective of his son. He'd sat with Kenny in his car at the bus stop for hours waiting for the school bus to arrive. He'd kept Kenny within arm's reach all day on the beach, on guard against riptides, sharks, and predators of the human variety. Every night he'd looked in on his sleeping son before he went to bed himself, though it was impossible for any kidnapper to enter his well-alarmed house undetected. But lulled into the false sense of security the theme park worked hard to create, he'd let down his guard during the few minutes when it really mattered. Shame swelled in his chest.

He pressed play.

On-screen, his distraught wife and confused son exited the Foto Hut. He joined them. His body stiffened. He dropped the tray of sundaes and they turned into a modern art project of splatters on the street surface. He grabbed his son by the shoulders. Fear bloomed on the boy's face. His wife said something and Drew shot her an angry, dismissive look. He shook the boy again. Harder. The boy responded and Drew jumped up to enter the building.

Drew paused the video and looked at this image of himself on-screen. He had the look of a madman.

Drew slumped back in his chair. No wonder Anna was so furious. She had every right to be scared to death to share a home, let alone a bed, with someone who looked, and acted, so crazed. It was going to take a lot of work to get his family set right again.

But it was going to have to start with catching a demon who looked like the president of some PTA.

CHAPTER THIRTY-THREE

After he finished his research through the law enforcement databases, Drew returned to the supposed comfort of the Starlight Motel. He turned on the television and watched a few innings of the Dodgers game for a mental break. The hotel television painted the Astroturf infield in shifting shades of pink. The announcer sounded like he was underwater.

A knock sounded at the motel room door.

Drew jumped off the couch and grabbed his gun from the table. There was a chance the demon had tracked him down here. There was an even greater chance that someone had seen the check-in records and mistaken his room for that of some witness the Sheriff's Department was trying to keep in hiding. What there was no chance of was that room service was out there with steak and champagne. He took a position to the right of the door.

Earlier someone had shoved a flyer for pizza delivery under the door. He scooped it up and covered the peephole with it. If anyone had a gun barrel pointed at the peephole, the sudden lack of light from the other side was the cue to pull the trigger and put a bullet in the room occupant's head. He waited.

No gunshot.

He leaned over and looked out the peephole. All he got was a fish-eye view of the crappy neighborhood across the street.

Another knock sounded at the door. Drew realized it was from knee level.

Now he looked down. An older man in a wheelchair sat in front of the door. He was groomed and in clean clothes, so he probably wasn't a homeless guy looking for a handout. That still didn't mean the man wasn't dangerous.

"Who is it?" Drew said.

"My name is Greg Wolter. I'm looking for Drew Price."

Drew flipped the safety off on his pistol. He'd counted on the motel manager to value the LASD contract too much to give him up. He might have been wrong about that one.

"What do you want?" Drew said.

"I used to work with Lincoln Jordan. I think we should talk in private."

This man in the wheelchair outside knew where Drew was and knew Drew was connected to Lincoln. Drew didn't have more tightly kept secrets than those. At a minimum, Drew wanted to find out where Greg had gotten his information.

He unlocked the door and eased it open, pistol still at the ready just in case. He looked down at Greg, then right and left down the balcony. Greg was alone. Drew opened the door the rest of the way and waved Greg in with a shake of his head. Greg rolled past him and Drew slammed the door. He locked it and spun around with his pistol pointed at Greg.

"Hey man, what the hell?" Greg said.

"Call it justifiable paranoia."

"That's an oxymoron," Greg said. He raised his hands. "But feel free to search me."

Drew assessed the man's demeanor, factored in his clothes and the near-new state of the wheelchair. He concluded that the consent for the search was as good as undergoing it for this man. He snapped on the safety and tucked his pistol into the back of his waistband.

"First question," Drew said, "who are you again?"

"Greg Wolter. I live out in Westlake. I was a sound man at the studios before I retired."

"And how did you know I was here?"

"I went to your house first," Greg said. "Your wife gave me this address."

"I'm sure that was a pleasant conversation."

"'Exasperated' would be the descriptor I'd use for her. I guess you two are on the outs."

"And I guess we're not going to talk about that." Years in law enforcement made Drew deeply suspicious by default about Greg's claimed connection to Lincoln. "If you knew Lincoln, what was the name of his car?"

"Gabriella. And honestly, the relationship there was borderline obsessive."

"People get attached to their Mustangs."

"It was a Chevelle. Are we done with the pop quiz?"

Drew dialed down his blaring distrust to background noise. "When you said you worked with Lincoln, you worked with him doing what?"

"Hunting demons."

"You know about that?" Drew said.

"One of the few who do. I'm like you. I have demon sight and see them as their true, terrifying selves."

There was an emancipating relief in hearing that there was another person in the world who shared his gift/curse. There had to be others, since Lincoln was aware that people like Drew existed, but Drew had never met one. He didn't really realize how alone that had made him feel until just now, when he no longer was.

"How did your partnership work?" Drew asked.

"I'd identify a demon for Lincoln, or he'd track one down based on his observations and information from the soulless. I'd make the final confirmation when we confronted it. Then he'd go in with the demon dagger and send the thing back to Hell. I rationalized that it was easier for him to confront the demon because he couldn't really see what it looked like. The damn things are terrifying."

"You've got that right. Who explained having demon sight to you?"

"My grandmother. She'd grown up in Eastern Europe. She was Romani. She had a book with a dead-on drawing of a demon in it. I started talking to her and it all came out. She said I had what they called 'the devil's eye' and it was revered in the old days."

"Nowadays, telling people you see demons would get you committed," Drew said. "When did you first meet Lincoln?"

"It was back in the late 1980s and I'm still working at the studio. I can see that this talent agent is possessed by a demon. The agent sure seems to always find fresh faces who skyrocket. I know that it must be making deals for souls. I figure any new prey needs to be warned, you know, before they make a deal.

"It hosts these blowout parties at his Hollywood Hills mansion where all the people desperate to be discovered come to meet it. The demon holds court in a big chair near the shallow end of a pool in the back. I slip past its security, cut a gap in the fence, and find my way onto the grounds. I set up in the bushes nearby the pool. I was a sound tech, so I had some good equipment to listen at a distance."

Drew assumed Greg could also walk back then, but he wasn't going to ask about it.

"All night," Greg said, "the demon's assistants rotate the potential victims up for review. The lighting isn't the best at night, so it's hard for me to tell if the assistants are shadowless and soulless and know what they're doing, or if they're just normals who think the agent is on the hunt for easy sex. Either way, I figure they're scum.

"I watch who's there, listen for an offer. A redheaded aspiring actress seems to be the one it picks. The party winds down and the demon tells her to wait for it inside. She probably thinks it's going to bed her. But I know better. There's only one thing demons want, and a one-nighter isn't it.

"So the agent is alone by the pool and I pick up noise from the other side of the yard on my headphones. A young Black man with a dagger sprints out of the shadows toward the agent. I figure maybe it's a robbery, or a pissed-off boyfriend, who knows what. But I do know that against a demon, this guy has no chance. No one would. According to my grandmother, you couldn't kill a demon.

"But as the guy closes on the demon, the dagger in his hand starts to glow. I've got no clue what that is, but it sure looks like he's brought something special to the party.

"The demon spots him and rises from its chair. It assumes a kind of crouch, ready to fend off the attack. The demon isn't afraid. Maybe it doesn't think the blade is a danger, maybe it doesn't think the guy wielding it is.

"When he's just a few feet away, the guy, who I later learn is Lincoln, throws angel's breath at the demon."

"What's angel's breath?" Drew said.

"A combination of herbs and some other repulsive things, like the mixture my grandmother told me they used to rub into doorways to ward off evil spirits."

Lincoln had never mentioned that little trick to Drew. Of course, he never mentioned Greg, either. He wished he'd had some angel's breath up his sleeve when he'd fought it out with Carrera.

"The angel's breath hits the thing in the chest," Greg continued, "and releases a big puff of smoke. The demon screams, drops to its knees, and starts trying to wipe the mixture off its chest.

"That distraction gives Lincoln the chance to get in close enough to use the dagger. But the demon is distracted, not incapacitated. The two start fighting, with the demon on defense as Lincoln tries to get the blade into it.

"But then I pick up another sound from the front of the building. The demon's scream has alerted its security. One of the men is on the way around the house to the pool area. If he gets to the pool before Lincoln lands the killing strike, the guard will just shoot him dead.

"I look over and the fight with the demon is even, at best. The glowing blade looks like it's given Lincoln some extra strength, but the demon is wicked powerful. I hear footsteps on the pavement coming closer at a run. I have to do something.

"Just as the security guard approaches where I'm hidden, I jump up from the bushes. My mic is on a boom and I swing it around and slam the guy square in the Adam's apple. He cries out and drops to the ground choking.

"His shout distracts the demon for a split second, but that's enough for Lincoln. He finds an opening and drives the dagger into the demon's chest. The demon screeches and falls back to the ground. Then, and this almost makes me puke, Lincoln uses the glowing dagger to cut the demon's heart out. He throws it aside, and then the heart and corpse glow red and melt into the ground.

"I'm so pumped on adrenaline that I can barely process what I just saw. But I can hear in my headphones that the rest of the security team has been alerted and is on their way to the pool, where Lincoln is standing over where the corpse vanished. The dagger has stopped glowing.

"I dash past the gasping guard and shout for Lincoln that security is coming and to follow me. Later he told me he reacted more on instinct than reason when he trusted some complete stranger in bulky headphones. We ran for the gap in the fence I'd cut, and we escaped while the security team searched the property for the employer they would never find. And that began our partnership."

"Lincoln never mentioned you to me," Drew said.

"But he told me all about you. We used the places you'd told him you'd seen demons as new hunting grounds. We damn near bought it a few times, but we took the demon population way down."

"I wondered why my sightings went to zero soon after I started meeting with Lincoln," Drew said. "I wish he'd told me what the two of you were doing."

"He wanted to keep what we did from you, because he knew you'd demand to be part of it."

"He had that right."

"And he knew you weren't ready at your age," Greg said.

"He probably had that right as well. You know that a demon killed him?"

"Are you kidding? I was there when it happened."

CHAPTER THIRTY-FOUR

Greg's admission shocked Drew. He'd long ago given up ever finding out the details of Lincoln's death.

"Can you tell me about it?" Drew said.

"That morning," Greg said, "we're in Lincoln's house. Lincoln is all excited about this USC professor he thinks can help us with our demon research. We talk about her a bit, then start going over what we thought you should learn that afternoon. Your education was much more organized than you might have thought."

"Apparently."

"I am also delivering something I'd acquired through my grandmother's contacts back in Europe, the Lance of Vladimir."

"What was that?"

"Reportedly, the nuclear weapon of demon killing. The head of a lance from the fifteenth century. The lore said it would dispatch archdemons, the most powerful ones."

"Lincoln never mentioned that weapon to me," Drew said, "or archdemons for that matter. Add in angel's breath, and there were a hell of a lot of important things Lincoln hadn't told me about."

"He would have, when you were ready. But his time was cut short." Greg returned to his story. "Lincoln tells me that he'd scared off someone who'd broken into the garage the previous night. He'd spooked him before he'd stolen anything, didn't get a good look at whoever it had been. But that had set him on edge, because his place was in a decent neighborhood back then. That's why he called you to postpone your meeting by a day."

Drew nodded, remembering the message on his phone.

"So we're talking over the plan for your training when he sees someone pass by outside the window. He thinks it's maybe the same guy trying to break in again. He goes to check the garage, and I go to the front door and step outside.

"I walk around the yard and I get this whiff of sulfur. I go instantly to high alert because that means demon. I turn to warn Lincoln and I'm face-to-face with the biggest demon I've ever seen. It has horns that meet on the top of its head and the stubs of wings poking from its shoulder blades. The thing is an archdemon."

That gave Drew a chill. Nicobar must be an archdemon.

"Before I can shout out a warning," Greg continued, "the thing swats me and sends me flying into the side of the house. I hit my head hard enough to see stars. When I get coherent, the front door is open. I have to go in after Lincoln. The Lance of Vladimir is still on me, so I pull it out and rush in through the door. Sure enough, Lincoln is locked in hand-to-hand with the archdemon in the garage. The demon trap isn't doing a thing."

"The person who broke into the garage must have found the demon trap and wiped away a section of it," Drew said.

"He was probably a soulless human compelled to break in to stack the deck against Lincoln. Anyway, the fight is trashing Gabriella, so I know that's just adding to Lincoln's fury. I watch Lincoln score hit after hit with the demon dagger. But the dagger wounds are barely slowing this archdemon down. The wounds are healing in moments. So, I charge in with the lance. Remember, Lincoln is the fighter, not me. I try to plunge the lance into the demon, but it moves and all I do is graze the thing. But that slash makes a hell of an impression. The thing roars and charges me. I retreat back to the kitchen. It follows me with Lincoln right behind it.

"I'll admit, I'm in full panic mode at this point. I swing the lance point at the demon and miss. It backhands me across the kitchen so hard that I fly into the refrigerator and dent the door. I hear something crunch in my back and the pain is excruciating. I drop to the ground and my feet feel numb.

"The thing laughs and turns back to Lincoln. Lincoln doesn't stand a chance. The demon doesn't want to kill him, it wants to *destroy* him. It pounces on him and literally tears him apart."

"I saw the aftermath the next day," Drew said.

"I'm so sorry you had to. When the demon finishes, it turns on me. I'm not even sure that I can stand up. I'm shaking and panic-stricken. It reaches down and grabs my shoulders. I still have the lance point in my hand but I'd fallen in such a way that I'm lying on it. As soon as the demon lifts me up, I drive the point into its chest. It wails and drops me. It staggers one step back and grabs the end of the lance with both hands to pull it out. But it cries out and releases it, like the lance point was white-hot to it. It drops to the ground.

"Every demon I watched Lincoln send back to Hell had to have its heart cut out. I assume an archdemon is no different. I crawl over to it and do the deed. Oh my god, it's so disgusting. But once I do, the demon takes on a red glow, and melts down into the ground. It leaves nothing behind but the lance point."

"That explains how Lincoln ended up like I found him and why the refrigerator was crushed."

"And so was my back. I can barely feel my feet. I can't have the police find me there. I'd have no explanation for how Lincoln died and they would just assume I killed him after he injured me in the fight. I have to get out of there.

"I crawl out of the house and back to my car. I can barely drive with the pain in my back, and my half-numb feet. I go to the nearest hospital, tell them I fell out of a tree. A few X-rays later they tell me I have shattered vertebrae and they need to operate. Turns out the bone fragments did some nerve damage. I could barely walk. Still can't much, so I use the wheelchair."

"Why didn't you get in touch with me then?" Drew said.

"I had enough physical issues with my spine and mental issues with what happened at Lincoln's house to keep me occupied. The archdemon was sent back to Hell, so what were you going to do about it anyway?"

Drew would have liked a little closure about Lincoln's death, but he understood that Greg's priorities were elsewhere.

"So why did you contact me now?"

"I saw that archdemon in MacArthur Park. If it's back, it needs to be stopped. You were the only person I knew with the demon sight and who might still have the skills to stop it, as long as you remembered all that Lincoln taught you."

"I don't just remember it, I've done it. I killed a demon with the same demon blade that Lincoln used."

"That's a relief," Greg said. "I was worried you'd never followed through on what he taught you. But an archdemon is something tougher. It's larger, stronger. The head is huge, with longer ears than normal and the two horns that curl up and over its head. The biggest difference is the torso. Much bigger, and almost see-through—"

"And you can see the consumed souls inside," Drew cut in.

"Yes! Exactly. You've seen an archdemon?"

"One stole my son's soul at Ducky World on Saturday. It told me it did it in retribution for me sending the demon Carrera back to Hell. Said its name was Nicobar."

"Oh, no." Greg collapsed in his chair. "It's already targeted you. Any element of surprise is gone."

"Well, so's my son's soul. Where's the Lance of Vladimir?"

Greg reached under the seat of his chair and pulled out a leather bundle eighteen inches long. "The Lance of Vladimir."

"You told me to search you? What if I'd found that?"

"Calculated risk that the offer to be searched would be enough, especially since the wheelchair generally gives the subconscious impression of vulnerability. You'd feel guilty searching a cripple."

"You use the word cripple?"

"Just to make people wince."

He handed the bundle to Drew. Drew unwrapped it and found what looked like the business end of a spear. The broken shaft was just a few inches long and the head was a four-bladed point of forged metal. The edges were sharp, the surface stained brown with blood.

"The legend is," Greg said, "that this was originally the tip of a spear from the army of Vlad III of Wallachia, a.k.a. Vlad the Impaler. And this spearpoint was one of the ones that earned him his moniker. But it was carried by a special contingent who hunted down witches and the like. Cloaked in spells long forgotten, this spearpoint can kill an archdemon."

"Wow."

"Yeah, all that may be crap for all I know. The point is that it will send Nicobar back to Hell lickety-split."

Drew moved it from hand to hand. "I don't feel anything from it the way I do with the demon dagger."

"It isn't active yet. No archdemon nearby."

"What is an archdemon anyway?"

"Supposedly an archangel cast out of Heaven during Lucifer's rebellion. Again, who knows. A lot of this lore might have just grown up into biblical references because that was how people framed it when the Bible was the only literature they knew. But the archdemon can ingest multiple souls, hence its greater powers. Being able to consume multiple souls means that it makes many more deals much more quickly. We don't want Nicobar to walk the Earth very long, considering what it did last time."

"Which was?"

"It ushered in the golden age of LA serial killers. Manson, Wonderland, Hillside Strangler, Freeway Killer, Zodiac, to name a few. Ever wonder why no one ever heard of serial killing and then all of a sudden Southern California has more serial killers than orange trees? Nicobar made deals aplenty. After we sent it back to Hell, no more media sensations. We don't need another wave of serial killers set loose."

"I've started to track it down, got some clues from the Dingbat Duck incident. But not many. This won't be easy."

"It never is. But at least with the lance point, you have a chance."

"So now I can send Nicobar back to Hell. How do I get it to leave my son's soul behind?"

"Umm, there's no way," Greg said. "When it comes to souls, gone is gone."

"I'm not going to accept that. I saw his soul cry out to me from within Nicobar."

Greg pondered for a moment. "I don't know. Maybe it's different with an archdemon. I know a guy, Marvin Vernon. He might be able to help. When it comes to demons, you never know how much you don't know. I'll go check with him."

"You want a ride home?" Drew said.

"I appreciate the offer, but the bus is better equipped to work with my chair than you are." He took out a pad of paper from one pocket, scribbled down his number, and gave it to Drew. "Send me all your details. We'll stay in touch and share whatever we find. I'm a little old, and a little broken, but we'll put that lance point to good use."

They shook hands and Greg wheeled himself out to the walkway. He spun around and headed for the elevator. Drew wondered if facing demons was safer than using the Starlight Motel elevator.

Drew closed the door and threw the locks. He inspected the four-bladed weapon in his hand. He needed to put this with the other demon-hunting gear in his car's spare tire well. This artifact was the ticket to send Nicobar back to Hell. Now he needed to find out how to do it without having the dying demon take his son's soul with him.

CHAPTER THIRTY-FIVE

Anna had been working from home long before it became common-place. With the unpredictability of what kind of day the Dragon would bring about, not having to sweat a Los Angeles commute each morning was a real gift. Her job was to proofread and complete the layout on training materials for a private training company. She took Kenny to the bus stop each morning, then as soon as he was safely aboard, she returned home and went to work.

This morning she was finishing a module for forklift drivers when her phone rang. It was her sister Cassandra.

"Hey, Cass."

"Oh my god, you weren't going to tell me about what happened Saturday?"

"Saturday?"

"Yeah, your whole family is, like, persona non grata at Ducky World now."

None of that had made any news as far as Anna knew. "How did you hear about that?"

"It's like all over the Ducky World community. Social media buzz was that a sheriff's deputy punched out Dingbat Duck, got nabbed by security. Then I saw the video one of the insiders posted and I was like, whoa, that's my brother-in-law."

"There's a video online?"

"It's from their security area. It's kind of blurry. But knowing it was an LASD deputy, I could tell it was Drew."

Anna was mortified that word had gotten out about the Foto Hut incident. The only good news was that if Cassandra could shut the hell up about it, it wasn't likely anyone else would ID Drew. Still, Anna needed to perform a little damage control because this was the kind of thing her sister would spread like measles.

"He didn't punch out the duck," Anna said. "He just went into the Foto Hut looking for the two of us. There was a misunderstanding, he went out the wrong door, ended up in an employee area by accident. Not a big deal at all."

"Don't tell me. He got all 'I'm a cop, I can do what I want' in their faces and it all went sideways."

"Something like that."

"I keep telling you the stats on cop divorces and you don't listen. You need to totally change your situation."

Cassandra was the kind of person who thought that Anna and Kenny leaving Drew and moving to a tent on the beach would be a great plan.

"Look, Cass, I have to finish a project this morning. I'll call you later."

She hung up before Cassandra could respond. Cassandra's last statement had ticked her off. Anna was mad at Drew, but despite demanding that he get out of the house, she wanted this separation to be temporary. She just needed him to be honest with her and she didn't want demons to be part of her life. Ever. Was that a lot to ask?

Now her sister had ticked her off and broken her concentration, which made her even angrier. She decided to start a load of laundry, then get back into her work. It was time to hold the Red Dragon at bay with some activity anyway.

She grabbed a laundry basket and began collecting dirty clothes in her bedroom. She picked up Drew's shredded uniform shirt, balled it up, and set it aside to be trashed. She went to Kenny's room, where finding dirty clothes frequently resembled a game of hide-and-seek. The kid had not mastered using a laundry basket.

She entered his room and scooped some clothing from the floor at the foot of his bed. She knelt down and looked underneath. There weren't clothes under there, but there was something.

She reached under and pulled out two stuffed animals, a bear and an elephant Kenny had for years, cute little characters from a children's book.

Both the heads had been torn off. Gray stuffing puffed from the necks like little dark clouds.

Her first thought was of her expensive shoe that Brutus had mauled the other day. This goddamn dog was turning into a problem. She could understand why the dog had hidden these two victims under the bed after she'd screamed at him about her shoe. She wondered if Brutus was going senile or something to make it attack these things.

"Brutus!" she called out.

The dog did not come. He wasn't going senile. He knew he'd done something wrong and was hiding. He was right to do that. Anna carried the decapitated stuffed animals out of the room with her. She wondered where the dog had taken the heads. She knew Kenny would be upset that these two toys were destroyed.

Kenny had behaved strangely, and now the stupid dog was acting out. Was it much of a stretch to say they were both reacting to the stress and dark emotions Drew had brought into the house?

Jesus, she thought. *Now I'm sounding like Cassandra.*

She sat at her desk and turned back to her project. Her phone rang again. She cursed and checked the incoming number. It was Kenny's school.

"Hello?"

"Ms. Price? This is Principal Lacoste. You'll need to come pick up Kenny. There's been a fight."

CHAPTER THIRTY-SIX

Once she got to the school, Anna had to ask directions to get to the principal's office. Until today she'd never even spoken to the man. She hoped he was going to help her get to the bottom of whoever attacked her son. She'd be livid if the man tried to cover it all up for some political reason.

She entered the administration area and the secretary sent her back to the principal's office.

She stepped into an office that looked nothing like the principal's offices she'd seen as a kid. A large window let in plenty of light. A minimalist desk sat in the center. It had no drawers and seemed to float off the ground on a bizarre collection of see-through legs. Shelves on the wall held copies of student textbooks as well as what looked like college texts. Several large diplomas hung on the wall behind the desk.

Pierre Lacoste sat at the desk. He looked mid-forties, with a deep tan and longish blond hair parted in the middle. He wore a blue button-down shirt open at the neck. Honestly, if Anna saw him surfing at Santa Monica he would not have looked out of place.

Kenny sat in a chair by the window. He looked up with a welcoming smile. "Hi, Mommy."

"Ms. Price," the principal said.

He came around his desk and shook her hand. "I'm sorry our first meeting has to be about a fight."

"Do you know who the boys were who attacked my son?" she said.

The principal looked confused. "I'm not sure where you got that idea. Kenny started the fight."

"Kenny?"

Anna turned to her son. He shrugged.

"I'm afraid he attacked a girl in the hall," the principal said. "Threw her down, started to punch her before the teacher pulled him away."

"That can't be," Anna said. "He's never gotten into fights."

"There were two dozen witnesses. The girl didn't do anything to provoke him. Doesn't even know him, in fact."

"Kenny?" Anna said. "Why would you want to hurt that little girl?"

"I don't know." His tone was quizzical, as if it was a mystery to him as well.

"That's about all I got from him," the principal said. "Now, I have some latitude here because he doesn't have any disciplinary history. But he is suspended for three days."

"Three days?"

All of this was spiraling out of control so quickly, and so unexpectedly, that Anna couldn't even think of what to say. This was the kind of thing that happened to someone else's kid, not her Kenny.

"Yes, that's the minimum policy requires. Has he exhibited any violent outbursts at home?"

"God, no."

"Anything changed recently at home that he might be reacting to?"

She sighed.

"Yes, his father and I are going through a rough spot. Nothing permanent, but I'm sure it's disruptive for him."

"He may be acting out in response to that. You should check with a psychologist."

"Really? Isn't that a bit drastic?"

"You might want to get ahead of things. We have a psychologist on contract." The principal handed her a business card that had been sitting on the top of his desk. "Dr. McNamara here can do a free phone consultation if you'd like."

Anna took the card in slow motion. All of this seemed so surreal. "He's never misbehaved like this before."

She realized, to her own horror, that wasn't true. There was his attack on the girl in the Ducky World Foto Hut.

"If Kenny returns and does something like this again," Principal

Lacoste said, "an evaluation will be mandatory. So will a home visit from Child Services. I'm not saying I think all that is necessary in this case. I'm just warning you what's ahead if you don't fix the root cause now."

This little meeting was a kick in the teeth for Anna. She'd always been sure she was raising her son properly. All she wanted to do now was extract Kenny and herself from this humiliating situation.

"I'll take care of it," she said. "Kenny, let's go."

"Great!" Kenny popped up from his seat and almost skipped to his mother's side.

"Thank you for keeping the suspension to three days," she said.

She walked Kenny out the door and through the admin office. She felt as if everyone there was staring at her as she passed, judging this failure of a mother, assessing her budding monster of a son. She just looked straight ahead and put her hand on Kenny's shoulder to keep him moving in the right direction. Passing out of the building to the parking lot felt like running a gauntlet.

On the way home, Anna didn't know what to say. She checked Kenny in the back seat through the rearview mirror. He watched the world pass by through the side window. His head bobbed to the music from the car radio.

"We should get ice cream on the way home," Kenny said.

"Kenny!" Anna wondered if her son had any clue how serious what he'd done was. "Why did you start hitting that girl?"

"I'd never been in a fight before. I wanted to see what it was like."

"Do you even know the girl?"

"Nope."

"Did you worry about hurting her? Think about how you'd feel if someone just started punching you for no reason?"

He gave a shrug. "I guess not."

"Hurting people is wrong. We don't do that."

"Daddy's a deputy. I see deputies on TV hurt people all the time."

Aha, she thought. *Drew is the root of this problem.*

"Deputies get into a fight as a last resort," she said, "with people who do bad things. And Daddy isn't that kind of a deputy, anyway."

The conversation didn't seem to be having any impact on Kenny. He wasn't comprehending the gravity of what he'd done.

"Your father will be back home very soon," Anna said.

"Okay."

No sadness, no happiness, no anticipation. Kenny's response was just an acknowledgement. Anna wondered how deep Kenny was burying the impact of Drew's recent bizarre behavior, and how long it would take to get her son to talk through the problems that were making him act out.

She was going to have to warn Kenny that Brutus had shredded his stuffed animals, but now sure as hell wasn't the time. Maybe he wouldn't notice they were gone. She already had enough on her plate. She couldn't help but think that if her husband hadn't started chasing demons, none of this would have happened.

"So, are we getting ice cream?" Kenny said.

CHAPTER THIRTY-SEVEN

Greg Wolter rolled his wheelchair up the ramp and stopped at his apartment's front door. Every day he gave thanks for the Boy Scout who decided that this ramp was going to be his ticket to making Eagle Scout. He unlocked the door, entered, and relocked it behind him. He sighed with relief.

From the moment he'd spotted Nicobar, dread had consumed him. He knew exactly what it meant to have this archdemon walking the streets of LA. He also knew that from this wheelchair, there was nothing he was going to do to stop him alone. But he'd found Drew and passed the baton to the next runner. Or only runner in this case. Greg had been so afraid that he'd need to try and face Nicobar alone.

He parked the wheelchair beside two cuffed metal crutches leaning against the wall. The doctors had told him that if he didn't work his legs and feet each day, however miserable the experience might be, he'd soon not be able to use them at all. So once he returned to the apartment, it was up and out of the chair to hobble around.

He made his way across the tile floor to the kitchen. He thought there was cake in the refrigerator that he could use to celebrate the day.

In front of the refrigerator, he stopped and balanced on one crutch. Halfway through his reach to pop open the door, he paused. Something stank. A lot like a rotten egg. A lot like…sulfur.

Hot breath brushed against the back of his neck.

His heart leapt into his throat. He whirled around and was face-to-face with Nicobar. The archdemon's glowing eyes locked on his eyes like twin laser beams. Charred skin peeled from its face in repulsive strips.

"Greg." Nicobar exhaled Greg's name with a sadistic smile. "Long time. No see."

In a flash, Nicobar sent one of the claws on its left hand plunging into Greg's right eye socket. With a snap of its wrist, it sent the eyeball popping out of Greg's head. Pain like having a steel spike pounded into his skull sent Greg screaming. Blood ran down his face. He dropped one crutch and reached up with that hand to stop the flow.

With a karate-chop motion, Nicobar sent the other crutch sailing across the apartment. Greg collapsed on the floor face-first. His front tooth chipped and a new, sharper pain lanced his head.

Greg started to pull himself across the floor, dragging his weak legs. Nicobar straddled him, with one blackened leg on either side of Greg's waist. Greg could see the shadows and ripples of the souls churning around inside Nicobar's broad chest. The oppressive smell like carrion and burned hair threatened to suffocate him. Nicobar bent down and spoke in Greg's ear. Its voice sounded like the roar of a firestorm.

"While I was suffering the eternal torments of Hell, images of your death filled my thoughts. So as soon as I escaped again, guess who I couldn't wait to come visit?"

Nicobar drove a fist down into Greg's back. His age-weakened bones crushed into pebbles. Greg's chest slammed into the floor and the pressure collapsed his lungs.

"Why, it was you," Nicobar said, "you pathetic human piece of shit. Now don't you feel special?"

Greg wheezed as he struggled to pull some air back into his deflated lungs. Nicobar grabbed his shoulder and flipped him over like a steak on a grill. Tiny red sparks flitted through the skin exposed beneath the peeling flaps of Nicobar's skin. It smiled to reveal a thick, black, forked tongue. Face-to-face with the demon, Greg shuddered with overwhelming terror.

"I'd offer you a deal," Nicobar said. "Trade your soul for access to a surgeon who can fix your legs, maybe set you up with a hot actress. Except that you sent me back to Hell."

It slashed Greg's chest with a claw. The wound felt like acid eating into his skin. Greg moaned, shocked that his body could still register new pain.

"I killed Lincoln for slaying my demons," Nicobar said. "You barely escaped the same fate, but I'm about to fix that. Every second between now and when you tell me where the Lance of Vladimir is will be spent in excruciating torment. That can be one second if you tell me now, it could be days if you try to hold out."

Greg knew he would soon be dead, unable to help Drew send this abomination back to Hell. One long-shot idea came to mind. Nicobar held many souls. If, as Greg died, he tried to—

Nicobar grabbed the index finger of Greg's left hand and broke Greg's concentration. With a quick twist the finger tore free. Greg screamed at this new current of agony from his hand. Nicobar tossed the finger into its mouth and gulped it down. It smiled again.

"Take your time," it said. "I literally have all eternity to entertain myself."

★   ★   ★

An hour later, Nicobar set down one of Greg's limbs. The demon nudged it into place with a claw. If memory served, and it certainly did, the limb was now in the exact position it should be.

To the human's credit, he didn't give up the location of the lance. Even a master of torture couldn't shake that fact loose from him.

But it hadn't been a total loss. Revenge had been exacted. And what Nicobar had just left on display in this apartment would send another reminder to Drew that his favorite archdemon was still up for fun and games.

CHAPTER THIRTY-EIGHT

Drew didn't need his special access to law enforcement records to find out that Greg had been killed. The story headlined the local news.

A neighbor in the old man's apartment complex had seen his door open and went inside. He'd found Greg murdered in his own kitchen. The body had been dismembered.

A horrid death in Los Angeles didn't automatically send Drew in search of a demon. But in this instance, he assumed it. There was no way Greg had human enemies ruthless enough to chop him up and then take no steps to cover up the crime.

The media's mini-obituary stated that the former sound technician had been wheelchair-bound since an accident in the 1990s. It said after retiring, he had become a 'fixture' in MacArthur Park, where he fed the birds every day.

There was no mention of his history of demon hunting. Of course.

The article stated that the police were asking any witnesses to come forward with tips. Drew wondered if demons left behind DNA and if so, how the forensics people would interpret it.

It didn't take him much searching to find some crime scene photos. The press wasn't publishing any of the gory pictures, but they were out there on the internet already. The neighbor who found the body denied having taken them, but the shots weren't professional enough to have been taken by the LAPD.

As he looked over the pictures, his blood ran cold.

The scene was a near-perfect match for how Nicobar had left Lincoln's body decades ago. Down to a knife gripped in the hand of a severed arm.

Drew sat back from his computer, closed his eyes, and took a deep breath. He had to rationally sort this out. Nicobar went there to avenge Greg sending it back to Hell. It would have been looking for the Lance of Vladimir so no one could ever do that again. Nicobar couldn't know that Greg had already given it to Drew. And no matter what Nicobar had done to him, Greg hadn't revealed the lance's location. Otherwise, Nicobar would have already burst into Drew's hotel room to retrieve it.

Unless Nicobar had gone straight to the lance's hiding place.

Drew jumped up and rushed out of his room. He popped the trunk of the car with his remote and by the time he stood beside it, it was wide open. He brushed some trash aside and pulled up the trunk liner, exposing the plastic tire well cover. The big wing nut that held it in place was still there. That was a good sign. Nicobar wouldn't have replaced it.

Or maybe it would.

Drew spun it off and threw the lid up.

Everything was still there. The notebooks, the tackle box, the manchineel box, and the leather bundle that contained the Lance of Vladimir. He even picked up the bundle to make sure he could feel the weight of the artifact within. Still nice and heavy.

He put the covers and liners back in place and closed the trunk. Still possessing the means to kill Nicobar was a relief, if it was really possible to feel relief with an archdemon walking the streets of LA.

He needed to find where the demon was holed up, and take the fight to it.

He had a good idea where to start.

★　★　★

That morning, Drew went over to Twin Towers Correctional. He'd opted for street clothes instead of his uniform. He wanted to keep this visit as low-profile as possible.

With LASD access, he could get into inmate files the public could not see. He checked through recent incarcerations for anyone who'd been referred to a psychiatrist after mentioning demons or soul snatching. Then he filtered for a background that included a particularly lucky break in the recent past. The severity of the crime was immaterial. The newly converted might do something minor, the longer-term soulless might have worked up to murder.

His research had yielded Alexi Novotney. Novotney was in for DUI manslaughter while on parole from a grand theft auto conviction. By itself that wasn't suspicious, except that Novotney was driving a new Ford GT, a quarter-million-dollar limited edition sports car, and it wasn't stolen. He'd legally won it in a Van Nuys dealership raffle. For a hard-luck, two-time felon in and out of custody since he was a juvenile, that stroke of splendid fortune was too good to be true.

The report from the arresting officer said that when Novotney had been pulled out of the car drunk, he'd told the officer he couldn't be arrested. He was under the protection of an archdemon and that Novotney was the demon's faithful servant. Later, when talking to the state's psychiatrist, Novotney blamed the alcohol for that outburst. The shrink believed him.

Drew didn't.

Drew checked in at Twin Towers and got an escort back to a secure area used for certain low-risk visits. The gray-walled room had no windows. A half dozen plastic tables and chairs dotted the floor. Novotney was the kind of nonviolent offender the jail would let use this room. Drew took a seat.

A guard led Novotney in. He wore a shapeless orange jumpsuit and his hands were shackled in front of him. Being low-threat wasn't the same as no-threat. And that was fine with Drew.

Novotney had a lean face, a hooked nose, and thick, long black hair. If he let his beard grow a half dozen inches longer, Drew could see him cast as a Svengali in some film. He double-checked the floor as Novotney's guard guided him to the table.

Novotney cast no shadow.

The guard sat him down across from Drew and then stood off to the side.

"I'm Drew Price."

Novotney slumped down in the seat. "Why do I care?"

"You told the police you were a servant of an archdemon when you were arrested."

"Yeah, I was so wasted, I didn't know what I was saying."

"You were saying the truth. I know that you sold your soul to that demon in exchange for some unbelievable luck."

Novotney sat back up straight. "I don't know what you mean."

"I mean that a demon who looks like a soccer mom made you an offer you couldn't refuse. Her perfume might have smelled like rotten eggs and burned skin."

Now Novotney looked scared. "Did she send you?"

"No. I'm trying to hunt her down."

"Well, you sure as shit aren't getting any help from me."

"I have connections with the LASD. I can help you out on the inside, make sure things go easier on you."

Drew had no intention of doing anything so illegal, but lying to a soulless felon didn't seem like anything to feel guilty about.

"Ain't nothing you can offer me. I'll be out of here soon enough. I'm protected."

"By...Nicobar?"

Novotney shrugged. "You said that, not me."

"That's not how a deal with a demon works. One soul, one payback. The damn thing's not on some retainer for you forever."

"Seriously, I don't know what you're talking about, all this crazy demon shit."

"You're in jail. Do you need more proof that Nicobar doesn't care what happens to you?"

"Awaiting trial, not convicted. This is a loyalty test. You're just a part of it. Tell her I passed with flying colors."

Drew couldn't believe how stupid some people were.

"Tell me where it approached you. I need to find it to save my son."

"Dude, you're just sounding crazy." He called over his shoulder. "Guard! I'm done here."

The guard walked over and escorted him from the table. They stopped at the door to the secure area and the guard called for the door to be opened.

"You tell her I passed the test," Novotney said to Drew. "All loyal, so come get me out of here."

A buzzer sounded. The guard led Novotney out of the room and the door slammed behind them with a thud and a click of the lock. As they disappeared, so did Drew's best hope at finding Nicobar. Drew could practically feel his son's soul slip further away.

CHAPTER THIRTY-NINE

Anna resolved that this second day of Kenny's suspension from school would be more regimented than the first.

Yesterday, when they got home, she'd sent him to his room and confined him there with no access to any electronics for the day. She thought that would be a splendidly draconian punishment. She checked on him a few times through the day, listening at the door. Once she heard him playing with his toys, the other times it was very quiet.

While he was under lock and key, she went on a search for answers. The poorly named site kiddiepsych.com actually seemed to have some well-documented information.

It said that kids under stress did not understand what they were experiencing and did not have the right coping mechanisms to deal with it. There was a list of possible responses a parent might see: sullenness, being uncommunicative, sleeplessness, expressing their fears in artwork. She cringed when she saw that picking fights was on the list. Her eyes went wide when under that, bedwetting was listed as a possible reaction. She could sure live without that.

She released him from confinement for dinner. The punishment hadn't produced a boy filled with remorse, or anger at his imprisonment. He just came out for dinner like none of it had happened at all.

If yesterday hadn't been hard enough to make suspension from school distasteful, she was going to make sure that today was.

Last night she had downloaded a bunch of assignments that Kenny's teachers had emailed her. This morning they sat in a pile on the kitchen table. As soon as Kenny finished breakfast, he would start tackling that work. Being home was about to become less fun than being in school.

She went to his room and listened at the door. Silence. He'd normally be asleep at this hour so that was good news. She steeled herself to adopt a pseudo-drill-sergeant persona and opened the door.

Kenny sat on the end of his made bed, fully dressed, staring at his closed closet doors.

Anna stopped short. Everything about this was bizarre. Kenny was awake, dressed, and had made his bed. The first two items were always a daily battle to get done. The third item he never did. There wasn't even an expectation that he might make his bed.

"Kenny?"

He looked over and up at Anna. "Mommy!"

The boy jumped up with a big smile, ran to her, and gave her a hug. For the first time ever, a hug from her son felt slightly unnerving.

"You're up and dressed," she said.

"It's time for breakfast," he said. He let her go and went to the kitchen.

Anna stood there absorbing this surreal moment. Maybe being ready early was his way of apologizing for getting suspended. Any other day, she'd have heaped praise on him, but today for some reason. it kind of creeped her out.

She was relieved that Kenny had not noticed the missing stuffed animals. Maybe he'd realized that he'd grown out of them. He hadn't said anything when she took the preschool stuff out of his room years ago.

Breakfast unfolded normally and Kenny went without complaint to the living room to start his schoolwork. He plopped down onto the couch under the gaze of a flight of plastic Halloween bat decorations. He began to read.

All of this behavior was wonderful, and it absolutely made her skin crawl.

As she was heading back to the bedroom she used as her office, she noticed Brutus making his third lap around the house, searching for Drew like Stanley on his quest for Livingstone.

"Yeah, it wouldn't hurt for him to be here now," Anna told the dog. "You could calm down and Kenny could stop acting out."

She hoped that Drew was getting his head together and his priorities sorted into the right order. She wanted the Drew she'd first married back in this house.

After a few hours of work, she took a break for some coffee to keep her awake and a little movement to keep the Red Dragon asleep. She looked in on Kenny first. She stuck her head in the living room and saw him lying on the couch asleep. Some half-finished worksheets were on the coffee table. She'd give him another fifteen minutes, then get him up and back to work.

She went to the kitchen and got a pot of coffee brewing. A glance into the laundry room reminded her that yesterday's clean clothes were still in a basket. A little folding and putting in drawers would be a good mental break while the coffee brewed.

Her first stop was Kenny's room. The freshly made bed made her smile. If that was his way of trying to make up for being suspended, good for him. Anna's mother had elevated bed making to an artform, and made a point of raising her daughter with the same appreciation. Anna made a note to commend Kenny for it and reinforce that act. He was the same age as she'd been when she took on that responsibility.

She plopped the laundry basket on the bed and noticed the perfect alignment of the comforter pattern with the mattress corner. That had been one of the signature touches her mother had taught her. Coincidental that Kenny had done the same thing.

She checked under the pillow. All the sheets were still tucked in tight without a wrinkle. She doubted Kenny had the strength to lift the mattress and drive the sheet ends in deep enough to make that happen. The more she inspected the bed, the clearer it became that Kenny hadn't made this bed. He'd never unmade it and slept in it.

She took a deep breath. This was just another manifestation of Kenny's stress, right off the list she'd read on that internet site. Still way better than bedwetting.

She opened the bifold doors to Kenny's closet. The light was on.

All the hangers had been swept to one side. Kenny's huge box of crayons was open and a dozen of the little wax sticks lay scattered on the carpet. She caught her breath when she saw the walls.

Crayon drawings filled the bottom three feet of all the walls. Dark figures drawn with ragged, overlapping strokes. The lines were haggard, angry.

On the left was a picture of a stick figure boy with a knife in his hand. A four-legged animal lay near his feet with a scribbled red wound in its chest. Big drops of blood dripped from the knife. Imagining her son drawing the picture made her chest tight.

On the longer back wall, Kenny had created a much larger picture. In the center was a creepy figure drawn with black and orange lines. Body parts were out of proportion, as in all children's drawings, but these were bizarrely so. The creature had arms and legs inconceivably thin, with three-fingered hands that ended in what looked like claws. The creepiest part was the eyes, furious red circles drawn with such intensity that the crayon blob stood out in raised relief from the wall. Beside the figure stood the stick figure boy again, holding hands with the creature.

Behind and above the duo in the foreground lay two prone figures. One had long hair, the other short. Both had crosses for eyes and jagged lines for mouths.

Strange drawings had been on the list she'd read, but she'd envisioned doodles in a notebook, not wall-sized frescoes. And certainly nothing this bizarre.

"Kenny!" Anna called over her shoulder. "Come in here."

Brutus's toenails clicked on the hallway tiles. The dog trotted through the doorway and looked into the open closet. He whimpered and dashed back out of the room.

Moments later Kenny stepped into the bedroom. He rubbed his sleepy eyes and then smiled. "Yes, Mommy?"

He wasn't the least bit fazed that his closet artwork was on display.

"What is all this?" she said.

"Drawings I made. Do you like them?"

No, they scare the crap out of me, she thought.

She pointed to the stick figure boy on the side wall. "What is this of?"

"A boy killing an animal." His tone bordered on condescending.

"Why is the boy killing the animal?"

"Just to see if he can." Kenny smiled with enthusiasm. "He wants to hear the screams."

Goose bumps danced up Anna's arms.

"What about this picture?" she said, pointing to the back wall.

"That was a dream I had. That person took me to a new place to live." He stepped up and pointed to the two prone figures in the background. "You and Daddy were dead."

Kenny's voice held no sadness, no embarrassment at depicting his mother's demise. Just delivered as matter-of-fact as Kenny would describe the weather. Anna didn't ask how she and Drew had died. She was afraid of the answer.

"I'm sorry you had that nightmare." It was all Anna could think of to say.

"It wasn't really scary."

Anna felt guilty, and then horrified at how uneasy she suddenly was in her son's presence.

"Go back and finish your schoolwork."

"Okay, Mommy. Can I ride my bike when I'm done?"

"We'll see."

Kenny sighed and left the room

Half in shock, Anna lowered herself onto Kenny's bed. Her pulse was pounding out a beat so strong she thought she'd make the mattress vibrate. She turned to look again at the gruesome pictures on the closet walls.

How had these things come from her own son's mind? She didn't let him watch any movies or television with anything like this in it. She had his internet access so locked down that it barely worked. Were the problems between her and Drew enough to spawn this kind of horror movie artwork?

Then she remembered part of Drew's recent revelations about his past. He'd been a kid in trouble, getting into fights at school, seeing scary things other people didn't see. Maybe there was some mental defect in him that he'd passed down to Kenny.

The website symptom list could not have included something this disturbing. She had a bad feeling this situation was going to get out of hand. For a split second she considered calling Drew, then dismissed it. She'd just tossed him out. She couldn't very well call right away, admitting she couldn't handle Kenny.

She marched to her bedroom and grabbed her purse off the dresser. She fumbled around in it until she found the card that the principal had given her. It was time to talk to Dr. McNamara.

CHAPTER FORTY

Anna took her phone into her bedroom and shut the door. She went to the far corner and sat on the floor so her bed would muffle the sound if Kenny tried to eavesdrop from the hallway. She felt guilty for feeling so scared of her own son. But not enough to get up and sit on the bed.

She dialed the number on the business card. A receptionist answered and, after a brief hold, Anna was put through to Dr. McNamara.

"Hello?" His deep, bass voice reassuringly reminded her of James Earl Jones, but from *The Lion King*, not from *Star Wars*.

"Dr. McNamara, my name is Anna Price. The school said I could call you for a consultation about my son, Kenny."

"Yes, the principal had your name on a list of potential callers. Hold on." His keyboard clicked in the background and then she heard him mutter as he read through something. "Looks like a fight at school got him suspended, and that this was the first time."

"Some other things he's done have been completely out of character lately."

Anna went on to recount the early morning stare-down, his bouts of emotional detachment, his apparent insomnia.

"I can't specifically diagnose anything over the phone," Dr. McNamara said. "But these are all common childhood reactions to home stress."

So far so good, she thought.

"His father and I had a fight," Anna said, "and he's moved out for the week, so I thought it might be that."

"If fighting between the two of you isn't common, it could be exactly that."

Anna hesitated. "And there was one other thing he did. Some… well…creepy drawings."

"Also normal. What about the drawings made you uneasy?"

"First, he drew them on the walls of his closet. Second, they had some pretty scary-looking figures in them."

"Children are rarely good artists. Even their depictions of happy family scenes can seem crude and unnerving. It isn't intentional."

"Can I send you a picture of them?"

"Certainly."

He gave her a number to text them to and she sent over the pictures.

"Why would he draw a picture of a boy killing an animal?" Anna said.

"Something like this is a way for the child to express having power in a situation where they currently feel powerless. It's not about actually killing a creature, it's about shedding a sense of helplessness, about being able to take control. The animal drawing doesn't represent an animal, it represents a force threatening him."

"Or threatening the family structure?"

"Exactly."

"Okay," Anna said, "but the second one. You can't say that one isn't scary."

The doctor paused. "What did Kenny say it was a picture of?"

"A new friend who was going to take him away. That's my husband and me, dead in the background."

"Is there anyone who has offered to take him away?"

"No."

"Again, my first interpretation would be that this is allegorical rather than literal. The figures of you and your husband, because they're together, represent your marriage, not the two of you as individuals. It shows he's afraid that your marriage might be over. I'm sure he's seen that happen to friends' parents."

"Absolutely."

"So, he's drawing that some unknown person will be there to take care of him if that happens. Because he doesn't know that person, the shape is vague, the colors dark. The point is that he's drawing this as a comfort against that fear of abandonment."

"With a figure accompanying him that's that creepy?"

"Has he been introduced to any unknown, dark personalities lately, new, different people or things? It could even be in movies or television."

"No, we don't let him watch anything like that."

Then she remembered his Halloween costume this year, a tiny demon, complete with pitchfork. "You know, there's some resemblance between that figure and his Halloween costume."

"That could be part of the inspiration."

She also thought about Drew telling her his demon stories. Had Kenny overheard that, and subconsciously injected something dark into his drawing?

"And you know," Anna added, "there might be something he heard us talking about privately."

"Which he'd interpret as part of the whole troubled marriage scenario."

"So, you've seen drawings like this before?"

"I've seen lots of strange drawings. I wouldn't get concerned about them just yet."

The tension eased from Anna's neck. "That's good to hear."

"Popular culture has so many parents worried that their kids are manifesting some behavior that foretells they're the next Ted Bundy, when that's virtually never true. The odds of a child being a psychopath are millions to one. The odds of having a bad day growing up are much better."

"That's also good news."

"Talk through the family situation with your son to ease his fears," the doctor said. "If in a week or so, he isn't coming around back to normal, call and make an appointment. Also call if there's anything extreme, if any of this fantasy violence starts to turn into the real thing."

"Will do, Doctor. Thank you."

"Happy to help."

Anna hung up and felt ridiculous cowering behind her bed. She stood and straightened out her shirt. Her first impression, that this was just a phase for Kenny, had been confirmed by a professional. There was more to the 'mother's intuition' thing than a lot of people gave credit for. She'd explain the family situation to Kenny in terms he could understand. By the time his school suspension was over, he'd be back on an even keel.

Best of all, she could handle this herself and wouldn't need to call Drew back to the house. She walked over and opened the bedroom door.

Kenny stood in the hallway facing her. He smiled.

Anna shuddered, startled.

"Hi, Mommy."

"Kenny? What are you doing out here?"

"Waiting to show you my worksheet." He held up a piece of paper filled with completed addition problems.

Tendrils of dread wrapped around her heart again.

"Fine," she said. "Back to the living room."

Kenny ran off ahead of her. She wondered how much he'd overheard of the conversation, or was she still letting her imagination run straight to darkness and disaster? She decided to go with the second option.

The rest of the day unfolded without any other strange behavior from Kenny. That night when she put him to bed, she decided to talk to him about Drew.

She got him into pajamas and under the covers. She was making sure he was positioned to go to sleep tonight, and she hoped that his bout of insomnia the night before would contribute to accomplishing that mission. She sat beside him on the bed.

"Kenny," she started, "I know it's tough having Daddy away right now."

"He's gone for work. He'll be back this weekend."

She couldn't tell if Kenny was mocking her by parroting back the story they'd told him, or if he actually believed it. He was smiling as he said it, but recently his smile had an artificiality to it that she could not help but interpret as sinister.

"How does Daddy being gone make you feel?"

Kenny thought for a moment. "Fine, I guess. But *you* feel bad."

"What?"

"You're all jumpy and stuff," Kenny said. "And you look at me weird."

"No, I don't. I'm just concerned about you getting suspended from school. Do you think that'll happen again?"

"No. I won't get in trouble again."

That was a different answer than saying he wouldn't get into a fight again. Maybe she was parsing a seven-year-old's semantics a bit too closely. She tucked the corner of his covers in.

"Sleep well," she said.

She stood up and noticed the bifold doors on the closet were cracked open. She stepped over and shut them tight. She wished she'd thought to scrub those horrible images off the walls today.

She left the bedroom and gave her son one last look. He lay in bed beneath the covers, staring at the ceiling. The hair on the back of her neck went straight up. She closed the door.

Anna beat a quick retreat to her bedroom and got ready for bed. One more thing had nagged her all day and she had to put that fear to rest before she could. She sat on the edge of her bed and took out her phone. She searched *child psychopaths*.

There were plenty of links. She selected one from a major university's medical school.

It said that the occurrences were exceptionally rare, just like Dr. McNamara had said. Symptoms included a lack of empathy, and no guilt or remorse for doing something wrong. If punished, the child reacted with complete indifference.

Rare or not, that dead-on description of Kenny's behavior made her ill.

It went on to say that true psychopaths had no problem hurting others to get what they wanted. And while they were callous, they could display convincing fronts of being caring or empathetic to manipulate someone else. In the true manifestations, the psychopath would kill or torture animals or people. The real proof was if they committed these crimes alone, without the pressure or reinforcement of peers. That proved their impulse to do harm came completely from within.

She could not imagine her Kenny doing any of those things. Of course, she could barely believe he'd done the drawings in his closet. She told herself that psychopaths were a fraction of a per cent of the population. Not her Kenny.

Her habit had always been to look in one last time on Kenny before turning in. Tonight she was afraid he'd still be in the exact same position as she left him, still staring at an empty spot on the ceiling. She opted not to leave her room.

And, for the first time ever, she locked her bedroom door.

CHAPTER FORTY-ONE

The next day, Drew followed the only lead Greg had given him before he'd been killed. Greg had planned on meeting a man named Marvin Vernon to get more information on archdemons. Drew needed to find Marvin.

He searched the DMV database and came up with only one Marvin Vernon. Age thirty-six. Active driver's license, active registration on a 1968 VW Beetle. The driver's license photo showed a man in his early thirties, balding, with ears about one size too large. He was a few inches shorter than Drew, but the same weight. He had no criminal record at all and there wasn't any indication as to why this particular man would have been of any help to Greg.

An hour later, Drew stood in front of Marvin's address. The houses on this street in Canoga Park were all well-maintained. The older ones, like Marvin's, were small and the garages had long ago been converted to living space. The front yard here looked positively manicured, with a circular bed of flowers in the center of putting green-quality grass. Marvin's Beetle was parked in the driveway. The cult following these old, underpowered cars enjoyed had never made sense to Drew.

Drew knocked on the screen door and waited.

"Be right there," said a voice from the other side.

Seconds later, the door opened. Drew stood face-to-face with a demon. Blackened skin peeled off a skull that oozed pus from two places. Its fiery eyes stared out from the untold depths of blackened sockets. Its mouth curled back in a semblance of a smile that revealed rows of jagged teeth.

Drew drew the demon dagger from his waistband at the small of his back. The handle turned hot and by the time he had the blade before him, it glowed bright yellow. The dagger's strength coursed through his body.

He yanked open the screen door and slashed at the demon. The blade cut its arm. It roared and retreated.

Drew pressed his advantage and jumped into the house. The spare furnishings were old and mismatched, but the place was well-kept. It looked like Marvin had taken pride in his home before this demon killed him. Drew would make sure this abomination paid.

The demon ran into the dining room. Drew followed and found the demon on the other side of the dining room table.

"That knife!" it said.

"Cuts demons like butter," Drew said. "Let me show you."

He jumped up on the table and went straight for the demon. He leapt off the other end and crashed into the creature. He pinned it against the wall and put the blade to the demon's throat.

"What did you do to Marvin Vernon?" Drew said.

"I *am* Marvin Vernon," the demon replied. "Don't kill me."

Drew paused. If there was one attribute a demon never displayed, it was submission. These things fought to the bitter end. A severed head kept biting, a crushed hand still didn't release its grip. They kept fighting with the demon blade plunged into them up to the hilt. If the demon was trying some kind of trick, Drew couldn't see what good it would do.

A mirror hung on the dining room wall. Drew looked over into it. A reversed image of him with a blade to Marvin Vernon's throat stared back at him. This thing had possessed Marvin. He pressed the blade harder against its neck. Skin sizzled along the blade's edge.

"You've possessed him. Why?"

"I didn't possess…. Wait, you think I look like a demon?"

"Just like Greg could have. That's why I know Marvin wasn't possessed. Greg wouldn't meet with him if he was."

"I am Marvin, and I'm not possessed. Stop cutting me and I'll explain it to you."

This thing was offering no resistance, though Drew knew that it could put up a hell of a fight if it wanted to. He let up on the dagger's pressure.

"Start talking," Drew said.

"Okay, first a little clarification. I'm not a demon. I'm a cambion."

"Which is?"

"The offspring of a demon and a human. My father was a demon, my mother its victim. To the whole world, I look human, except to people like Greg. And apparently you."

Drew gave Marvin a closer inspection. He did have some less than demonic physical traits. His ears were almost normal. His tongue was still black, but not forked. His right hand had four clawed fingers instead of the usual three. His left hand had the usual demonic three.

Drew took a step back and gave Marvin a little room to stand on his own. But he kept the knife at the ready.

"So how much demon are you?" Drew said.

Marvin put a hand to the slash in his arm and squeezed the charred flesh back together. "Enough that that thing in your hand hurt like hell. What is that?"

"Demon dagger. Use it to cut out a demon's heart, and the thing goes back to Hell."

"Ugh, I've heard of those. Well, if you could keep it away from me, that would be wonderful. It's the first thing that's ever hurt me. So, I'm at least that much demon. I'm stronger than the average human, but nowhere near as strong as a demon, according to Greg."

"And how do you, well, stay alive?"

"Meaning do I eat souls? No. Steak and bacon kind of man, really. And raw meat is better. I'm like the anti-vegan. You can imagine I don't eat out much."

Drew accepted that Marvin was no threat. He took another step back and returned the demon dagger to the small of his back. The power of the dagger ebbed from Drew's body, and his amped-up aggression did as well.

"Your records say you're thirty-six years old," he said. "How have you not been detected before?"

"How many people do you think there are with the demon sight? I can tell you that Greg searched his whole life and never found another."

Greg knew about Drew and hadn't told Marvin. Drew was thankful Greg had taken that extra layer of precaution.

Marvin continued. "My mother survived the attack and rape by a demon. My genetic makeup didn't mesh with hers. My birth was unbelievably difficult, and she barely survived. To everyone in the world, I looked like a human baby, but she knew I was different. She kept me away from the rest of the world, away from medical exams that might give inexplicable results."

"You've had contact with demons, though?"

"No way! They're about as open to cambions as humans are. A demon would slaughter me on sight as an abomination."

"Then how do you know about the demonic world?"

"Demons have a collective unconscious, for want of a better phrase. It's like how some animals are born knowing how to do things, but much more complicated. There's a lot of demonic history comprehension that just comes to a demon. I have a big chunk of that. Not all of it, because I'm not all demon, and some of it kind of seems like I'm reading it in a funhouse mirror, but even with that, I have a lot I share with Greg."

"You know that Greg is dead, don't you?"

Marvin froze. His demonic face was difficult to read, but Drew thought he could see distress.

"What happened?"

"Hunted down and killed by an archdemon named Nicobar."

"Nicobar?" Marvin's speech started coming rapid-fire. "Oh, that's bad. That's really bad. Demons are bad, but archdemons, they are *horrifically* bad. And wow, Greg had sent Nicobar back to Hell once. Of course it would be out for revenge."

"It's still looking for more revenge. It stole my son's soul to punish me for hunting another demon."

"Wait, it's targeted you and your family? And you came here? It might find me now if it's watching you."

"Don't worry. It didn't. You're safe. I have a weapon that will send it back to Hell."

"The Lance of Vladimir?"

"You know about that?"

"That's what Greg used before."

"And it's what I'll use again. But I want my son's soul back when Nicobar disappears."

"There's no soul to get back. Demons consume them."

"Demons do," Drew said. "But archdemons can consume and hold several souls, right?"

"True."

"Nicobar was specific when it confronted me that it was going to keep my son's soul alive for decades so I would always know he was living in a demon. That means Nicobar wouldn't be consuming it. I even saw my son's soul inside Nicobar."

"Hmm," Marvin said. "A soul in an archdemon. There might be a way to rescue it."

"How?"

"There are certain things that act as magnets for souls. A demon isn't one of them. It has to actively hold the soul as it consumes it. But if the demon returned to Hell leaving behind an unconsumed soul, it'll naturally gravitate to the strongest pull. The strongest magnet is the soul's original body. That's why it takes death to release it without a demon ripping it free. Maybe if your son's body was in the vicinity when Nicobar is dispatched, his freed soul would return."

Drew rejoiced at the possibility that Kenny would be made whole again. But he didn't like the idea of his son being anywhere near Nicobar, especially when he and the archdemon would be locked in mortal combat.

"Even if that theory worked," Marvin continued, "it's risky putting his soul back into his body. Nicobar isn't to be believed. It may have consumed part of Kenny's soul. Putting back a partial soul would make a serious mess. But even if your son's soul was still in Nicobar unconsumed, trauma may have seriously damaged it. There is no telling what you'll get back. Having a damaged soul can drive a person insane."

Drew's heart sank. A raving lunatic? Would that be better than becoming the living heartless killer a soulless person was likely to become? What the hell kind of choice was that to have to make?

"I don't see another option," Drew said.

"It's a moot point, really. What we're talking about would be nearly impossible, cornering Nicobar, piercing it with the Lance of Vladimir, all with a little boy at your side."

"It's a long shot. But it's way better than no shot, which is where I was an hour ago. You helped Greg do this kind of thing. Can I count on you to help me out?"

"That thing killed Greg," Marvin said. "And it plans on torturing your son's soul for decades. And an archdemon would hunt a cambion down for sport. So, I'm in. Let's figure out how to save your son."

CHAPTER FORTY-TWO

1995

Drew tightened the last lug nut on Gabriella's front wheel and stood up. His back creaked a bit. He kicked the rolling floor jack out from under the car.

"Ta-da!" he announced.

"Congratulations," Lincoln said from the workbench. "Now you know how to change brake pads. No point being able to make a car go if you can't make it stop."

Lincoln pulled a notepad out of the workbench drawer and flipped it open to a clean page. He began to write.

"What's that?" Drew asked.

"A record of the work done. Everything I do to the car gets written down."

"It's like Gabriella's medical records," Drew said as he stepped up to the bench.

"As I get older, I don't understand it, but time sure slips away faster. I'll swear that I just changed her oil and look at my notes here and see it was two years ago. Plus, if something with a lifetime warranty breaks, I have the installation date noted. Companies that do lifetime warranties don't count on someone actually owning a car for a lifetime."

Drew thumbed through some pages. Some of the records were from before he was born.

"There's something else I need to show you," Lincoln said.

Lincoln went to the drawer where he kept the demon-hunting tools. He opened it and pulled out a kid's school composition book, one of the ones with the cardboard covers speckled in black and white. He brought it over and tossed it on the workbench.

"Once I decided to give demons a run for their money, and started doing research, I realized that I'd never remember it all. So, just like for Gabriella, I've kept a record, a combination of a logbook and a homemade encyclopedia."

"And you did it in a schoolkid's notebook?"

"Did you expect some leather-bound book inscribed with fancy scrollwork? You watch too many horror movies. These notebooks are cheap, durable, and never attract any attention if someone sees one."

"You're right. I'd never be curious enough about it to open it."

"Well, open it now."

Drew slid the notebook closer and flipped the front cover. The first page started with a date from years ago and a location. There were some notes about a place on the coast north of Malibu, along with several names. The scrawled handwriting often passed through the blue lines on the page and there were numerous strike-throughs and corrections scribbled in the margins.

"So, this is like, a record of a demon hunt? It's a little cryptic."

"Damn, I wrote it as notes for me, not an autobiography. And yes, that was a demon I hunted. Those were names of the soulless I used to help me track it down."

Drew flipped through a few more pages. He got to some that were filled with strange designs.

"What are these?"

"Sigils. Those are marks that, when applied to a wall with the proper kind of paint, mask the people inside from a demon's senses. I have them on the walls of the house here. A demon isn't going to know whether I'm here or not, or even if I live here at all."

Drew thought that was a pretty wise precaution.

"If you need to use these someday," Lincoln said, "you know where this book is to copy them from. There's a lot of other things I've discovered written down in this book. Some of it I know is true, some of it I've proven false, some of it is still just a myth. So be careful what you rely on when you take it from this notebook. It's done chronologically so there's no organization to it. You want something, you'll need to poke around to find it."

Drew closed the book. "I'll just ask you instead, and let you go look it up."

"At some point, I won't be here. Maybe temporarily, maybe for good. Then you'll need to take everything in this drawer with you, including the notebook, and do with it the best you can."

The idea of fighting demons alone made Drew a little weak in the knees.

"That will be a long time from now," Drew said.

"I sure hope you're right."

CHAPTER FORTY-THREE

Present day

The idea of having to sneak up to his own home made Drew sick to his stomach.

But he had to retrieve something important he'd left behind, and this was not the time to start talking with Anna. She'd be in no mood for it, and he hadn't resolved his demon problems enough to deserve to begin that discussion. So, like the kind of petty burglar his fellow deputies regularly arrested, Drew had parked his car far from the house and walked to the property.

His faint hope that Anna might not be home evaporated when he saw her car in the driveway. Keeping out of the line of sight of the windows in the house, he walked up the edge of the property line and made his way to the garden shed in the back. He popped the lock open and went inside.

Drew took Lincoln's old notebook from its hiding place and brought it into the light from the open door. The years had faded the black-and-white flecked cover to shades much closer to gray. The cardboard cover had grown soft, the pages yellow and brittle.

Right after Lincoln's death, Drew had dived into the journal-cum-encyclopedia, eager to glean any facts that would help him find Lincoln's killer. But the book's byzantine lack of organization and the frequent illegibility of many entries made him so frustrated he'd given up and tucked it away. But if Greg's memory served, one of the final entries might tell Drew what Lincoln was working on just before he was murdered.

Drew flipped to the last page with an entry on it. The entry contained the words *MISSING SPANISH MISSION* in big, underlined letters. Underneath that were the words *EXORCISM PRIESTS*. Then it said *Professor Elizabeth Brawley, USC*, with a date and time to meet. That had to be who Greg had been referring to when he talked about Lincoln scheduling a meeting with a professor. The meeting date was several days after Lincoln's murder, so he hadn't made it.

Drew hoped that the old professor was still alive. He returned the Starlight Motel and sat at his laptop. A flurry of keystrokes brought up USC's website and a page listing active faculty. Elizabeth Brawley's name wasn't there.

Drew ran a broader internet search. A string of links came up that had titles with the words *mission*, *possession*, and *exorcism* in them. All were articles posted on the same website with Elizabeth Brawley's name in the title. Drew started checking links. None of them went to an active webpage. The website itself was no more. Brawley had no listed social media links. Maybe she'd died.

Drew ran a search through the DMV database. The old professor still had an active driver's license, with an address in the city. That was Drew's next stop. He hoped that Professor Brawley could remember what that broken meeting with Lincoln was supposed to be about all those years ago.

If this woman was an expert historian on Californian Spanish missions, Drew didn't want to walk in to talk to her about them in complete ignorance. He'd seen historical markers for them around the state, but never visited one or knew much about them. He found a website dedicated to their history.

A quick overview revealed that the Spanish government commissioned a string of twenty-one missions up along the California coast in the mid-1700s, while the territory was still part of the colony of Mexico. Their task was to help settle the land and to convert the Native Americans to Christianity. The Franciscan order was in charge of the missions and their coat of arms was two overlapping arms superimposed over a Christian cross. The missions spread agricultural skills, provided a place to live, and proselytized.

Drew saw that he could quickly get lost in the weeds reading all the competing assessments of whether the missions were a net positive or negative. Some certainly seemed to treat the Native Americans better than others.

After Mexico gained independence from Spain, the missions were all secularized by the new government in 1832. By the time California became part of the United States, many had vanished or been put to other uses.

Since nothing he read mentioned anything supernatural, Drew wasn't sure how the missions were linked to demons and exorcism. He hoped the professor could help him solve that mystery.

While he was hunting through Lincoln's notebook, he tried to find a reference to the demon-incapacitating powder Greg had mentioned using when they'd sent Nicobar back to Hell last time. Eventually he found a passage near the middle of the book labeled *ANGEL'S BREATH*. Lincoln noted that he'd copied it from a medieval text.

A list of ingredients followed that included oxidized iron, silver, and a host of odd plants and seeds. The instructions were to grind them with a granite mortar and pestle (Drew wasn't sure why the type of stone mattered) and to sprinkle the resulting ground-up concoction with human tears. Wrap it in a silk cloth. When the cloth hit the demon, the reaction of the materials with the demon would incapacitate it.

A healthy dose of angel's breath would certainly give Drew the chance to get in close with the lance and kill Nicobar.

Drew copied down the recipe. After he spoke to the professor, he was going to need to make a few of these.

★　★　★

Later, when Drew pulled up to the address on the professor's license, he had to double-check it. Instead of a residence, the address was a storefront occupied by an antiques shop. A spinning wheel and an old-fashioned school desk were displayed in the front window beneath a faded sign reading *YESTERDAY'S NOVELTIES*. Drew parked in the lot by the shop.

When he entered the store, the door rang an actual brass bell and creaked as it opened. He stepped inside to a scene of chaos. Antiques filled shelves on both sides of the shop. Toys and china and faded books sat jumbled side by side with no attempt at organization. More artifacts cluttered a table in the center that had been fashioned out of an old farm tiller. In one corner of the shop stood a wooden wardrobe made of dark oak. The open doors revealed a half dozen fur coats on hangers. The room smelled of dust and mold and ancient wood.

An older woman sat behind a glass counter at the rear of the store. Drew recognized the former professor from her driver's license photo. Her silver hair was cut short and her lined face spoke of years exposed to SoCal sunshine. A pair of bifocals perched on the end of her long nose as she read a thick hardcover book with time-yellowed pages. Drew went straight back to her.

"Can I help you?" Her voice had a smoker's rasp and Drew noticed nicotine stains on the fingers of her right hand.

"Professor Elizabeth Brawley?"

"Not called by that title for a very long time. Now it's just Elizabeth."

"My name is Drew Price. I wanted to talk to you about some research a friend of mine was doing twenty-five years ago. I'm trying to restart it. His name was Lincoln Jordan. I was hoping you'd remember him."

"No, can't say that I do. That was a long time ago, in another lifetime. I was still teaching at USC back then."

"You got tired of the academic environment?"

"It got tired of me. I wasn't tenured and the dean of the history department didn't like some of the things I taught."

"Such as?" Drew said.

"You wouldn't be interested."

"If they had to do with demons, I'd be very interested."

Elizabeth raised an eyebrow.

"So was Lincoln," Drew continued. "I think that was why he wanted to meet with you. He was killed before he could. By a demon."

Elizabeth closed her book and sat up facing Drew. She slid her glasses up to the top of her nose with her middle finger. "How do you know it was a demon?"

"Eyewitness account, the body was torn to pieces, the crime scene reeked of rotten eggs."

"What did the police think?" Elizabeth said.

"They thought it would be convenient to convict someone offering a false confession."

"Of course they would. The same story has been happening for hundreds of years."

"Which is why I think that Lincoln was looking for the Missing Mission."

Elizabeth smiled. "Indeed? What do you know about it?"

"Just that it's missing. The notes Lincoln left behind were worse than vague."

Elizabeth pointed to a stool by the counter. "Have a seat."

Drew settled in. He got the feeling that Elizabeth had been waiting to talk about her history theories with someone for a very long time.

"Back when the Spanish still laid claim to California," she began, "standard history says that they accelerated colonization of the area to counter threats from encroaching Russian fur traders out of Alaska. Now, let's take a look at that idea. Russians are going to set up cities all the way from the Bering Strait, down the Pacific Coast, to Baja California? This is the same Russia suffering under dismal leadership after Peter the Great dies, the Russia all tied up in Europe and China? Hardly believable.

"Plus, why would they? Alta California, as it was called back then, had almost no economic value before finding gold in 1848. That's why it was still unexploited."

"Before all the irrigation and water diversion projects," Drew said, "the state *was* pretty much a desert."

"Let's say all that conventional history is true, and the Spanish needed to counter a possible Russian military threat. Who would you send?"

"The military?"

"Absolutely. But they also send Franciscan friars. Because the threat they were countering from the north wasn't the Russians. It was demons and the soulless criminals they created. They kept showing up in Spanish cities, always from the north."

"And people just accepted that demons walked the Earth?" Drew said.

"It was a different time, with different beliefs. Witchcraft was taken for granted as being a real thing. Even veteran sailors believed in mermaids and sea monsters. So, starting in 1769, the Spanish set up a series of missions all along the coast, twenty-two in all. The missions were all positioned a day's travel apart, because no one wanted to transport a demon at night."

"Why would they be transporting demons at all?"

"Because the friars found the source of the demons who escaped Hell for Earth, and it was in what is now Los Angeles. Mission de San Uriel Arcángel was founded in 1770 in the mountainous area north-west of the city, away from farms and the local population. I believe that mission had a purpose different from all the others. Demon containment and exorcism."

Drew thought containment was possible, but he knew from Lincoln that the exorcism thing was a load of crap. "You had proof of all this?" he said.

"Did I have a signed document from the governor of Mexico authorizing a secret plot to eliminate demons from Alta California? Surprisingly, no. But there was plenty of circumstantial evidence, a lot of pieces that didn't fit the puzzle using the conventional wisdom, and a lot of Native American lore that backed me up.

"There was one pretty good piece of evidence I found. The remains of a burned book I believed to be from Mission San Uriel, a kind of ledger. It listed names, a date of arrival, a date of death, with some Latin phrases by each name. The dates ran from 1772 to 1812. I believed it was the equivalent of an inmate roster and the exorcism rituals used on each demon. Some of the rituals appeared to take months."

Drew thought that since the exorcisms didn't really work, the imprisoned demons simply starved to death without being able to consume souls. The priests wouldn't know the difference since the result would have been the same.

"That find sounds compelling."

"Other historians thought it was a hospital roster, with a list of the prayers said to each patient before they died. Missions did provide whatever crude medical care was available at the time. At any rate, none of the evidence I gathered was good enough for the academics to embrace, or even tolerate."

"So, they booted you out?"

"And blackballed me. Then I started this store. I decided if I couldn't teach history, I'd surround myself with it and pass it on to people who'd appreciate it."

"Why was the Mission San Uriel lost when the others weren't?"

"I could never find that out. An 1806 list of the missions when San Juan Capistrano was founded contains the mission. An 1817 list after the founding of San Rafael Archangel does not. At some point between those two dates, Mission San Uriel disappears."

"Maybe there was a fire."

"The mission disappears physically," Elizabeth said, "but it's also scrubbed from all the records. One theory is that the new Mexican government found out the true purpose of the mission system, and wanted to erase the one location whose anti-demonic purpose could not be denied. Maybe the secular government was embarrassed by what could be seen as superstitious nonsense."

"And the other theory?"

"Demonic containment failed. Some supernatural power from inside the mission, or even a natural disaster from outside, leveled it in one cataclysmic event. Whatever caused the mission to cease to exist, the event was abrupt, and complete. I could never find the actual site to do any archaeological investigations."

"Do you believe that people possessed by demons walk the Earth?" Drew asked.

"Absolutely. But, as I told my former colleagues, it doesn't matter if I believe it. It matters that the people running the missions believed it. We don't believe that the Greek god Apollo exists, but we don't use that to deny that the ruins of temples to him are all around the Mediterranean Sea."

Drew hoped that finding those mission ruins might give him some kind of advantage over Nicobar. "What would the mission location likely look like?"

"It would need natural access to the Los Angeles basin, like through a dry streambed in a valley, so that no overt roads would be created to give away the location. It would need enough land for several buildings and some farmland for trees and fields to help support the mission. It would need access to a lake, or a well, or enough spring runoff from snowmelt to give the mission a water source."

"Seems that a place like that would have been paved over and built on at some point over the past two hundred years."

"My fear exactly. I'm afraid that Mission San Uriel, and the answers to its mysteries, are lost forever."

CHAPTER FORTY-FOUR

An hour later, Drew returned to the Starlight Motel. Elizabeth's theories had him preoccupied throughout the drive home. The idea that demons had been roaming Southern California for so long validated what Lincoln had told him about places where the fabric was weak between here and Hell. It was a little staggering to think that Los Angeles had been a battleground for humans and demons for centuries. Even more staggering to think that the responsibility for keeping that fight going now lay on his shoulders.

As he settled into his room, a knock sounded at the door. He got up and peered through the peephole.

The sight of Marvin on the other side sent a wave of panic through him. Marvin looked human to the rest of the world, but Drew saw him as he was. It was going to take a long time for the sight of the demon-like cambion not to fill him with the same fear he'd felt as a child seeing demons. Maybe it never would. Maybe that was a good thing, because at one point soon, it would be a demon he faced, not Marvin.

He opened the door and ushered Marvin in. Marvin stepped in and gave the furnishings a sideways look. He ran a finger over the top of a chair back and then inspected it for dirt.

"Don't tell me," he said. "You moved out of your house *and* decided to atone for all your sins at the same time? What do they charge per hour for this room?"

"It's actually a much better place than it seems. It's clean and the water's hot and the towels are new."

"I'm sure that the Ritz-Carlton sends people over to take notes."

"Get serious. We need to find a lost Spanish mission," Drew said. "This history professor I met thinks the missions were set up to fight demons and the lost one was where they sent them back to Hell. Have you ever heard any of that?"

"Not a word."

"Well, she seemed credible. She said it disappeared from records between 1806 and 1817 and she was never able to find the location. If we can, maybe there's something there that can give us an edge when we take on Nicobar. Records, artifacts, who knows."

"You seriously think we can find a building that's been missing for almost two hundred years?"

"I think we have to try. She said that it was called Mission San Uriel Arcángel and it was in the mountainous region north-west of present-day Los Angeles."

Marvin shivered. "Wow, that's totally weird."

"What?"

"Okay, it's hard for me to explain to a human the demonic collective subconscious I'm tapped into. The closest I can get is saying it's like overhearing simultaneous conversations between a lot of people. There are specific facts about demons that I've learned, but there are also some vague things passed down through generations. For example, demons should shy away from silver for some reason. Another of those general rules is to stay out of the Angeles National Forest."

"A demon-slaying center would be a good reason for that. That's the general area Elizabeth mentioned. She said she never had the time to look for the ruins. Maybe we can leverage some technology she didn't have back then and find something."

Drew went to his laptop and called up a map of the area. He switched it over to the satellite view. The preserve was a series of hills and steep ravines with almost no roads.

"How would someone get to a mission built up there in the 1700s?" Marvin said.

"Elizabeth said to look for a place where mules or horses had access up a dry streambed in a valley."

The two of them pored over the map. Marvin pointed to an area in the corner on a hillside. In a sea of random vegetation, it looked like a grove of trees were lined up like soldiers on parade.

"Look at those trees growing in rows," Marvin said. "That's bizarre."

Drew zoomed in on the area as much as the application would allow. While there were large gaps in the lines, indeed it did look like there had once been a grove planted there.

"Elizabeth said the mission planted fruit trees to help keep themselves fed," Drew said. "That could be an old grove if there was a water source nearby. That looks like a stream running above that spot."

"Maybe in the spring. The rest of the year it would be bone-dry."

Drew shifted the view to the area nearby the grove. "Look right there," he said. "You can almost see two circles on the ground with barely any vegetation inside them. There's no way that's a natural way for things to grow. Those could be the remains of cisterns to catch the spring runoff."

"And you said this mission disappeared sometime between 1806 and 1817?" Marvin said. "Zoom out."

Drew zoomed out until the national forest boundaries showed up. Marvin reached over and opened a new browser window. He typed in an address and a website dedicated to California seismology came up.

"What's that?" Drew said.

"An earthquake website. It's been something I've been into forever. When, as a kid, you learn your father is a demon escaped from Hell, getting an obsession about earthquakes and volcanoes is just natural."

He called up a map that showed the dates and locations of past major earthquakes. Red dots marked each event and they made several crooked lines across the map of the state. Drew recognized many locations of famous earthquakes. San Francisco, Oakland, North Ridge.

"Older records are always suspect," Marvin said, "taken from local newspapers and such. But see how the quakes line up along faults like the San Andreas? Well, look at this one out here all by itself."

Marvin pointed to a dot north-west of Los Angeles, far from any fault line. The date on it was 1812. The location was near the spot they'd identified as possible ruins of the mission.

"So, an earthquake might have destroyed the mission?" Drew said.

"Or destroying the mission caused an earthquake."

"Sounds like we need to hike out there and take a look."

"Hike?" Marvin said. "Seriously? Do I look like the trek-through-the woods type?"

"To me, or to everyone else?"

"Oh, you are just hysterical, aren't you? Walking from my car to the beach is as much hiking as I do."

"This location isn't that far from the road," Drew said. "I think you'll enjoy it."

"That's what my mother told me about spinach."

CHAPTER FORTY-FIVE

1995

Drew and Lincoln stood beside Gabriella in Lincoln's garage.

"Sit in the driver's seat," Lincoln said.

Drew sat in Gabriella and settled in. The old vinyl felt hard and cold. "New cars have heated seats."

"New cars also have cup holders. It isn't called the drinker's seat. It's called the driver's seat. Because you're supposed to be driving. To further that point, look down near your feet."

Drew checked the bare floorboards. There were three pedals instead of the usual two.

"The left pedal controls the clutch. You press the pedal and the clutch disengages the transmission so you can shift gears."

"Why would you do that when automatic transmissions will do it for you?"

"Because the point of driving the car is to drive it. To listen to the engine and change gears when it hits the peak of the power band, to guide the vehicle to a place of optimal performance. With an automatic transmission, you let some engineer at a desk make that decision for you. Now press the clutch pedal in and move the gear shift lever into the center. Then release the clutch."

Drew pressed the clutch pedal. It took a lot of effort. He pulled the shifter back and it felt like it popped free. He wiggled the shifter back and forth and then let out the clutch.

"That's neutral," Lincoln said. "You're not in any gear. Rev the engine all you want, and the car won't go anywhere. Once she's up and running, I'll teach you how to drive a stick."

"Awesome."

"Today I'm going to teach you how to put a demon into neutral. Step out of the car and look up."

Drew got out and checked the garage ceiling. A red circle stretched from wall to wall. Inscribed within was a five-pointed star. Between each point was a symbol that looked like a cross between a Greek letter and an Egyptian hieroglyph.

"That's a demon trap," Lincoln said. "There are specific dimensions and the characters must be copied precisely. Once a demon steps inside, it can't step out, not unless the paint in the outer circle is broken."

"How does it work?"

"Like most things in the demonic world, I have no idea. But I can tell you that the paint has to be a special mixture. Oil-based, mixed with specific amounts of ground silver, berries of deadly nightshade, and human blood."

"Human blood?" Drew said.

"I recommend you volunteer to be the donor. It's not something you can easily recruit for. Once the demon steps in, it's like its transmission is in neutral. It can rev all the horsepower it wants, but it isn't going anywhere."

"Then it's easier to kill?"

"Hardly. Don't confuse being confined with being powerless. The demon is just as strong as ever. Step inside there unprepared to tangle with it, and the demon will still tear you to pieces."

"You'd think that demons would know about these traps," Drew said.

"Oh, they do. And that's the challenge. How do you get one inside a trap? The trap needs to be hidden away, under a carpet, that kind of thing. And the smaller they are, the more powerful. Cut one into a cornfield like a crop circle and it's so weak that it's useless."

"So, this one on the ceiling?"

"For emergency use if one surprises me in the garage. I can get out, but it can't."

"Great, as long as you have time to get out."

"Nothing is guaranteed. You just have to have enough layers of preparation that you hopefully have the advantage. And nothing is going to give you a better advantage than a demon trap."

CHAPTER FORTY-SIX

Present day

Angeles National Forest didn't live up to its name.

The Angeles Crest Highway snaked through the hilly preserve, often passing through narrow cuts blown through the rocky hills. Any traveler expecting trees in this national forest would be disappointed. Only scrubby desert vegetation covered the hillsides, mostly succulents and wiry bushes made to tolerate the arid climate.

Even though they were climbing higher with each twisting mile, the temperature continued to rise as the sun beat down from a clear blue sky. In the last half hour Drew and Marvin had seen three cars going in the opposite direction and been passed by a pair of apparently suicidal racing motorcyclists doing twice the speed limit. It was quite a contrast to the usual war of attrition waged on LA freeways.

"I always thought it funny how just a few miles out of overdeveloped LA you can be in such a desolate, unpopulated place," Marvin said.

"Saved from development by steep slopes and a lack of water," Drew said.

"You'd better slow down." Marvin checked his navigation app. "Our turnoff should be coming up on the right."

Moments later, Drew caught sight of a sandy turnout up ahead. He slowed and pulled off the highway. He was able to continue about fifty feet downslope before the grade got too steep and the dirt road devolved into two deep ruts. He stopped the car.

"Time to start hiking," Drew said.

Marvin didn't respond. He sat upright in the passenger seat, eyes wide.

"It's just a short walk, really," Drew said. "We can practically see the location from the car, I'm sure."

"It's not just my aversion to hiking," Marvin said. "Something feels… dark."

"Maybe your collective subconscious kicking in."

"Could be. Well, let's go get this over with and see if this is your mission."

Each of them grabbed one of the two collapsible shovels they'd brought and got out of the car. Drew used his compass app to shoot an azimuth in the direction of what he hoped was the old mission site. There was already a faint trail through the scrub in that direction. Not from recent usage, but more like a game trail that animals had used over time.

"Looks like this place might not be all that secret to the animal kingdom," Drew said.

He set out with Marvin a few steps behind him. Except for the steep downward slope, the going was relatively easy through the low scrub. The game trail meandered a bit right and left, but a few checks with the compass confirmed it still went in the right direction. The sun warmed Drew's skin and the breeze brought the sweet scent of sage with it. Under other circumstances, this would have been fun.

He kept having to pause and check on Marvin. He made slower progress, displaying whatever the opposite of sure-footed was. He really hadn't spent much time off concrete paths and beach sand.

As they closed on the potential location, Marvin moaned. Drew stopped and turned to see Marvin bent over at the waist, hands on his knees.

"What's wrong?"

"This is definitely a bad place," he said. "The collective subconscious just waved a big red warning flag. You know how you get scared standing near the edge of a cliff, because you innately know it's dangerous? That's how I feel right now."

"Maybe we're onto it, then. Can you keep going?"

Marvin straightened and took a deep breath. "I'll suck it up. Let's go."

They continued downslope and entered a checkerboard pattern of stunted trees. It looked like there had been splendid rows at one point, but now gaps yawned in the ranks where trees had died. Younger trees grew off-center between the older ones where fallen fruit had left seeds to volunteer as replacements. Weeds carpeted the ground between the trunks.

"This is what the game trail leads to," Drew said. "This stand of old fruit trees and free food. This is what we saw on the photo maps. The rest of the remains would be on the other side of what's left of this grove."

Drew led Marvin through the trees to the open space beyond. The slope here had been terraced into a level location. From eye level, it didn't look any different from the scrubby hillsides around it.

"This doesn't look at all like the aerial picture," Marvin said. The tremor in his voice implied that he was ready to admit defeat and head back.

"No, it doesn't. But we know it has to. Maybe the vegetation was growing differently in the season the picture was taken."

Drew started walking south and stubbed a toe against a rock. But it wasn't any rock. It was a cut stone, set in the ground as a foundation. An intermittent line of the blocks ran east to where they made a right-hand turn.

"Hey, check this out!"

Marvin joined him. The two followed the foundation in opposite directions. They tracked the perimeter of a building that had been about three thousand square feet.

"Some sort of something used to stand here," Marvin said.

Several charred four-by-four beams lay half-covered in dirt inside the foundation. Drew speculated that if this had been the mission, maybe it had burned down, or one of the annual California wildfires had consumed it after it had been abandoned.

He unfolded his shovel and scraped away the dirt at a spot inside of the walls. He uncovered a floor of brown ceramic tiles. Every sixth one contained a picture of two overlapping arms superimposed over a Christian cross, the same Franciscan coat of arms he'd seen on the California missions website.

"I'd say we found it," Drew said. "The main mission building."

"Then the cistern remains must be over here," Marvin said.

He stepped out of the foundation and walked across the terrace. He paused, moaned, and put his hands to his head.

"This feels much worse here," he said. "Now, not just fear. Actual pain, sickness." Marvin dropped to one knee.

Drew went to his side. "Why don't you head back?" he said. "Whatever leftover mojo is here from the Franciscans isn't doing you any favors. The half-demon part of you must be reacting to the place."

"Give me a minute to see if I can get used to it." Marvin smiled. "I mean, who knows what kind of a mess you'd make if I left you out here alone, bereft of my outdoorsman skills."

Drew patted him on the back and resumed his search. After a few minutes, he was ready to give up. Whatever circular structure the satellites had seen from the sky wasn't apparent here on the ground.

Then he noticed a set of two partially filled ditches that ran down the side of the hill. If there had been cisterns here, those were the kind of crude aqueducts that would direct spring snowmelt water into them. Both depressions led in his direction.

He looked around more closely. A ring of larger scrub surrounded him, but within it grew weeds and much smaller vegetation. From eye level outside the circle, it all looked the same, but once he was inside, he could see that something was keeping plants that needed deeper roots from growing here.

"I think I found it!"

Drew knelt down and began driving his shovel into the ground. He tossed shovelsful of dirt and sand over his shoulder and soon hit something hard. He dropped his shovel and swept away a thin layer of dirt to expose a red adobe tile. It was the buried cistern roof. He glanced over at Marvin. The cambion seemed to have recovered some and was standing a hundred feet to his left.

"This is definitely one of the cisterns here. You're probably standing in the other one."

Marvin looked around. "Maybe." He unfolded his shovel and put the spade point on the ground. He raised a foot and drove the shovel down.

The earth around him collapsed. A cloud of brown dust blew skyward, and the ground swallowed Marvin.

CHAPTER FORTY-SEVEN

Marvin bellowed from within the hole that had taken him. His cry sounded more animal than human, more pained than angry. Drew ran to the opening.

As he got closer to the hole, the ground moved beneath him, wood creaked under the earth. He froze before the collapse of whatever he was standing on could expand from where it had consumed Marvin and swallow him as well.

"Marvin?"

"Drew!"

His friend sounded weak. Marvin had told him cambion were almost indestructible, and the fall into a relatively shallow cistern should not have hurt him.

Drew dropped down to his chest and inched forward until he could pop his head over the edge of the hole. Unlike the tile that covered the other cistern, the roof of this one was simple wooden slats. Time and insects had rotted them. Jagged, splintered ends ringed the hole where the cover had collapsed. A trickle of fine soil poured through a gap between boards and into the open space like sand in an hourglass.

About eight feet down, Marvin lay sprawled on the ground in the spotlight of sunshine that came through the hole. The floor of the cistern looked like it had been carved out of the hillside bedrock. Marvin didn't look too banged-up and there wasn't any blood on the ground.

"Are you okay?" Drew called down.

"Nothing's broken, but I can't move. It's like the ground here is sucking the life out of me."

Drew peered into the shadows surrounding Marvin. As his eyes adapted, the outline of a demon trap chiseled into the floor took shape.

"Are you affected by demon traps?"

"I don't know. I never thought it was a smart idea to make one and step inside to find out."

"Well, you're in one now. This second cistern may not have been a cistern at all. Maybe this was where they held demons."

"This trap is doing more than keeping me from leaving," Marvin said. "It's pinning me here, crushing me. I can't even stand up."

With the trap a permanent part of the floor, there wasn't going to be an easy way to break it and make it powerless. "I'll come down and pull you up out of it."

"Hurry. The pressure…it's growing."

Drew scrambled away from the hole and out of the cistern circle. He needed a way down and back, and he'd have to be able to bring Marvin with him. Nothing in his car would be of any help, and it was too far away anyhow. Whatever a demon trap did to a cambion, it looked like it might turn fatal.

He thought of the charred beams in the mission building. He could stick one of those into the cistern, climb down, and then climb back out. Provided that the burned, several-hundred-year-old wood was up for the task. He grabbed his shovel and ran to the old building's foundation.

One of the beams seemed less buried than the others and looked to be long enough to extend out of the cistern from the bottom. One end stuck out of the ground, supported by a few rocks, at a thirty-degree angle. He could see an unburned bit of surface and could tell it was made of redwood. Wood didn't come much more durable. This might work.

Drew stood facing the end and dropped his shovel. He bent at the knees and wrapped both hands around the beam. He took a deep breath and lifted. The dense wood's weight made the muscles in his back sing.

The beam broke free of the dirt. Sunlight lit up a den of rattlesnakes. The snakes had slithered in using the space between the rocks and the old beam. They lay in a spaghettilike pile, a swirling mass of brown and tan scales. Drew couldn't count how many there were, but even one was more than he wanted to see. A chorus of angry rattles buzzed like the crackle of high-voltage wires.

Hissing snakes exploded out of the hole in all directions. Drew dropped the beam. It landed on a rock as one of the rattlers tried to cross it. The beam crushed the snake just past the neck and cut off the head like a clumsy guillotine.

But others had already escaped, and two were heading for Drew.

He scooped his shovel up off the ground. The lead snake rocketed across the sand, straight for Drew's leg. Drew raised the shovel and brought it down on the snake with a mighty swing.

And missed. The snake darted left as the blade plunged into the ground a fraction of an inch from its side.

Now the second snake was in striking distance. It closed on Drew and then coiled to attack. Drew yanked the shovel out of the ground and took a blind swing in the second snake's direction. It launched itself at Drew's thigh. The snake sailed over the rising blade, jaws gaping wide.

But the shovel caught it mid-flight an inch from Drew's leg. It sent the snake sailing out into the bush.

The wild swing had put Drew off balance. He flailed his arms in circles as he tried to stay upright. But he failed and dropped flat on his back.

The first snake had not given up. Drew looked up between his feet to see the serpent racing across the sandy dirt, its glistening eyes locked on his. It hissed and sprang straight at Drew's face.

On instinct, Drew blocked the snake with his left foot. The snake bit hard onto the sole of his shoe. The rest of its body whipped by past his foot and coiled around Drew's leg.

Drew shook his leg, but the snake would not, or could not, release itself from his shoe.

He clamped both feet together, pinning the snake's body between the sides of the soles of his shoes. The snake uncoiled from Drew's leg and whipped back and forth, trying to free itself from between Drew's feet. If it wriggled free, it would strike before he could get back on his feet.

He raised the shovel, gripped the handle with both hands, and flipped the blade to point straight down. With a flex of his knees, he tucked his feet closer. The snake's tail whipped up a sandstorm and the rattle slapped him across the face.

Drew drove the blade down hard between his legs. The edge caught the snake and chopped it in two. The tail went dead and dropped to the ground. The rest of the snake jerked back and forth and sent a spray of blood across Drew's chest. Hot droplets splattered his face.

Then the severed serpent went limp. Drew relaxed his legs and the snake dropped to the ground.

"Drew!" Marvin croaked from the open cistern.

Drew breathed deep and used the shovel to push himself to his feet.

"I'm coming," he called back.

He went back to the beam and pulled it free of the ground. He rested one end on his shoulder and dragged it to the edge of the cistern circle. He laid it down, and then pushed it out toward the hole. When the end extended over the hole, he stopped pushing and began a slow crawl across the weakened roof. With the extra weight of the wood on it, he had a bad feeling that he'd be tumbling into the cistern at any moment.

He crawled across the dirt. A cactus scraped against his calf and sent pricks of pain up his leg. He cursed and kept going. At the edge of the hole, he stopped and stuck his head into the opening.

"Marvin, I'm here."

"Good...." His voice was weak, his breathing labored. "Hurry."

Drew rose to his knees, angled the beam down into the cistern, and lowered it, hand over hand. Charred bits broke free with each grip of the wood, and it was all he could do to keep the beam from slipping out of his grasp. Finally, the end struck the cistern base. He maneuvered it so the corner rested in a crack in the floor. He swung his body around, and climbed down the beam.

At the bottom, Marvin lay still, his eyes closed. Drew shook him.

"Marvin, let's go."

Marvin's eyes opened. He forced a great inhalation and pushed himself off the floor. Drew grabbed him under the armpits and lifted him up. The cambion was much denser than a human the same size. There was no way Drew was going to crawl up the beam carrying him. He leaned Marvin against the beam.

"You climb and I'll push, Marvin."

Marvin nodded and began to pull himself up the beam. Drew leaned a shoulder under Marvin's butt and pushed him up. As he rose, Drew shifted to the other side of the beam and wrapped his hands around the soles of his shoes. Then, like he was curling an immensely heavy barbell, he pushed Marvin up the beam. Marvin reached the top, and pulled himself up and onto the roof. His feet still hung over the hole.

"Now crawl back to the cistern edge," Drew said.

"Crawling's all I can do right now."

Marvin's feet disappeared. Common sense told Drew to wait until the cambion was on solid ground before following him. He pulled out his phone and clicked on the flashlight app. He took a closer look at the demon trap on the floor. The chiseled pattern in the floor had been painted red, and then some sort of glossy glaze layered over that. The Franciscans weren't taking any chances here.

The cistern was maybe thirty feet across, with a ten-foot gap between the outside edge of the demon trap to the wall. He ran the flashlight around the top of the perimeter wall. There weren't any spouts to fill this space with water. It might have been dug so the workers thought they were building a second cistern, but the plan had always been for this space to hold something far more volatile than water.

A crumbled stone staircase ran up the wall in one location. The remains were so narrow that the only way a person could use it now would be if they did it with their back against the wall. A trap door at the top of the steps opened through the roof. Since neither he nor Marvin had seen it on the ground, blowing dirt must have buried it over time.

Looking up from underneath, it was easy to see why this roof was so rickety. It had been slapped together with mismatched boards and irregularly spaced timber supports. The top of the cistern wall was blackened and glazed. Had the fire that swept through the mission building burned the roof off the demon prison? Or had something in the demon prison blown the ceiling out and caught the mission building on fire? He'd never know. But whatever had happened, at one point someone had tried to make this space usable again. He wondered if they had known its original purpose.

He walked the perimeter wall. Chiseled sigils were spaced at equal intervals. These had been finished in white. Drew recognized some of them as the same ones he'd used to ward his house. The others were unfamiliar. Elizabeth Brawley would certainly be thrilled to visit this place and then throw it back in the face of her former dean. Too bad there was no way Drew was going to let that happen.

He put his phone away and climbed up the beam. He peeked over the edge to see Marvin resting against a tree far outside the demon prison circle. Drew climbed out, crawled across the groaning roof, and joined him.

"Doing better?"

"Much. The question of being affected by demon traps is answered, for sure. You want to play around over there again, you're on your own."

"I understand that," Drew said. "We've definitely rediscovered Mission San Uriel, and it was definitely built to kill demons."

"You can't guarantee that trap kills demons," Marvin said. "I'm sure that with a little more time, it would have killed me, but any demon trap might do that. I'm only part-demon, not as strong as they are."

"And an archdemon is even stronger. Still, we came out here hoping to find some clues about fighting an archdemon. I think we found something better, a place that will help us kill one."

"I don't think Nicobar will respond to an invitation to visit the pit," Marvin said.

"Nicobar needs to think coming here is its plan," Drew said. "And I have an idea about how to make that happen."

CHAPTER FORTY-EIGHT

That night, Drew sat in one of the visiting room alcoves and tapped his finger on the countertop. He had to use this room at Twin Towers to see Novotney this time since visiting hours were long over. A string he could pull being a sheriff's deputy. He came in uniform to make the visit look more official than personal.

He had the entire room to himself. He couldn't decide which was more depressing, being here all alone, or being in a room filled with strung-out girlfriends and little kids who'd never seen their father except through shatterproof glass.

A door buzzed open on the other side of the glass. A deputy brought a shackled Novotney in and sat him down in the seat opposite Drew. Novotney looked bemused. He picked up the handset and Drew followed suit.

"Well, imagine my thrilled reaction when I'm told I have another audience with Drew Price." Novotney gave Drew's uniform a once-over. "And you're an actual sheriff's deputy. Big surprise there. I was going to decline the offer of your company, but I didn't want to give up the change of scenery walking down here."

"Anything I can do to make your extended stay here more enjoyable makes me so happy," Drew said.

"I told you before, I don't know anything about your crazy demon stories. And my stay here won't be very extended."

"So, your lawyer hasn't told you about the crystal meth?"

"What meth?"

"The forensics guys found it in that Ford GT you wrecked when they started picking through it."

"Bullshit. I wasn't carrying no meth."

"Sure you were." Drew tapped the badge on his chest. "Or later today you will be. Remember those connections I told you I had? They're never above planting some evidence for the right price. And that price is low. I'll make sure there's enough there to turn this into a federal case."

Drew had no intention, or ability, to do any of that. But again, lying to a criminal like Novotney wasn't going to bother him at all.

Novotney's face paled. "You wouldn't do that."

"You know how often I already have? Now you need to do something for me and I'll forget to call my forensics pals."

"I'm still not giving up Nicobar."

"I don't want you to. Word on the street is it's offering a big reward for something it says it's lost."

"Yeah, some Lance of Vladimir thing. No one knows what the hell it's talking about."

"I do. And I'll let you collect the bounty by calling and telling Nicobar where it is."

Novotney sat back in his chair. "I'm in jail. How could I do that?"

"With one of the dozens of smuggled cell phones tucked away in there. You call and get the reward and Nicobar's renewed trust. The Ford GT never gets a second search, and you're the big winner."

"What if Nicobar doesn't act on the message?"

"It will. And I'll make sure that you collect if it doesn't."

"Hmmm. A deal that's too good to be true usually is. Especially a deal from a cop."

"Your decision," Drew said. "I have forensics on speed dial. Nicobar hasn't sprung you from local custody yet. I'm sure Nicobar will do more for you in federal."

"You think you can get a jump on Nicobar? You don't know who you're dealing with."

Actually, Drew thought, *you're the one who has no idea who you're dealing with.*

"That will be my problem, then," he said. "Deal?"

"You have a deal."

Drew gave him the latitude and longitude of the Mission San Uriel. Novotney repeated the numbers back.

"Tell Nicobar someone's going to bury the lance there for safekeeping Saturday after sundown."

"It won't be pretty for you if Nicobar catches you there with the lance."

Drew hoped it wouldn't be pretty for Nicobar.

Minutes later, Drew was back in his car outside the jail. Marvin sat in the passenger seat.

"The trap is set," Drew said.

Marvin fingered a painted wooden copy of the Lance of Vladimir sitting in the center console. "And the bait is ready. You think Nicobar will come for it?"

"It despises humans. No way it would miss the chance to destroy the only thing on Earth that can kill it."

"I hope you're right."

So did Drew.

CHAPTER FORTY-NINE

The next morning, Anna woke up and for a moment felt rested and relaxed.

Then a dark cloud of dread descended on her. She remembered she was on her third day home alone with Kenny, and she had no idea what she'd be waking up to. This needed to be a nice, normal day so she could trust sending him back to school tomorrow.

She checked the clock. The stupid dog should have already been whining at her door about breakfast. Brutus let her sleep in. Maybe the day was starting on an up note after all.

She sat up and the Red Dragon roared. Dragon's breath lit up the base of her spine. She cursed the destructive little bastard and pushed herself up on her feet.

She shuffled into the master bathroom and glanced out the window into the backyard. Golden morning sunlight lit the area beside the little patio. A big fat raccoon and two smaller versions were digging a hole in the yard.

"Son of a bitch."

The little trash pandas were becoming a community scourge. The neighbor three doors down had decided to make his cat an outdoor animal. The food bowl attracted a raccoon, and it seemed like that animal immediately invited his extended family into San Fernando. Maybe the morning wasn't starting on a high note after all. No way she was letting these giant rats think they could move in here.

She downed her morning medication and lurched to her bedroom door. The click and snap as she turned the handle reminded her that she'd set the lock last night in fear of her own son. A ripple of shame went through her heart.

She went to the back door in the kitchen and threw on a hoodie hanging there on a hook. She stuffed her feet into a pair of flip-flops on the floor. Her fingers burned under the Red Dragon's breath as she grabbed a broom from the corner. She was ready to do battle.

She headed out the door and across the patio as fast as her searing joints permitted. The three intruders had excavated themselves a decent-sized hole. They paused to look up at her. The mother looked more irritated than scared. She bared her sharp, white teeth.

"You think you're the number one badass momma?" Anna said. "Guess again."

She raised the broom and charged the three raccoons. The mother reared up on her hind legs, front paws spread wide to intimidate. When Anna did not stop, the raccoon thought better of it. She turned and began a lumbering sprint for the redwood backyard fence. The two youngsters squeaked in terror and dashed after her. The three of them scrambled up the fence and disappeared into the neighbor's yard.

Anna skidded to a stop at their little work site. The sprint had left her panting and her hip joints screaming. She bent over and tried to catch her breath. She wondered what the hell the raccoons were trying to bury.

A look in the hole made her realize they weren't burying something. They were digging it up. Something matted and black lay half-exposed in the hole.

She flipped the broom around and probed the edges of the mass with the handle's end. She wedged it under the thing and tried to lever it up out of the dirt. It resisted. With a harder push, it broke free and popped out of the hole.

Anna screamed and dropped the broom.

Brutus's corpse lay at her feet. Earth caked his fur, but a long cut from his neck to his back legs split his abdomen wide open. Glazed eyes looked at her from beneath half-closed lids. Dried blood coated his lower jaw.

An image of the animal execution scribbled on Kenny's wall flashed through Anna's memory.

In the dirt underneath where the dog had been buried lay the two severed heads of Kenny's stuffed animals.

"Hi, Mommy!" Kenny said behind her.

She spun around to see Kenny standing on the patio. Mud caked his bare feet. Dirt and grass stained his pajama bottoms all the way up to his knees. A smear of dried red blood painted over the cute monkey on the front of his pajama top. He gave her a broad smile and his little teeth looked white as bleached bone.

"Kenny." She exhaled his name and it felt like all her energy passed out with her breath. "What have you done?"

"I killed Brutus. He was old."

The smile never left her son's face. It was like he was telling her he brought home a good report card.

"I buried him where I'd buried the stuffed animal heads."

Her fear increased. Her son was a budding psychopath.

She wanted to step toward him, but the combination of Kenny's actions and his reaction absolutely repelled her. It was as if whatever was standing on the patio wasn't her son at all.

"I put the pancake mix out so we can have pancakes," he said.

Pancakes! Yeah, let's just sit down with Brutus's organs smeared on your jammies and dig into a little of Aunt Jemima's best.

"Honey, you need to get clean and dressed first. We both do. I'll meet you in the bathroom."

"Okay, Mommy."

Kenny went back inside. As Anna stepped back on the brick patio, she noticed the puddle of dried blood on the far side. One of the big knives from the wooden block on the kitchen counter lay beside it. Blood coated almost every bit of it.

She closed her eyes and rested a palm against her forehead.

Please let this be a nightmare. Please let this be a nightmare.

She reopened her eyes and the horrific reality of the last few minutes was still there. This was out of control, definitely out of *her* control.

That million-to-one shot the psychologist had talked about had come true. She'd won the lottery no parent would ever want to win.

She wasn't going to cash in this ticket alone.

Screw pride, screw principles, screw what's right or what's wrong. Anna was ready to scream from the rooftop that what she was in the midst of now was more than she could handle alone.

She was calling Drew.

CHAPTER FIFTY

Drew's phone rang. Anna's number displayed. This was her first call since he'd moved into the Starlight. He'd hoped she would, but this was just about the worst possible time for her to have done it. He contemplated letting it roll to voice mail. Then he imagined the hole that would dig him on Anna's end. She'd be so mad she'd hunt him down.

But the overriding reason to pick up was that he wanted to hear her voice.

"Hey, Anna."

"Drew, you need to come home. Now."

Her tone didn't sound like a request for permanent reconciliation. It sounded like an emergency order.

"What's wrong?"

"It's Kenny. Something's wrong with him." Anna sobbed. Tears choked her voice. "Since we fought, since you left, he's acted so strange, so wrong."

Drew's heart ached. The manifestations of Kenny losing his soul must have started. He'd hoped to have his soul returned and everything back to normal before that happened.

"Anna, we'll take care of this. I'll take care of this. I'm sure that if you keep an eye on Kenny—"

"Jesus Christ," Anna cut him off. "He killed the goddamn dog! Come home now."

She hung up.

Killed the dog? Brutus? What the hell?

Nicobar had told him it had not only taken Kenny's soul, but left a bit of evil behind in its place. If that was enough evil to kill the family pet, what more could it make Kenny do?

He dropped what he was working on and headed for his car.

A half hour later he pulled into the driveway. Anna stood in the front window, watching for him. When he pulled in, she disappeared, then came out the front door. She slammed it and the big Halloween spider on it detached and dropped onto the porch. Anna was halfway to the car by the time he opened the door to get out. She raised one hand at him.

"Don't get out."

The way she walked told him she was having a bad bout with the Red Dragon. She went around to the passenger side and got in.

"What are we doing?" Drew said.

"Close the door. I don't want to have this discussion where Kenny might hear us."

Drew eased the door closed. Anna looked awful. Crying had turned her eyes bloodshot and puffy. Her skin appeared gray and lifeless. He doubted she'd been sleeping well.

"Tell me what's going on," he said.

Anna recounted a list of horrors that had unfolded over the last few days. Kenny staring at her in bed one morning, picking a fight at school, making creepy drawings in his closet. Then she broke down as she described finding Brutus in the backyard and their son happily caked in dirt and blood.

"I bathed him," she said. "Scrubbed the blood off him, cleaned Brutus's guts from under his fingernails. He acted like it was any other bath."

Drew reached over and held Anna's hand. She gripped his tight.

"We'll get everything back to normal," he said.

"You need to talk with him. Tell him you're okay, that the family is okay. That'll snap him out of it."

Drew didn't think it would. The desperation in Anna's voice said she didn't think so either.

"Let's go inside," Drew said.

They left the car and met at the front door. Drew pushed it open and they went inside. Kenny sat at the kitchen table, eating pancakes.

The room smelled of butter and maple syrup, comforting scents that seemed completely out of place.

"Hey, champ!" Drew said.

Kenny looked up. "Hi, Daddy."

His voice had no enthusiasm, no excitement, no anticipation. If he'd been missing Drew the kid wasn't showing it. Though it was the reaction Drew had expected, it still made him sad to hear it. Knowing that having his soul ripped from him was the reason made Drew feel even worse.

"That special assignment is over and I'm back," Drew said.

"Mommy's going to be very happy."

Drew and Anna stepped back out of the kitchen. Anna looked crestfallen.

"I'd hoped for a bigger, more positive response than that," Anna said.

Drew hadn't kidded himself about what to expect. "Let's look at those drawings in his closet."

Anna led him to Kenny's room. Inside, she opened the bifold doors like a model on a game show.

"Ta-da," she sighed.

Drew's eyes went wide and his pulse rose. The drawing on the back wall, crude as it was, was unmistakably one of a boy standing beside a demon.

"What did he say about this picture?"

"It was of a new friend who would take care of him. That's supposed to be the two of us in the background there. The psychologist I spoke to said the picture represents—"

"He's wrong. He has no idea what that's a picture of. That thing next to him is a demon."

"Drew, please. Kids' drawings can look like anything."

"It doesn't look like anything else, it's a demon. Proportionally and anatomically correct."

Anna looked horrified. "How could he know what they look like? Do you think he sees them like you do?"

"No. It's worse than that."

There was no way around telling her now. He closed the door to Kenny's room and took a deep breath.

"At Ducky World, that wasn't a man wearing the Dingbat Duck costume who I chased. It was a demon, an archdemon, to be more precise. I was after it because it took Kenny's soul."

"No. How could it? I was right there in the room."

"There's no flash of lightning or peal of thunder when it happens. It's just gone. You'd never know. Even the victim feels nothing."

"No. Kenny couldn't understand what he was doing."

"He doesn't have to understand the significance, just the concept of a trade. The thing gave him that stupid toy duck."

Anna's eyes fell to look at the floor. Then fury caught fire behind them. She looked at Drew.

"You," she seethed. She charged at Drew and began to pound her fists against his chest. "You did this!" she shouted. "You brought all of this under our roof. You brought a goddamn demon into my son's bedroom."

He stood and took the beating he richly deserved. He'd done exactly that, hidden the most important part of his past from the woman he loved, and in doing so opened up the path for evil to steal away his son.

Anna tired and stopped hitting him. She leaned in against his chest. He wrapped his arms around her as she started to cry.

"I did do it," he said. "But I can fix it."

"You can?"

"I have a plan. Marvin, a friend of mine, is helping set a trap. When we do, we'll kill the archdemon who did this and free Kenny's soul."

"Then where will the soul go?"

"Up to Heaven, or whatever the afterlife actually is."

"And that will make Kenny better?"

"No. He'll grow into an ever-darker psychopath without his soul. I could try to get it to return to him, but he'd have to be there when I killed the archdemon. I mean I'll have to have him *right* there with me."

Anna pushed away from him, stood up straight and sniffed back her tears. "Then that's what we have to do."

"There's no *we* in the plan," Drew said. "Just me and Marvin."

"And Kenny, because he's getting his soul back. And that means I'm going too."

"Anna, I don't know how dangerous this will get. I can't risk having you there."

"The only way you're taking Kenny out of here without me is to chain me to the water heater. I'm going."

The steel in her voice told Drew she wasn't using hyperbole. After all these years, he knew the moment when further argument was worthless. Anna looked scared and determined at the same time. That was going to be a perfect, potent combination for what they'd need to do.

"All right," Drew said. "We all go."

CHAPTER FIFTY-ONE

Anna took Kenny's empty plate from the table and dropped it in the sink. She leaned against the counter and watched her son as he drained the last of his juice.

He looked no different than he had before all of this insanity had erupted a week ago. But now that Drew had told her that Kenny had no soul, she saw her son completely differently, as something evil and empty. Fear spread its tentacles through her when she looked at him, and she hated herself for feeling that way. That little boy was still her Kenny. She hoped.

"Kenny, go brush your teeth and play in your room," she said. "I have to clean the kitchen."

"Okay, Mommy."

Kenny hopped out of his chair and went down the hall. Having her son disappear from the room brought a sense of relief, followed by a crushing tidal wave of guilt. She couldn't live like this, loving and fearing her only son, caring for him and repulsed by him at the same time. They needed to make Kenny whole again, and do it quickly.

Drew finished a muted phone call in the living room and stepped back into the kitchen.

"Since my friend Marvin's going to help get Kenny's soul back," Drew said, "you should meet him. He's on his way over."

Anna was already ticked off about the slew of secrets Drew had been keeping from her. Now he was telling her a stranger was coming into their home instead of asking about it first. She clenched a fist and forced herself to sound calmer than she felt.

"Is he someone else who sees demons?" she asked. "Or someone else who hunts them?"

"Neither, really. I got him involved with this, but he has a family connection with demons."

"Which means?"

"Don't overreact," Drew said.

Very few of Drew's pet phrases got under her skin faster than his admonishments to not overreact.

"I only say that," he continued, "because I know I overreacted when I found out what I'm about to tell you. He's what's called a cambion, the offspring of a demon and a human."

Anna's self-control boiled away. "Are you kidding me? You're inviting a demon into the house after what one did to Kenny?"

"Half-demon. And that half is buried very deep. If you met him, you'd never know he was anything but normal. I can see he's different, but you won't."

"And why do you trust him?"

"He's helped other humans in the past, people I trusted. He's no happier being part demon than we are about it. He wants to do what he can to keep demons out of this world."

"Jesus, Drew, what the hell?" Anna said. "Working with a half-demon? You have more goddamn secrets to reveal than a magician."

"Anna, I trust him. You meet him. If he makes you uncomfortable, outside he goes. Fair enough?"

"Fair enough."

"Keep in mind we can't do this alone."

Twenty minutes later there was a knock on the door. Drew answered and invited in a balding, middle-aged man. Anna had to admit that this half-demon wasn't anywhere near as imposing as she'd expected.

"Marvin, this is my wife, Anna."

Marvin smiled at her and then his face fell. He turned to Drew.

"Oh my god. I can see it in her face. You told her what I am. You didn't say you were going to do that."

Anna was embarrassed. She thought she'd masked her reaction to him.

"I thought she needed to know," Drew said.

"I spend every waking minute keeping my personal life a secret, and as soon as you know, you start telling everyone. Don't you appreciate how dangerous that is for me?"

Marvin wasn't at all living up to Anna's expectations as an aggressive denizen of Hell.

"You can trust Anna," Drew said. "She won't tell anyone. If I thought she would, I wouldn't have told her."

"He's right about that," Anna said. "He's a master of keeping secrets from me."

"Well," Marvin said, "maybe I should have been part of the decision about opening my life up to the rest of the world."

Anna couldn't believe it, but she was feeling sorry for this half-demon. Drew had described demons as indestructible, but this cambion seemed, if anything, fragile. She stepped over and placed her hand on Marvin's arm. He jerked, startled at her touch.

"Marvin," she said, "I'm sorry for my reaction. Sorrier for my husband not telling you that he would reveal your secrets to me. His communication skills have been a big pile of crap lately."

"I picked up on that when he tried to kill me before he even said hello."

"Please come and sit down," Anna said.

She led him into the living room. Marvin looked around the room, gave the plastic Halloween bats on the mantlepiece a sideways glance, then scratched at the back of his neck.

"I'm going to go check on Kenny," Drew said, and he disappeared down the hallway.

Marvin sat on one of the living room chairs, perched on the edge like a bird ready to take flight. Anna took a seat on the couch. She could almost smell the tension and fear he exuded.

"Sorry that the house is warded with sigils," she said. "I know that must hurt."

"Sigils hide what's inside a place from a demon," he said. "They aren't a demon repellent. And I'm not a demon, anyway."

"Sorry!" she said. "I'm afraid I'm new to all of this supernatural stuff."

"Your husband has taken us both into places we didn't want to go." He gave the room a very nervous once-over. "I'm not used to being in other people's homes like this. I've never gotten out much."

"Why is that?"

"My mother kept me kind of isolated, afraid of what my demon half might do to other kids. That only got worse as I grew older. I didn't fit in, wasn't sure what could go wrong if I tried to. I know how much stronger I am than a human. I was afraid what harm I could do with that strength. As I got older, it seemed easier to keep to myself."

"But you never did anything bad?"

"No, but the San Andreas fault hasn't sent us a major earthquake lately either. That doesn't mean it won't tomorrow."

Anna thought that was a terrible way to see yourself in the world.

"So according to my husband," she said, "demons look like normal people to everyone, except him."

"And some other people with his special sight."

"How does a demon look to you?"

"I don't know, and I don't want to know. I mean, I know what they truly look like. There's this collective subconscious thing that's given me an image of demons. But I don't want to ever actually see one. They'd kill me on sight, the way you'd kill a cockroach. I'm an atrocity to them."

"That's sad," Anna said.

"Humans would be no different if they knew. Luckily, I look human to all of you."

"How does Drew see you?"

"As I am, mostly demon. When he first met me, he took a demon blade to me without asking a question."

"So how do you see yourself?"

Marvin paused. "No one ever asked me that before. I see myself as Drew does."

"How did you manage that growing up?"

"I didn't know I was different. I thought everyone saw what my mother referred to as 'my special self' when they looked at themselves. It wasn't until I was older that she told me the truth, when I was mature enough to understand. Understanding didn't make it any less of a shock to deal with."

"You don't seem very demonic," Anna said.

"I'll take that as a compliment."

"What do you do for a living?"

"I lived with my mother until she died. She'd insured herself for millions so I'd be set up for life when she passed. Well, we guessed set up for life. It's not like anyone knows how long cambion live."

"Thank you for helping us put my son back together."

Marvin shrugged. "He doesn't deserve what happened to him. I can put my demon self-loathing to good use."

Anna reached over and patted Marvin's hand. She already liked this half-demon more than most human beings she knew in LA.

★　　★　　★

Drew eased open the door to Kenny's room. His son sat on the floor playing with a fire truck. He sat down beside his son.

"How do you feel, champ?" he said.

"I'm okay, I guess."

"No, I mean since we went to Ducky World, how have you been feeling?"

Kenny knit his brow, as if focusing on some internal self-diagnostic. "Different."

"Different good or different bad?"

"Kind of bad, I guess. Like, empty."

Drew guessed that if he was seven years old trying to explain the lack of a moral compass due to losing his soul, he couldn't do any better.

Drew pointed to the closet doors. "The new friend you drew on the wall in there. You saw him? You dreamed him?"

"No. I just know him."

Because that bastard Nicobar left something of itself in you, Drew thought.

"We're going to fix it so you don't have to go with him. We'll stay together as a family. The way we've always been. And you won't feel empty anymore."

"I'll be like I was?"

"Exactly. Do you remember when we went camping in the summer, and the storm came at night?"

"We were in the tent and the kerosene lantern smelled bad and there was thunder and lightning and rain and it was scary."

"But you were brave and we got through it. What we're going to do will be like that."

"I won't be afraid."

Drew wished he could promise his son the same thing. He wrapped an arm around Kenny's shoulders and kissed his head.

Drew returned to the living room. Anna and Marvin sat around the coffee table. Marvin looked up at Drew with a smile on his face.

"This is a special one you have here," he said.

"Tell me something I *don't* know," Drew said. "She's been amazing since the day I met her."

Now it was Anna's turn to smile.

"We need one more thing," Drew said. "It's called angel's breath. It will knock a demon on its ass long enough to drive a blade into it."

He took the recipe he'd copied out of his pocket and showed it to the other two.

"Will it work on an archdemon?" Anna said.

"I have to hope that it will."

"I'm officially un-volunteering to mix that," Marvin said. "No telling what touching that will do to me."

"No problem," Drew said. "Once I have Nicobar in the trap, you just need to get it down to me in the cistern. I'll mix it up."

"No," Anna said. "I'll do it. You have enough to prepare."

"Are you sure?"

"I need to contribute," Anna said.

"I have a few old coins I can file down into flakes for the silver,"

Drew said. "And I can scrape plenty of rust off the garden tools. But some of the other ingredients are kind of obscure."

"The place Cassandra lives over carries every weird root, berry, and pollen you can think of," Anna said. "She'll be happy to help fill the order if I tell her I'm trying some New Age remedy for my RA."

Both Marvin and Anna had determined, optimistic looks on their faces. Drew dared to hope that with all of them working together, they just might send Nicobar back to Hell.

CHAPTER FIFTY-TWO

Marvin had been home for about an hour after meeting Drew and his family. In all that time he hadn't been able to sit still. His anxiety about what they were about to do had him bouncing all over the house. The stress about what was going to unfold in the ruins of Mission San Uriel felt like it was going to turn *him* into ruins as well. He needed to get out and get away from it all.

He had just the place to go.

He stepped out of the house into the bright sun and fragrant scents of Southern California. He was about to smile when a blanket of dread enveloped him. He sensed something dark and unseen outside, something that was aware of him, and waiting.

Across the street, Mr. Garcia stood in his bathrobe, watering his flower beds with a hose. One door down, a woman walked a poodle on a pink leash down the sidewalk. Robins flitted from tree to tree in his yard. He chided himself that the most threatening things out here were the weeds sprouting around his azalea bushes.

As a cambion, he had little to fear. He was physically stronger than any human, and able to take much more punishment. He wasn't bulletproof (at least he didn't think so), but he'd made a few catastrophic mistakes with knives and fire over the years that had healed almost instantly. Nothing out here was going to hurt him.

This unjustified anxiety was stress playing a trick on him, and the exact reason he needed to head out for some relaxing open space. He locked the door to the house and headed for his car.

A while later, he turned off the Pacific Coast Highway and into the unimproved parking lot for El Matador Beach north of Malibu. His was the only car, normal for a weekday.

The parking lot perched on a bluff overlooking the Pacific Ocean. This was the kind of hiking he'd told Drew about, not wandering around a national forest. A series of steps and switchback paths led down the cliff face to several small beaches at the base. Sea stacks and a stone arch along the shore attracted professional and amateur photographers, especially at sunset. But the minimal actual beachfront limited its tourist popularity, which was exactly why Marvin was here.

He left his car and went to the edge of the bluff. A consistent breeze blew refreshing salt air into his face. He wasn't sure how it worked for full demons, but cambion definitely had heightened senses compared with humans. A blessing and a curse. A trash dumpster in the summer sun nearly made him gag. But the invigorating smell here more than made up for it.

Out before him, the empty ocean stretched out to the horizon. No white caps dotted the placid waters. Today the sea lived up to its name, Pacific.

He started down the trail to the beach, picking his way between the low brush and watching for loose stones. When he set foot on the first step, the wind shifted to blowing offshore. Marvin caught a new, unpleasant scent. Like a barbeque grill, where meat had been burned onto the metal. Plus something metallic, like the smell electricity leaves when it arcs through the air. Then a whiff of natural gas, no, the sulfur added to natural gas.

His connection to the demonic collective subconscious sent up a bright red warning flare. Shivers of fear racked Marvin's body. He'd never caught this scent before, but he knew exactly what it was.

Archdemon.

He whipped his head around and looked at the top of the bluff. The silhouette of a figure stood atop the cliff. Human-esque, but clearly not human. Far too large, with too massive a chest, and with withered arms and legs. Marvin did not need a closer look. That was an archdemon, and there would only be one walking Southern California. Nicobar.

He dashed down the steps toward the sea. He hoped that against all odds, the archdemon had not seen him. Once at the base of the cliff, he could hug the rocks and stay out of sight. He risked a glance over his shoulder.

The archdemon bounded down the trail in pursuit. Its strength and grace defied the perceived limitations of its spindly legs and outsized torso. As it came closer, the twin horns on its head were plain to see. So was the glowing fury in its eyes.

Marvin practically tumbled down the last flight of steps. His feet hit the sand and he sprinted south along the kelp-strewn beach. Up ahead, two families sat on blankets under large umbrellas. Several small kids played with shovels and buckets where the waves kissed the land. Marvin's heels dug into the sand as he jerked to a stop.

If he ran past them, there was no telling what the demon might do. Slaughter them because they were witnesses to its hunt, or maybe just kill them for fun. Whatever awful plan this archdemon had for him, those innocent people did not deserve to become part of it.

Marvin spun around and ran north up the beach. Above him, Nicobar had made it to the last set of stairs. Any chance of hiding was gone. Marvin's heart pounded and he sprinted as fast as he could.

He passed the stone arch and hazarded a look over his shoulder. The archdemon launched itself from halfway down the steps. It landed in the sand, raising a cloud of dust. Then it sprinted toward Marvin.

Marvin looked ahead and realized he'd made a mistake. A few dozen yards up, the beach ended at a cliff wall. In his panic to save the beachgoing family, he hadn't thought this second choice through. He looked out to the sea. Maybe demons couldn't swim. He wished he'd learned how to.

To his right, a cave opened up in the cliff. Incoming waves rolled up the beach and rushed into the opening. Then water ran out when the sea retreated. The opening was six feet high and slightly wider.

Marvin searched for a ray of hope from this discovery. Maybe the opening wasn't natural. Maybe storm water pipes ran down to the sea through this hole bored into the stone. Maybe they would be narrow enough that he could get through but the larger archdemon could not. Maybe he'd survive this encounter and get a million miles away from Los Angeles.

He ran into the cave. Within a few feet, he realized the heart-crushing truth. The sea had washed out the shallow opening and the cave came to a narrowing end twenty feet ahead. He stopped. His panting breath echoed off the walls. The light from the opening behind him dimmed.

He turned around to see Nicobar's silhouette in the entrance, backlit by the sun. Its shadow reached into the cave and touched Marvin's feet.

"Cambion," Nicobar growled. "A loathsome scent that demons can smell from miles away. Humans are disgusting, but even worse is having something of them corrupt demonic purity."

Marvin backed up until his head hit the cave ceiling. Though he had rarely been afraid of anything his whole life, paralyzing terror gripped him for the first time. Sweat wept from his pores and he smelled the ripe scent he knew predators celebrated. Fear.

Nicobar stepped into the cave and stopped a few feet from Marvin. Now the archdemon's face was easily visible with charred skin peeling from the cheeks and forehead and the elongated, misshapen ears on either side of its head. A wave of water surged into the cave and covered their feet. As the water rushed back out Marvin wished it could have taken him with it.

"Just get it over with," Marvin said. His attempt at bravado definitely came out sounding more like whimpering.

Nicobar grabbed Marvin around the chest with both hands. It picked him up and slammed him down back-first into the sand. Another wave rolled in and splashed Marvin in the face. He choked and spit out the salty water.

"I would," Nicobar said, "if I was just another demon and you were just another cambion. But it gets more complicated when you're my son."

The shock hit Marvin like a sledgehammer. Its son? Could he be related to something this horrific? He'd accepted that he had been sired by a demon, but could it have been this most evil of the evil? Could something of this monstrosity be part of himself?

Nicobar picked Marvin up and slammed him back down, so that Marvin was sitting on dry sand.

"Yes, nine months before you were born, I took your mother out of vengeful anger, not out of love, or even lust. I'd assumed the way I left her she'd soon be dead. But some idiot found her, and I hadn't counted on the power of the seed I left in her trying to survive. Right after I became aware that the both of you were alive, two humans got lucky and sent me back to Hell."

Marvin remembered the story Greg had told him about sending an archdemon back to Hell before Marvin had been born.

"So imagine my surprise when I smell cambion upon my return, and one with a familiar scent. Of course, my first task had to be killing the pathetic creature who sent me back to Hell. But after that, what kind of father would I be if I didn't look you up, say hello, maybe take you to a Dodgers game?"

Marvin saw one bright side. Nicobar didn't know that he'd been working with Greg or Drew.

"And when I do find you," Nicobar said, "what do I see?"

Nicobar backhanded Marvin across the face. The impact nearly snapped his neck. The whole cave took a swift spin and then stabilized.

"You're buddies with a demon hunter."

Marvin's gut sank. Drew thought he would be able to hunt Nicobar, but Nicobar was still hunting Drew.

"So while I should kill you," Nicobar said, "instead I'll do you a favor, my son. Your problem isn't that you're too much a demon to fit in on Earth, it's that you aren't enough demon to reign over these mortal bags of shit. Let's fix that."

Nicobar clamped one hand around Marvin's throat and squeezed. Marvin choked and fought for air. With the other hand, Nicobar extended one finger and placed its claw against Marvin's chest. Nicobar drove the claw into Marvin and then slashed downward, leaving a gaping six-inch wound in its wake.

For the first time in his life Marvin felt true pain. Not the inconsequential annoyance of conventional injuries, but excruciating, white-hot, searing pain. The combination of the physical agony and the psychological shock made him roar in a way he'd never known he could. The bass cry thundered off the wall of the cave.

Nicobar placed the claw in its mouth against its upper palate. With a flick of its wrist, it sent drops of black blood sailing over Marvin's head.

Nicobar hung its open mouth over the rip in Marvin's skin. A black, viscous liquid dripped out and into the wound. Each drop sparkled with flecks of red. As they hit Marvin's body, he could feel them burn as they seeped inside him. After several eternal seconds, Nicobar closed its mouth. It placed a hand over the wound and Marvin's skin knit back together. The demon relaxed its grip on Marvin's neck.

Marvin sucked in a gallon of air to feed his starving lungs. The pinpoint burning sensation from whatever Nicobar had introduced into his body subsided to an uncomfortable warmth that spread across his torso.

"That ought to kickstart the demon in you," Nicobar said. "A drop of my blood on a soulless human, and I can compel them. Do you know what I can do using more blood injected into my own offspring?"

Marvin's head swam. The sound of Nicobar's voice seemed to reach inside him, overpower him.

"What you're going to do for me," Nicobar said, "is kill the demon hunter's wife."

Marvin thought of Anna and how kind she'd been to him.

"Never," Marvin mumbled. "I'll die first."

"No, you won't. You'll wait until the opportunity is perfect, and then you'll tear her apart. You won't remember anything that happened in this cave, any hint that the desire is anyone's but your own. All you'll feel at that moment is that killing her is an obsession that must be appeased."

The idea of being this thing's murderous puppet churned Marvin's stomach. He struggled against the archdemon's grip, fought against the haze that clouded his mind.

"No!" he moaned. "I won't. I'll remember this. I'll remember."

"You'll remember what I let you, and nothing more."

Nicobar placed its free hand over Marvin's eyes and forehead. A sensation like he was being deconstructed swept through Marvin and everything went dark.

★   ★   ★

Marvin blinked. He stood in the cave, looking at the entrance. He'd just run in here and thought he'd seen a silhouette in the opening blocking the light. But there was nothing there. He went to the upper reach of the cave, crouched down and waited. Nicobar wasn't far behind him. It would be in the cave in seconds.

Marvin waited.

The archdemon did not arrive. A minute later, a man in a bathing suit walking a Doberman passed by.

Marvin made his way to the cave entrance. The only thing on the beach was the man and his dog. He stepped out and looked south down the shoreline. The two families were still enjoying a morning in the sand. Nicobar was gone.

Maybe the archdemon hadn't seen the cave opening. Maybe something else had spooked it off. Maybe it was afraid of the ocean. Marvin didn't really care what the reason was. He was just thrilled with the results. He wasn't dead and the demon was gone.

He climbed back up the stairs to the parking lot. There was one other vehicle in the lot now, a small white SUV with an *I LOVE DOBERMANS* bumper sticker.

Marvin collapsed against the banister in relief. That had been close. Too close. He was going to have to keep a better watch on his surroundings, and be alert if that sensation he'd had in his front yard manifested itself again.

For now, he needed to get out of here. All this terror had worked up an appetite. And he needed to tell Drew what had happened. Nicobar was after them both. He had a feeling even Drew's wife might be in danger.

CHAPTER FIFTY-THREE

Drew checked the clock on the kitchen wall for the dozenth time. Marvin should have been here by now. If they didn't get to the old mission site before Nicobar, the whole plot would fail.

He'd spent most of the morning getting the site ready, then the afternoon in the garage touching up the fake Lance of Vladimir. Side by side, the copy was a close match for the original. Only when he picked it up could he tell that it was made of wood and that the weathered appearance was all paint tricks.

"He'll be here," Anna said.

"Huh?"

"Marvin will be here. Checking the clock more frequently won't get him here faster."

"We need him tonight. Without his strength helping out, I doubt I can get the Lance of Vladimir into Nicobar."

Mentioning the lance reminded him of something. He made a quick trip to their bedroom. He returned and handed the demon dagger to Anna.

"You should carry this tonight," he said.

"This is that knife that kills demons."

"It's the only thing I can give you that will help you keep Kenny safe if something goes wrong trapping Nicobar. It won't kill an archdemon, but it will hurt it enough that you can make an escape."

"And run to where?"

"Let's hope we don't have to figure that out."

Drew left the kitchen for the living room. He looked out the front window just as Marvin pulled up outside in his old VW Beetle. Drew met Marvin at the door.

"Any problems?" Drew asked.

"No, just traffic, the usual."

Anna arrived with Kenny in tow. Kenny gave Marvin a suspicious look.

"You're different," Kenny said.

"Kenny!" Anna said with embarrassment. She stepped back behind her son and waved her hands back and forth as she mouthed, "I didn't tell him anything."

"Kenny, this is Marvin," Drew said. "He's going to help us. He'll keep you safe."

Kenny looked wary, and stepped back next to his mother's leg.

"I have this irresistible magnetism when it comes to children," Marvin deadpanned.

"I made two doses of angel's breath this morning," Anna said to Marvin.

"No trouble finding the ingredients?" Marvin said.

"My sister was a big help. She can't wait to hear how my miracle cure for RA works out. Anyway, they're wrapped in silk like the instructions said, then they're double wrapped in shopping bags on the kitchen counter. No way they can touch you."

"Couldn't find a more considerate person to hunt demons with," Marvin said.

"We'll take my car," Drew said. "Anna, sit in back with Kenny. Marvin's up front with me. Let's go take care of Nicobar."

A half hour later they parked in the turnout that Drew and Marvin had used when they discovered the lost mission. Drew led them down the same game trail. He carried the kerosene lantern the family had taken camping. Anna carried the bag of angel's breath.

Kenny followed right at Anna's heels. He didn't seem as nervous and worried as the rest of them. Was that because he didn't understand how dangerous all this was, or because being soulless had numbed him to it? Drew didn't know. Once he'd reunited Kenny with his soul, the answer wouldn't matter.

"How are you feeling this time?" Drew asked Marvin.

"No problem," Marvin said. "I feel much stronger, or maybe I've gotten used to the general uneasiness of the place. But I'm still staying out of that demon trap."

"The plan is to keep you well away from it."

Before they got to the mission ruins, Drew led the group off to a spot where they could watch the cistern area from behind some bushes.

"You'll all watch from here," Drew said. "That open area out there is the demon trap pit. I've covered the hole in the center with a tarp and dirt. Nicobar will arrive and see me on the other side of it. I'll act startled and leave the fake lance on that tarp. It'll go for it, and fall through the hole into the demon trap below. Then we'll all use the trap door and staircase to get to the safe area around the demon trap. Marvin will toss me down the angel's breath. I'll hit it with that, then take it down with the Lance of Vladimir, and then we'll get Kenny's soul back."

The plan sounded simple as he reviewed it. He had a bad feeling that executing it would be anything but simple.

CHAPTER FIFTY-FOUR

The sun dipped below the western horizon and cast the mission ruins in long, purple shadows. Nicobar would be due soon if it took the bait. As if the daylight had kept Drew's anxiety at bay, the darker it got, the more worried he became about his plan.

Drew stepped around the edge of the concealed hole in the cistern roof. He struck a match and lit the old kerosene camping lantern. He adjusted the wick to produce a good glow and then set the lantern down at his feet. He took the fake Lance of Vladimir from his pocket and tossed it onto the center of the dirt-covered trap. The lantern's light lit it up nicely, and that was the whole point. Nicobar wouldn't walk into the trap if it couldn't see the prize.

Drew backed away a half dozen feet, picked up a collapsible shovel, and dug a shallow hole in the ground. After a few shovels full, the blade thudded against the old roof. The wood felt soft and spongy. He stopped digging.

He was perfectly lined up. Nicobar would come down the game trail, see the fake lance in the lantern light, and see Drew digging a hole to bury it just beyond. The two would rush for the lance. Drew would make sure the archdemon won the race, and it would fall into the demon trap below.

He sat back on his haunches and listened. The silence was striking compared to the continuous cacophony he was used to in the city. There was always some noise in LA, a car, a neighbor, a helicopter, a distant siren. But here, it was still. An insect chirped a few times, then fell quiet, as if it realized how wrong it was for disturbing the peace.

A faint glow from behind the hills to the west told him that the city was still there in all its concrete and incandescent glory. Up above, the clear night sky was host to uncountable stars and the moon shone down, a quarter-way through its nightly trek across the expanse.

Drew realized that this was what the priests at Mission San Uriel experienced every night over two hundred years ago, except with much less civilization waiting for them at the bottom of the mountains. Did they feel alone and isolated up here, or did they feel closer to God? As they slept in the mission building, were they confident that the demons in this prison were contained, or did they live in fear that they might escape?

He couldn't hear his family and Marvin, but he knew they were watching from off to his left. He was grateful for Marvin's help. Knowing he was there to protect Anna and Kenny meant Drew could focus on dropping Nicobar into the trap.

From uphill, he heard the sound of a car engine and the crunch of rocks under tires. A brief flash of headlights lit the hilltop and then the area went dark again. That would be Nicobar, probably parked right behind Drew's car. He could imagine the demon smiling, thinking that it had its prey trapped, when actually, the situation was the other way around.

He listened for any noise from along the game trail. Every minute or so, he shifted a shovel full of dirt around the hole he'd dug. He wanted Nicobar to hear exactly where Drew had left the bait even before it could see the lance.

Something rustled in the brush uphill from the cistern. Drew stood still and peered into the darkness beyond the lantern's yellow light. More leaves scraped leaves and rock ground against sand as something stepped on the trail. The scent of charcoal and sulfur drifted in around him.

Drew stepped back from the hole, making sure that Nicobar would be able to beat him to the center of the cistern when the demon made its rush. He reached behind him with his free hand and gripped the shaft of the real Lance of Vladimir in his back pocket.

On the other side of the cistern, two eyes reflected the glow of the lantern's light.

Drew's fingers tightened around the lance. Time for Nicobar to go back to Hell.

The eyes in the gloom widened. The light gave them a decidedly yellow glow. A guttural growl sounded from the darkness.

Drew held his breath.

The eyes advanced and a coyote stepped into the farthest reaches of the lantern's light. It bared its white teeth and snarled.

In any other circumstance, meeting a wild canid at night in a set of deserted ruins would have scared the crap out of him. But since he was awaiting the attack of an archdemon, the coyote was a relief. Drew exhaled.

Then he got mad. This animal was a distraction he couldn't afford, a wild card that might spook his wife and son and reveal their position. He couldn't let that happen.

He let go of the lance and scooped some rocks off the ground. He hurled them at the coyote's feet, then jumped up and down waving his arms over his head.

"Beat it!" he yelled.

The coyote flinched and ducked its head in submission. It took a step back, then turned and fled into the night.

"You're so scary," a voice said behind Drew. Hot breath blew across the back of his ears. The scent of sulfur stung his nose.

Drew spun around and was face-to-face with Nicobar. The lantern cast ghastly shadows up across the demon's face and its eyes glowed a rich red against the dark of the night. Drew stepped back as a scream caught in his throat.

"You almost frightened me away," Nicobar said. "Almost."

The demon lashed out with one hand and struck Drew in the chest. The blow knocked him off his feet and he slid backward closer to the covered hole in the cistern's center. Nicobar smiled and stepped nearer to him. The demon paused and scanned the ground.

"What do we have here? Feels like a demon trap buried underground. Do you think it could affect me from that far away? You know even less than I gave you credit for."

Drew jumped to his feet and drew the true Lance of Vladimir from his pocket. The blade took on a red glow and an amazing strength suddenly coursed through Drew's body.

"You're going to take me on with that?" Nicobar said. "You won't even get close to me."

"I'm not fighting alone."

"You mean you have a cambion and your family over there in the bushes? You might as well be fighting alone."

How did it know? Drew thought.

"I can sense them, smell them, especially the cambion. Did I mention I've gotten him working for me? He doesn't know it but he'll be finding that out about now, and then so will your wife."

A whole new level of terror engulfed Drew. What had Nicobar done to Marvin? Was he about to ambush Drew's unsuspecting Anna?

A little angel's breath would have come in handy now. But it looked like he was going to have to do without. He brandished the lance and charged at Nicobar. The demon smiled and stood its ground. Drew positioned the blade for a deep strike up into the demon's chest and closed on the creature.

Nicobar lashed out with an upper cut that caught Drew between the neck and chin. His head snapped back as he sailed up and away from the demon.

At the last second, he realized where he was going to land.

He hit the tarp covering the trap flat on his back. The tarp collapsed into the demon prison. The fall seemed to take forever, with the ends of the tarp flapping around him like a set of broken wings. He hit the ground hard enough to knock the wind out of him. The impact also knocked the Lance of Vladimir from his hand.

He lay in the center of the demon trap. He searched but could not see the Lance of Vladimir. His wife and son were about to fall victim to a creature strong enough to shred them without effort.

Nicobar peered over the edge of the hole in the cistern roof. The lantern lit its face from one side, leaving the rest in shadow. Its eyes glowed like the coals in a blacksmith's forge.

"How sweet to add experiencing the death of your wife to the pain you'll carry through life," Nicobar said. "Listen closely and I'm sure you'll hear her scream."

CHAPTER FIFTY-FIVE

The plan was for Anna and the others to wait, hidden, until Drew called them over after trapping the demon. But Anna struggled against the temptation to pop up and keep an eye on her husband as his plan to trap the archdemon played out.

Apparently, Kenny felt the same way. He rose to his feet to watch his father. Anna grabbed his shoulders and yanked him to the ground.

"Kenny!" she whispered. "Stay down."

"But I want to watch," Kenny said.

He stood back up. Anna went to her knees to pull him back down, but didn't have the leverage and didn't want to stand up and expose herself even more than Kenny was doing.

"Marvin," she said over her shoulder, "help me."

No answer. She turned to look at Marvin. He sat a few feet away, knees tucked up to his chin and arms locked around his legs. Even in the moonlight she could see his lower lip quivering. What she didn't need the moonlight to see was his eyes. They glowed an unnatural red.

"Something's wrong," Marvin said. "I'm having…urges. I don't…."

Kenny's attention on the cistern area didn't waver. "There's someone else over there."

Anna dared not take her eyes off Marvin to see what her son was talking about. Something terrible was coming to a boil inside the poor cambion.

"Anna." Marvin's voice deepened into a gravelly rumble. "Run!"

Anna didn't need a second warning. She jumped to her feet, grabbed Kenny's hand, and ran downhill.

"Mommy, what's happening?" Kenny wailed as she pulled him behind her.

"Run," she said. "As fast as you can. Marvin is...sick."

Anna's heart pounded, and she gripped her son's hand so tightly she was afraid she'd break it. But she was not letting go of him, not now, not ever.

She could barely see in the moonlight. Her shoes skidded on sand and rocks. Unseen brush scraped at her jeans and threatened to entangle her feet. She didn't know where she was going and it didn't matter. Just away from Marvin and his glowing eyes.

Feet pounded the ground behind her, not the thrum of a running human, but the thunder of a racing horse, steps so fast and so heavy that no human being could make them. She and Kenny would never outrun the cambion.

Branches snapped and the pounding came closer. She remembered the demon dagger, her only hope to survive this attack. She grabbed the knife with her free hand.

It was too late. Marvin leapt from uphill and pounced on her back. The demon dagger flew out of one hand. Kenny slipped from the other. She went sprawling face-first into the gritty soil. Sharp stones sanded her right cheek as she slid forward.

Marvin flipped her over. His eyes now burned bright red. His face had contorted into a gargoyle-like visage of uncontrolled fury. If there was some part of Marvin inside of this thing on top of her, Anna could not see it. All she saw was a rage-driven killing machine.

Marvin snarled and clamped both hands around her throat. He squeezed and her throat collapsed. Her face flushed as her lungs began to burn for fresh oxygen. She let out a garbled cry.

"No!" Kenny cried.

He jumped on Marvin's back and wrapped his arms around the cambion's neck. Marvin growled, released his left hand from Anna's throat and reached back for the boy. Air flooded Anna's lungs, but her relief was short-lived. Marvin grabbed Kenny and plucked him off his back like pulling lint from a sweater. He tossed the boy aside.

"You get to watch," Marvin said, "and live with what you'll see."

His left hand shot back to Anna's throat. Both hands squeezed even harder than before. Anna choked. She struggled to break free, but Marvin seemed to weigh a thousand pounds. The edges of the world began to go dark.

Memories rushed through her mind. Old and new, sad and happy, jumbled and confused. Childhood memories fast-forwarded to high school to college and then to her job and married life as a mother. It was all about to vanish forever, her life gone like the flame of an extinguished candle. The only thing she'd miss, the only thing that mattered steamrolled all other thoughts. Love. Love for her son, and for Drew.

Her field of view shrank until all she saw were Marvin's glowing eyes. The pressure on her throat grew. Everything went dark and she surrendered to whatever lay beyond life's veil.

CHAPTER FIFTY-SIX

Somewhere above and outside the demon prison, Anna cried out in terror.

Drew jumped to his feet inside the demon trap. Above him, Nicobar cupped a hand to one ear with a theatrical flourish.

"Sounds like Marvin is finishing off your wife," Nicobar said. "I should give him a hand before all the fun is over."

Drew couldn't do anything about Marvin, but he could do something to stop Nicobar from touching Anna. One of the beams that had broken when the roof collapsed earlier lay at his feet. He scooped it up from the floor.

"Sorry I can't join you down there," Nicobar said.

"I insist you do," Drew said.

He swung the beam at the ceiling support under where Nicobar stood. The decayed wood exploded into splinters. The roof swayed and the archdemon shifted to keep its balance. Drew swung at another support. It broke in two and the roof began to collapse. Nicobar dropped to its knees.

Drew shuffled backward but no place was safe. The roof collapsed in a cascade that widened in both directions. He threw himself against the cistern wall and covered his head with his arms. A waterfall of old timbers and dry earth fell into the demon prison and filled the pit with a choking cloud of dust.

The kerosene lantern dropped straight down onto the stone floor. The glass shattered and sent a spray of kerosene in all directions. Flames exploded with a whoosh as tinderbox-dry wood went ablaze.

The fire lit the pit in a hazy orange glow. The dust settled to reveal a dirt-covered lump near the center of the pit. The earth shifted, and

Nicobar rose from the debris. The archdemon shook like a dog and sent a spray of dirt and shards of wood in all directions. It scanned the perimeter until it spied Drew against the wall. Its glowing eyes narrowed and locked on him. The surrounding flames lit its angry face.

"You worthless pouch of mortal shit," Nicobar said. "You're like a mouse scurrying by a tiger, thinking you can survive while pissing off an apex predator. News flash: you can't. Now you've made keeping you alive and tortured not nearly as enjoyable as killing you."

Nicobar charged at Drew. Burning debris blocked the route between the demon trap and the outer wall to the stairway beyond. Drew had nowhere to run.

Nicobar closed to within a few feet of Drew and stopped like it had hit an invisible wall. At its feet, the symbols in the demon trap flared bright red. The pentagram burst to life and blew dirt and debris off the trap's outer edge. Nicobar roared and bounced back into the trap.

Relief swept through Drew. He relaxed against the wall. The first part of the plan had worked after all.

Nicobar stepped up to the edge of the demon trap across from Drew. It pressed a palm against the air above the demon trap's outer circle. The air crackled and the demon trap lit up. Nicobar winced but did not jump back. It drew its hand away. The sizzling stopped. The glow of the trap ramped down, and stabilized a bit dimmer than it had started.

"You think a trap for common demons can hold me forever?" it said. "The people who made this place barely knew what they were doing. I'll have this trap discharged in no time."

This time Nicobar put both hands against the demon trap's outer limit. A current surged through the air that made the hairs on Drew's arms stand on end.

To Drew's right, he spied the Lance of Vladimir against the wall. Another wave of relief washed over him, even though burning timber blocked him from it.

Drew spun around and kicked the burning wood into the demon's trap. With the path clear, he dove for the lance. He grabbed it with his right hand, smiled, and jumped to his feet. Nicobar stood at the edge of the demon's trap, hands extended, trying to discharge the trap. The archdemon faced away from Drew, exposed and undefended. One thrust of the lance into the demon trap, and Nicobar would be as good as dead.

Drew dashed over opposite Nicobar. He reared back to deliver the fatal wound.

Something was wrong. The blade wasn't glowing.

Had the fall broken it? Was there something in the demon trap that sapped its power? Did Nicobar have some kind of defense?

Then Drew checked the heft of the blade. He was holding the fake.

If he'd realized that a second later, after he'd thrust it uselessly into the demon trap, Nicobar could have pulled him in. That would have been the end of the story.

On the opposite side of the demon trap, the true Lance of Vladimir stuck out of the debris from the roof collapse. The lance wouldn't be his salvation. Burning timbers too large to move blocked him on either side, so he'd need to run past Nicobar to get the blade. And even if he did get the blade, Nicobar had somehow turned Marvin against him and his family. He could never overpower Nicobar alone.

Nicobar dropped its hands from the wall and the crackling stopped. The sigils in the demon trap went dimmer still. Nicobar rested its hands on its knees and panted.

Flames spread across more of the fallen timbers. Small, dry plants that had ridden in on the collapse combusted from the heat and puffed into little balls of flame. The growing flames of the burning wood began to heat the stone walls like a fireplace hearth. Sweat broke out on Drew's forehead.

"It will be a shame," Nicobar said between breaths, "if the flames cook you before I can break through and kill you."

CHAPTER FIFTY-SEVEN

Anna's last thought before death's abyss engulfed her was a memory of cradling her son in her arms just after he'd been born. That sense of accomplishment, of love, of completeness was the closest to total bliss she'd ever felt. She wanted that sensation to usher her into whatever awaited after this life.

Marvin cried out. The pressure on her throat went away. Her vision returned. Something very bright glowed in front of her face.

Her eyes focused to see the point of the demon dagger sticking out through Marvin's chest. His eyes were wide in surprise. Both his hands grasped the wound around the knife.

The blade slipped back through Marvin's chest, then erupted again through his shirt, this time higher. Blood sprayed over Anna's face and chest. Marvin's eyes rolled up in his head. The blade disappeared again. Marvin slumped over to the left. Anna scrambled out from underneath him.

Kenny stood over the body with the glowing demon dagger in his hand. Blood dripped down the hilt. Droplets speckled his shirt. His expressionless face betrayed nothing; no joy, no fear, no wonder that he'd just taken a life.

Anna went to his side. She took the knife from his hand without any protest from her son.

"That wasn't like killing Brutus at all," Kenny said. "I was much faster this time."

Anna barely had time to be horrified at the pride in her son's statement. Uphill, flames lit the mission ruins from within the demon prison. That sure as hell hadn't been part of the plan to fix her son.

She took Kenny by the hand and led him upslope. The demon

dagger went cool and dull in her hand. She stopped at the edge of the terraced section. The formerly covered demon prison now looked like an open pit barbeque with flames licking up from its sides.

She pulled Kenny over to the side of the pit. The roof to the demon prison had collapsed and now a ring of fire consumed its timbers. A woman she assumed was Nicobar stood inside a glowing red demon's trap. The archdemon's soccer mom look threw Anna for a loop. She'd been expecting…well, something else.

Nicobar pressed against the trap's edge and its hands made a noise like frying bacon. The demon trap flared to a brighter red. The demon dagger in Anna's hand began to glow again.

Drew was trapped between Nicobar and the wall with fire raging on both sides of him. She'd never seen him look so panicked.

"Drew!" she shouted.

He looked up and his face brightened. He pointed across the pit. "Get the lance!"

Opposite Drew, at the base of the stairs, the lance sat point-down and embedded in the debris of the collapse. No one was killing Nicobar without that.

"Kenny, you stay right here," she said. "Don't move."

Anna couldn't wait for an answer. She sprinted around the cistern wall to the now-exposed top of the stairway.

Nicobar stepped back from the demon trap's edge. The illuminated circles and sigils dimmed to a very low glow. Anna didn't think that could possibly be a good sign. Nicobar looked up and saw her running.

"Why the hell aren't you dead?' it said. "This is what I get when I send a cambion to do an archdemon's job."

Anna made it to the top of the stairs. There was no way she could run down those narrow remains of the steps. She leaned back against the cistern wall, and began to descend sideways.

Nicobar screamed in frustration as it saw what Anna was doing. It rushed to that side of the pit. Anna was almost halfway down.

A pile of burning roof wreckage lay near the base of the steps. The rafters that had supported it extended into the demon trap. Nicobar grabbed the flaming rafter ends and lifted them over its head. Anna paused, stunned. The whole blazing structure had to weigh over a thousand pounds. But Nicobar lifted it with ease, and showed no pain handling the wide, burning rafter ends. Then it shoved the whole pyre up and into the steps.

The blazing wood crashed into the wall inches from Anna's face. Sparks flew and embers burned holes in her clothes. Smoke and sulfur and a stench like burned hair assaulted her senses. The pile of wood broke apart on impact, but the extra exposed surface just made it burn hotter. She climbed back up two steps. A jumble of fiery boards now covered the bottom third of the stairs, and blocked any hope of her getting to the Lance of Vladimir.

The right side of Anna's body began to blister from the heat. She had no choice but to retreat. She climbed back up out of the pit and stood beside Kenny. She looked down at Drew.

"I can't get to it!" she yelled over the sound of the flames.

Drew nodded in acknowledgement and resignation.

Nicobar smiled and went back to Drew's side of the pit. It slammed both hands against the area over the demon trap's edge. The sizzling noise returned, weaker than before. The glow of the demon trap intensified, but Anna had a bad feeling that when Nicobar took its hands back this time, the glow might be gone, and the demon trap would just become another decoration on the ground.

CHAPTER FIFTY-EIGHT

The air crackled and sparked around Nicobar's hands. The demon trap was about to fail. Drew had no doubt that Nicobar would drain the last of its power with this attack, and then the archdemon would tear him to pieces. But everyone else didn't have to die because his plan failed.

"Anna!" he called up to his wife. "Get back to the car! Get out of here! Save yourself and Kenny!"

"You think I won't hunt her down?" Nicobar said over the buzzing hum its hands created on the failing demon trap. "You think I won't compel your son into becoming the greatest serial killer the world has ever seen?"

The archdemon was right. There was nowhere to hide from the supernatural. Demons would always win. In the end, Lincoln learned that. In the end, Greg learned that. In the end, Drew saw he was about to learn that.

Anna and Kenny hadn't moved. She stood with the glowing demon dagger in her hand.

"We're not leaving you," she said.

"That's going to spoil my hunt," Nicobar said.

This time the archdemon didn't drop its hands. The splattering hum of the violated trap subsided. The glow of the rings and sigils faded to black. Nicobar smiled.

"Humans plan," it said, "and then demons laugh."

It reached for Drew.

A cry sounded from up above. Marvin appeared at the cistern's edge. He pulled the demon dagger from Anna's hand on the run and leapt from the edge. He sailed through the towering flames and crash-landed on Nicobar.

Marvin's weight drove Nicobar to the ground. He raised the demon dagger and plunged it into Nicobar's chest. It penetrated the skin and Nicobar roared. The dagger wasn't going to kill it, but being stabbed sure pissed it off.

Drew wasn't about to let this opportunity slip by. He ran past the two and went straight for the Lance of Vladimir. He pulled it from the ground. The lance burst into a bright red glow. Energy blasted up Drew's arm and then across his body. He gritted his teeth and sprinted back for Nicobar.

Nicobar tucked a foot up and against Marvin's chest. With one thrust it sent the cambion flying through the air. Marvin passed through a curtain of flames and slammed into the wall outside the demon trap.

Drew dove onto Nicobar before it could rise. The demon dagger still protruded from Nicobar's chest. Drew drove the Lance of Vladimir into a spot beside it.

Nicobar shrieked the cry of a wounded animal, the terrified shout of one feeling absolute agony. The archdemon grabbed Drew and threw him aside.

But Drew kept his iron grasp on the lance. He hit the ground and bounced back up with the lance in hand for a second attack.

Marvin was one step ahead of him. He came charging at Nicobar from behind. He leapt and landed on Nicobar's back, and put it in a headlock.

Nicobar reached both arms up and behind him and grabbed Marvin's shoulders. It pulled him off its back with the ease of taking off a t-shirt. Nicobar slammed Marvin to the ground on his back and stomped a foot across Marvin's neck. The cambion choked out a groan.

Drew rushed the two of them and slid in low behind the archdemon. He slashed Nicobar's calf with the lance. The blade did far more damage than the demon dagger still embedded in its chest. The lance cut away a swatch of flesh and muscle, clear down to the bone.

Nicobar screamed and dropped to one knee with the other foot still on Marvin's neck. Drew slid into the wall foot-first, inches from a pile of burning wood.

Nicobar drew the demon dagger from its chest. The wound around it closed instantly. It raised the dagger overhead to drive the blade into Marvin.

"You bastard!" Anna shouted from above.

She'd recovered the angel's breath and gripped one silk bundle in her hand. She wound up and hurled the pouch at Nicobar. The bundle hit it square in the back of the head with an explosion of brown dust and silver flakes.

Nicobar's skull smoked and sizzled. The archdemon howled and dropped the demon dagger. Both hands went to its head to scrape away the agonizing concoction.

Drew launched himself at the archdemon. He ran into Nicobar from behind and plunged the Lance of Vladimir into its back. The archdemon wailed. Drew pulled the lance free, and this time drove it into the back of the archdemon's skull. Bone crunched and black blood gushed out all over Drew's arm. Nicobar shuddered and fell to the ground.

Drew knew the lance could hurt the archdemon, but the thing wouldn't be truly dead until he carved out its heart. Only then his son's soul would be free. He pulled out the lance and rolled the archdemon over.

The heat from the fires around the pit baked Drew's skin. The smoke had caked his lungs and breathing was a chore. Battling the archdemon had exhausted him. He steeled himself to complete the final task. He dropped down and straddled the archdemon's waist.

"Anna," he called, "bring Kenny around to this side."

"Already here," she said from above him.

He looked up and saw his wife's beautiful face splattered with blood and dirt. She was still the most enchanting sight he'd ever seen.

He drove the lance into Nicobar's abdomen. He sawed a circle about eight inches wide. The lance cut through flesh and bone with ease. He finished and pulled away the excised section of the archdemon's chest with a viscous slurp. Its still-beating heart pumped in a cavity of obsidian liquid. A slow swirl of glowing red flecks swam in the blood.

Without hesitation, Drew reached in with both hands and grabbed the heart. The archdemon's blood coated his skin, seemed to seep into his pores. The taste of ash and sulfur coated his mouth and he nearly gagged. He ripped the heart free of the creature's torso and threw it aside.

An immediate change began. The archdemon's shape grew red and hazy. Straddling its chest, he could feel the demon becoming less corporeal. Great news, but he needed something else to happen first. He needed his son's soul back.

Is Kenny close enough to attract it? he worried. *Did Nicobar eat the soul at the last minute out of spite? Should I have already done something else to release the soul first? Did this whole thing even work or was it just a misguided guess from Marvin and his collective subconscious?*

Dispatching Nicobar was a victory, but if he didn't get Kenny back, *his* Kenny, then he couldn't help thinking he'd helped the world and completely failed his family.

Nicobar dissolved beneath him like melting snow. Drew ran his hands through the mist of the vanishing corpse, as if his fingers might sift out a soul before the archdemon disappeared. But he came up empty.

Drew remembered the face of his son pressing through Nicobar's back, crying out for Drew to save him. His son had counted on him, and now....

The mist dispersed and seeped into the ground. Drew's heart shattered.

Then a tiny ball of light emerged. It hovered over the ground for a second, then shot straight up and into Kenny's chest. The impact rocked the boy back on his heels. Then he dropped to his knees. Anna caught him on the way down.

If that wasn't a soul transfer, Drew didn't know what was. His rush of elation made him feel like he was floating. He looked over to Marvin lying on the floor of the pit. The cambion looked exhausted and guilty.

"Drew, I'm so sorry. I…Anna…I couldn't control myself. Nicobar, it infected me."

"I know. I'm just glad that you came out from under whatever that spell was."

"A few stabs with the demon dagger seemed to burn out the demonic elements," Marvin said. "But I'll pass on getting knifed again if it's all the same to everyone else."

Marvin swayed as he rose to his feet.

"Jesus, Marvin. How can you stand up?"

"Cambion constitution. Can't be beat. It would be worse if Nicobar hadn't shorted out this demon trap. Get me out of here."

Drew wrapped one of Marvin's arms across his shoulder and led him past smoking timbers and out where the burning roof still blocked the stairway.

"I got this," Marvin said.

He sighed and stepped over to the pyre. He swept enough aside to clear the steps, then slapped his burning hands against his legs to put them out. He waved Drew forward and sat down against the wall.

"On second thought," he said. "I think I'll take a break here. You go ahead."

Drew hobbled up the steps with all the spunk of a septuagenarian. At the top, he took a deep breath and staggered over to Anna and his son. Kenny knelt facing the demon pit, leaning against his mother, eyes closed. She held his hand. Drew dropped down on his knees before Kenny.

"Our poor sweet boy," Anna said.

Drew put a hand against his son's cheek. His skin was so soft, his body too young to have been put through all of this. He held his son's other hand. Was Kenny strong enough to survive all of this?

Kenny moaned.

"Hey, champ," Drew said. "Doing okay?"

Kenny's eyes flickered open. "Daddy?"

"Yes, it's Daddy. Are you all complete again?"

"Yes." Kenny smiled. "It's me in here."

Then Kenny's head shook back and forth in an inhuman blur. His face contorted and his eyes narrowed. The smile on his lips transformed into a wicked grin. He spoke again, this time in a gravelly growl.

"I'm in here too. Hopped a ride on Kenny's soul."

Drew's mouth went dry. "Nicobar?"

"Can't keep a good archdemon down."

Kenny shoved Drew back with tremendous force. Drew rolled backward and over the edge of the demon pit. He landed on the sloped, burning collapsed roof. He rolled through flames and felt his hair and eyebrows catch fire. He spun over hot timbers until he hit the floor within the demon trap.

He slapped at the flames on his head, then his arms. Drew looked up at the edge of the pit through tearing eyes. Kenny looked down at him with a maniacal smile. Anna stood beside him shaking and looking like she was about to go into shock.

"His body isn't prepared," Nicobar said. "So I'll burn through this boy pretty quick. But what fun I'll have doing it!"

CHAPTER FIFTY-NINE

Kenny had finally been whole again.

His soul had reunited with his body. Like incomprehensible puzzle pieces finally fitting together, the partiality both had felt apart had at long last made perfect sense. He struggled against the confusing sensation of parallel memories. One set was a nightmare land where he'd teetered on a column in the center of a sleet storm, the other a dark version of the world where he'd killed their dog and attacked a girl at school. It had felt reassuring to be beside his parents instead of surrounded by the wailing specters of dying souls. As he'd knelt at the edge of the demon trap, holding their hands, he'd been exhausted, relieved, and very happy.

Then all of a sudden, like being caught by a giant vacuum, he'd been sucked away from consciousness. Now he stood alone in the dark, cut off from the rest of the world, in fact devoid of any tactile sensation. The joy of being whole crumbled to dust, and all the fear and dread he'd felt in that awful netherworld rushed back and consumed him. Having just been reunited with his family, this time the isolation was even more crushing.

Two massive red eyes blinked open above him in the darkness, the same terrifying eyes that had stared down at him over the Canyon of Souls. Kenny wasn't being lashed by icy rain and high winds, but the same chill he'd felt then struck him to his core.

The eyes shrank and descended out of the abyss. When they reached a normal size, a body formed around them. As it solidified, Kenny recognized the form. Long, spindly arms and legs, an oversized head and chest, three fingers on each hand tipped with black claws. Bony stubs protruded from its shoulder blades. This was the creature from his subconscious, the one he'd drawn on his closet wall, the one that was going to take him away from his parents.

"Hey, boy," the demon said. "Did you miss me?"

Kenny tried to run away. His legs moved, his arms pumped at his sides, but he didn't go anywhere. The demon walked up beside him. Each step it took closer seemed to double the rising panic Kenny felt. The darkness around him grew blacker, heavier, more inescapable. He stopped running, dropped down, and tucked himself into a ball. He began to rock, whimpering.

The demon stood beside him and looked down. It grasped Kenny's head with one hand. The three fingers nearly encircled Kenny's skull. They squeezed and the tips of the claws pierced Kenny's skin. Each wound screamed in burning pain.

"Now, you sit here nice and quiet," the demon said. "I'm going to have fun with your parents, and when your body flames out, I'll swallow you whole."

CHAPTER SIXTY

Drew rolled over on the floor of the demon pit. The fall had done some damage. His left leg felt like it had been put through a wringer. His knee and ankle had been twisted so badly he doubted he could stand, let alone climb back out of this pit.

"Drew!" Marvin called from the side of the pit.

"I'm okay," Drew lied.

Marvin looked up to the precipice of the pit and grimaced. "I feel Nicobar," he said. "Kenny was vulnerable when his body opened up to return his soul. It's in there with Kenny."

At the edge of the cistern, Kenny stared down with an evil look of satisfaction.

No, Drew corrected himself, *not Kenny. Nicobar.*

But he'd spoken to the real Kenny, whose soul was back in there, somewhere. But how the hell was he going to eject the demon from Kenny before the thing tore his son apart from within?

Anna knelt behind Kenny and wrapped her arms around his shoulders.

"Kenny, Kenny?" Anna said. "What did you do to my boy?"

Nicobar snapped Kenny's head straight back into Anna's face. Her nose made a crunching sound. She screamed and let go. Blood gushed down over her chin and she gripped her nose with both hands.

"You bastard!" Drew shouted. "You want someone to torment, come on down here. I'm the one you hate."

"I can torment you much better from up here," Nicobar said. "Kill your wife, add in some nice mutilation, then let you watch your son's body start to die as I burn it out. Don't worry, I'll leave before he dies, but not before he's reduced to a painful, vegetative state."

Hatred boiled inside Drew, the kind of deep, all-consuming loathing that only the violation of one's child can bring out. He tried to get up. His leg wouldn't have it. Moving it sent blinding waves of pain through him. He sagged back down to the ground.

"Can't get a good view?" Nicobar said.

It went back to where Anna sat choking on her flowing blood. The archdemon grabbed her by the hair and dragged her to the edge of the pit. The demon's power was clearly running through his son's body. Nicobar yanked Anna's head back.

"I'll make sure that you have a front row seat, catch every sight, sound, and smell. No worry. Across all eternity, I've never disappointed."

Nicobar raised a hand to strike Anna, and stopped mid-swing. It looked confused.

"What the hell?" it said.

CHAPTER SIXTY-ONE

The demon had vanished and left Kenny alone in the darkness. Was this worse than the sleet storm he'd been trapped in before? It felt that way. Before, he was miserable and afraid he'd die in the Canyon of Souls. Now he was terrified and knew this time his parents would die as well. The worst thing was, with the demon in charge of his body, his parents would think he did it.

A trail of silvery mist flew in from the abyss. It circled around him, stopped, and swelled into a human shape. It solidified and Kenny recognized it as one of the souls he'd seen when he was trapped in the demon. The older man had a broad face and short, curly hair. He looked much more substantial than he had before. He wasn't scary like the demon had been.

"Who are you?" Kenny said.

"My name is Greg. I'm a friend of your father's. How about we push the demon out of you?"

"You bet!"

"It's going to be hard and you'll need to do what I tell you to do, no matter what."

"Okay."

Greg explained a plan and told Kenny exactly what to tell his parents. He made Kenny repeat it back. Then the surface of whatever it was Kenny stood on vibrated like there was an earthquake.

"The archdemon knows I'm here," Greg said. "It'll be coming back. I'll keep it distracted. That's your chance to take back control."

"Okay."

Nicobar came charging out of the darkness, red eyes burning hot as the sun. Rage contorted the archdemon's face. It saw Greg and stopped. It breathed out so heavily, Kenny was sure the breath would turn to fire.

"You?" Nicobar said. "How did you get here?"

"When you killed me," Greg said, "and set my soul free, I skipped heading to the big white light, and hid inside you, tucked between the other souls you had trapped, hoping for a chance to hurt you from within. That chance came when you slid in here on Kenny's soul. I slid in on yours."

"There's not enough room in here for all of us," Nicobar said. "Time for you to go."

Nicobar grew to a half again larger size. The horns on its head took on the same color glow as its eyes. The exposed skin between the charred elements shifted to a ruddy hue. Despite this reality being devoid of sensation, Kenny was certain it just got hotter.

Nicobar charged Greg. Greg threw himself headfirst at the archdemon. When they collided, the two burst into flame. They turned into two dark shapes wrestling in a swirling, fiery tornado. Greg's voice called out from within.

"Go, Kenny!"

Kenny could feel the way back to consciousness the way a swimmer can sense the direction to the water's surface. He closed his eyes and travelled there.

★　　★　　★

Kenny released his grip on Anna's hair. She dropped down to her hands and knees.

"Mommy?" Kenny said.

She choked back the blood and mucus running down her throat and looked up at Kenny through bleary eyes. It was her son looking down in confused sadness at her, not the archdemon within him. She cried out in joy.

"Kenny! You're back."

"You need to help." Kenny teetered back and forth. "Hurry. Stab me with the Lance of Vladimir."

His mother looked shocked. "What? No. Fight the demon. Push it out of you."

"It's too strong." Kenny winced. "This is the only way. Greg says use the lance."

As far as she knew, Kenny didn't know what the Lance of Vladimir was. And she had no idea who Greg was.

"Anna," Drew called from the pit. "What's going on?"

"Kenny's back. He's not making sense. He said Greg wants me to stab him with the lance."

"Greg? But he's…." Drew paused. "If his soul is in Kenny as well, he has a plan. He knows how the lance works. You have to do it."

Drew crawled over to where the Lance of Vladimir lay in the dirt. He grabbed it and struggled up on one knee. He reared back and threw it up to Anna. It landed point down in the dirt beside her.

"Do it!" Drew shouted. "Greg knows what he's asking."

"I can't stab our son," she said.

Kenny began to shake. He touched one hand to her shoulder.

"Please, Mommy. Send it away before it makes me kill you."

Anna grabbed the lance. The blade glowed red in her hand and she felt its power surge up her arm. She could sense that the lance point itself had a mission. It felt like she was holding a magnet as the point turned to aim at Kenny. The blade demanded to be buried in her son's heart, to be given the chance to dispatch the demon it had failed to kill.

"Mommy?" Kenny begged. "Do it now!"

"I love you," she whispered.

She drove the lance into the center of her son's chest. He collapsed onto her.

★　　★　　★

Kenny returned to the abyss. Greg and Nicobar were locked in combat, two flaming outlines of themselves. Nicobar pounded Greg with a right cross and Greg staggered back. The archdemon pursued and grabbed Greg by the neck with both hands. It raised Greg up off his feet.

"I should have done this years ago," Nicobar said.

Kenny saw that Greg's plan hadn't worked. The lance was supposed to help Greg, and it didn't. Nicobar was about to destroy Greg even though his mother—

My mother just stabbed me in the chest, he realized. *We're all going to die.*

Then Greg's body began to blaze hotter. His red flames turned to a bright blue. He grabbed Nicobar's wrists.

The surface under Greg went from black to soft white. The light below him intensified. The blue flames that consumed his body crawled down Nicobar's arms. The archdemon roared.

"What is this?" Nicobar said.

It tried to release its grip on Greg's neck. Greg kept its hands in place. The blue flames crept down Nicobar's arms to its chest. The flames blew out around the lower half of Greg's body and from the waist down he looked normal again.

Nicobar cried out in frustration. Greg released its wrists and Nicobar dropped him. Nicobar teetered and spun its arms in useless, fiery windmills. The blue flames reached its waist and then raced down its legs.

Greg's whole body returned to normal. The blue flames ran up Nicobar's body like the demon was dry tinder and consumed its head. It grabbed its temples and screamed.

A glowing white version of the Lance of Vladimir appeared on the ground. It flew up into Greg's waiting hand.

Greg charged the burning archdemon. He wrapped his free hand around the back of the demon's neck and pulled them chest to chest.

"This is for Lincoln," he said. "I should have done *this* years ago."

He plunged the lance up into Nicobar's chest. The demon threw its head back and shrieked. Then the two of them burst like a pair of pom-pom fireworks, one blue and one white. The white sparkles consumed the blue and then faded away to nothing.

A dot of bright, snowy light swelled over Kenny's head. Then the Lance of Vladimir appeared in Kenny's hand.

"Don't let go of that," Greg's voice said. "No matter what. And *don't* go to that light up there."

★   ★   ★

Anna felt numb as she eased the body of her son to the ground. The horror of what she'd just done was incomprehensible. She gripped the end of the Lance of Vladimir, the tip buried in her son.

A red mist surrounded Kenny. She'd seen this happen just before Nicobar vanished. Kenny was about to do the same.

But the mist fell to the ground and disappeared without taking Kenny with it. Anna checked Kenny's pulse with her free hand. It was weak, but still there. In the flickering light of the flames burning in the pit, she could see his eyes dancing back and forth beneath his closed eyelids. She still hadn't dared release the glowing Lance of Vladimir, not knowing if she was helping whatever was going on inside her son.

Suddenly, Kenny opened his eyes. He sucked in a deep breath.

The glow of the lance diminished to nothing. All the power she'd felt running through her body evaporated.

Does that mean there's no demon in him to activate it? she thought. *Leave it in? Take it out?*

An old first aid class had taught her the answer but now all she could remember was that only one action was correct.

Kenny gagged. A sucking sound came from around the wound. She acted on instinct and pulled out the lance.

As she did, the wound healed. The blade carried no trace of blood. The incision shrank as Kenny's skin knitted together without a scar. He began to take deep, regular breaths. He looked at Anna and smiled.

"They're gone," Kenny said. "Now it's just me."

Tears ran down Anna's cheeks. She hugged Kenny tight.

"Anna!" Drew called from the pit. "Are you okay?"

"I'm fine," she called back. "We're both fine."

A siren wailed far up the hillside and red lights strobed the sky over the main road. A blaze like the one in the demon pit wouldn't go unnoticed against the darkness of the National Forest. Someone must have called it in, and there would be firefighters crashing around here in no time.

That meant a lot of explaining to do, a lot of lies to create and stick to. And first responders would be there before they'd have time to get the story straight.

CHAPTER SIXTY-TWO

The relief Drew felt at seeing his wife and son safe almost made him forget about how much his leg hurt. Almost.

He dragged himself around the burning timbers. The demon dagger lay on the ground to his right. He picked it up and put it in his pocket. He crawled to where Marvin sat propped up outside the demon trap by the stairs. Marvin stood up as Drew got there, but from the pained look on his face as he did, it took some effort. Marvin pulled Drew clear of the closest flames and propped him up against the wall.

"Thank you," Drew said. "Feeling better?"

"I'll admit I've healed a lot faster than this. Looks like you've managed to end up worse for the wear."

"My leg. It's not broken, but it's pretty torn up."

Marvin reached down and scooped him up. The cambion's strength, even injured, amazed Drew. Marvin walked him up the stairway one step at a time.

"This is the second time I've helped you get out of here," Marvin said. "Fall in again and I'm leaving you there."

At the top of the stairs, Marvin laid him down in an open spot. Anna and Kenny rushed over. Kenny's soft eyes and tired face told Drew Nicobar was gone for good.

He touched Kenny's uninjured chest. "The lance stabbed you...."

"And sent the demon away," Kenny said, "and then helped me stay here. Just like Greg promised."

Drew looked up at his wife and smiled. She knelt down and hugged him around the neck.

"Your face is so bloody," he said.

"I'm positive that demon broke my nose," she said. "What's wrong with your leg?"

"Twisted it up in that fall." He looked past her to Kenny. "You said that Greg told you about the lance?"

"He was there with me in the darkness," Kenny said. "He fought the demon and then they both disappeared and I came back to you."

"What did Greg look like?"

Kenny described Greg to perfection. Drew grinned. The old man had somehow defied the odds and saved the day. Some of his soul must have still survived inside Nicobar.

Voices and the jangle of equipment came from the direction of the animal trail. Flashlight beams swept back and forth across the ground.

"What are we going to tell them?" Anna said.

"I have no idea," Drew said.

Several firemen in full battle gear came to the edge of the cistern. Plenty of the roof still burned brightly. One of them grabbed a mic from his shoulder and radioed some commands and equipment requests back up to the truck on the highway. Another firefighter approached the group. Before Drew could say anything, Marvin stepped forward.

"Oh, thank god you're here!" he said. He'd ratcheted up his voice at least an octave and sounded exasperated and helpless. "His stupid idea almost got us killed."

Drew had no clue where this was going, but keeping quiet seemed to be the best plan. Before the firefighter could respond, Marvin launched back in.

"So, Drew's plan is to go out to see coyotes at night, which isn't like my first choice in entertainment. Then he drags his whole family along, using a kerosene lantern that's like fifty years old or something, like before batteries existed. We're walking along and then this whole roof over whatever this thing is collapses. We fall in, the lantern lights the place on fire, and we almost die!"

Drew had to give Marvin credit for whipping up a plausible story on pretty damn short notice.

The firefighter looked down at Drew. "Are you hurt?"

"Twisted up my leg in the fall. I can't walk on it."

"Understood. We'll get a stretcher down here and call in an ambulance." He turned to the firefighter who'd called back to the truck. "The fire is contained down there. Make sure it doesn't spread. Let it burn itself out." He turned back to Drew. "Pretty unsafe adventure to take your family on, don't you think?"

"Trust me," Drew said, "we won't be doing anything like this again."

Out of the firefighter's line of sight, Anna showed Drew that she had the Lance of Vladimir. Drew still had the demon dagger in his pocket. He hoped they would never have to use either again.

But he'd keep them safe in case they did.

CHAPTER SIXTY-THREE

Three weeks later

The long Saturday morning drive up to Bakersfield was the first time Drew had been somewhere other than work or his house in the weeks since they had sent Nicobar back to Hell. Those days had been well-spent.

The deputies who'd responded to the fire at Mission San Uriel gave Drew a hard time about doing something as stupid as a night hike with a kerosene lantern. But they hadn't taken any action about it, so that was good. The LASD grapevine had spread the word of his misadventure with blinding speed. He arrived at work on Monday in a leg brace and the whole office chided him about it. Every officer thought it was hilarious to ask if he needed to borrow their flashlight.

With the threat of criminal prosecution dismissed, the biggest worry was for Kenny. He'd been through a mind-bending experience with evil incarnate. Drew had dealt with demon contacts far milder and at a much more mature age, and he came through it with more than a touch of PTSD. He and Anna were terribly afraid that Kenny would never be the same.

But in a tribute to the resilience of youth he was. The boy was back to normal, and a bit better. The experience seemed to have strengthened him instead of scarring him. Kenny acted more loving, more focused, much older for his age. Drew wondered, if Nicobar had left traces of its corrupted soul in Kenny before the encounter at the mission, maybe Greg had been able to do the same with his generous spirit afterward.

What most amazed Drew and Anna was Marvin's reaction to the experience. He came by most days after the fight at the mission. That experience had bound them all together. Without a second thought, Marvin became Uncle Marvin to Kenny and part of the family. Everyone was glad to have him there, and the loner cambion was thrilled to be unconditionally accepted for the first time in his life.

Drew had left the three of them at the house as he went on his quest today. It was one he'd hoped to make for a long time, and each year became surer that he'd never complete it. But this week one of the many alerts he'd programmed into his browser finally sent the message that there was an answer to his prayer.

He exited off Interstate 5 and followed a dusty, two-lane road for a dozen miles. This area in the Central Valley was still as agricultural as Los Angeles was urban. Fields of crops stretched out all the way to the hazy base of the mountains to the east. He finally arrived at the address he'd programmed into his navigation app.

The small ranch house looked like it had been here since irrigation had first turned this dry land arable. The blue paint had faded to the color of a robin's egg. A disorganized collection of cacti landscaped the front yard and the gravel driveway looked like it had never been paved. Brighter rectangles on the roof betrayed where some of the old shingles had blown away. A clapboard one-car garage just to the side of the house had a decided leftward cant as if it had slowly bent to the common westerly winds.

A woman a few years older than Drew stood between the garage and the house. She wore a business suit that had no place in this dusty farmland. The breeze blew a dead leaf into her short dark hair and she brushed it away, annoyed. A silver two-door Mercedes was parked behind her.

Drew pulled into the driveway and got out of his car.

"Hi, I'm Drew."

They shook hands.

"I'm Renna. Thanks for working around my schedule to meet. It's a haul driving down from Sacramento and I already had other things to settle in town today for my father's estate."

"No problem," Drew said.

Renna led him to the garage. The two hinged doors in the front opened outward. She grabbed one.

"You'll need to give me a hand. The way the garage leans, these are hard to open. Don't worry, it won't fall down on us."

Drew gave her a hand and the two of them manhandled the heavy door open. Sunlight illuminated a car-shaped tarp covered in dirt. It looked like the wind had delivered tractor-driven dust through the cracks in the garage walls for some number of years.

"I can't tell you much about it," Renna said. "My father bought it in a probate auction years ago. I don't think he did anything but look at it since then. I found the title and have all the documentation to transfer it to a new owner."

"Mind if I uncover it?"

She pointed to her suit. "I'm not doing it dressed like this."

Drew pulled the tarp back off the hood of the car. Dirt flew skyward and put the garage in a temporary brownout. Renna coughed and stepped out of the garage.

When the dust settled, the nose of a 1970 Chevelle poked out into the sunshine. Drew pulled the hood release and raised the hood.

"You know your way around an antique car better than I do," Renna said.

"I had a friend who would have bristled if you called a car this young an antique."

Drew went over to the base of the windshield, pulled a small flashlight from his pocket, and lit up the VIN number on the dashboard. It matched the one he'd memorized long ago, the one he'd plugged into his internet search.

He shone the light around the engine bay. Brake master cylinder. Power steering pump. Exhaust manifolds. He recognized every part. He should, since he'd been the one who installed them. He'd finally found Lincoln's car.

"I'll take her," Drew said.

"Her?"

"Yes. Her name is Gabriella."

Renna gave Drew an odd look. "The car has a name?"

"All cars have a name. Sadly, few people ask the car what it is."

"Are you sure you don't want to check it over more? It will need a lot of work."

"That's no problem," Drew said. "It's going to be a project I'll share with my son."

AFTERWORD

Usually when I start a novel, I either have a cool beginning that inspires me, or a killer ending I can't wait to write myself to. In this instance, my inspiration was the middle.

I live in Florida and love our theme parks. They are a great place to escape the world for a day and have fun. But the costumed characters, the silent ones with the giant heads, well, they kind of creep me out a little.

The local myth is that there's always a woman playing Mickey Mouse because he's relatively short. I have no idea if that's true. Being a horror writer, I had to extrapolate that possibility into something chilling. Who knows what kind of person is wearing that giant head? Worse, what if it wasn't a person at all? What if some awful entity used the costume as a way to get close to people who've let their guard down in the ultra-safe theme park world?

My ability to turn any happy experience into a scary story is why I never get invited anywhere.

So the idea of a demon in a theme park costume blossomed. Who would that demon want to target? The son of a demon hunter, of course. Then the story unfurled in two directions from there, ahead to the final showdown between the hunter and the demon, and back to how Drew got into demon hunting in the first place.

Here are a few more notes about the story for you:

All the basic auto mechanic skills Lincoln teaches young Drew are generally correct. So, ha ha, you learned something reading this book. I have restored several classic muscle cars, including a 1970 Chevelle like Gabriella, but she's a red-and-white convertible named Valerie. Writing a scene where a demon tears up a classic car was traumatic.

The 1901 experiment by Dr. Duncan McDougall that Lincoln refers to really happened and fired his claim for a soul weighing twenty-one grams. The subsequent experiment on convicts in 1982 is something I made up.

I love to visit Southern California, so I thought I'd set the story there. Many of the places mentioned are actual locations, like MacArthur Park, Angeles National Forest, Topanga Canyon, and the park in San Leandro where Anna takes Kenny. El Matador Beach, where Nicobar traps Marvin, is also a real park near Malibu. If you're in Los Angeles, you should visit it and see the cave where Marvin was turned more demon.

The history of the Spanish missions in California is correct, but there were definitely twenty-one, not twenty-two, and they were not set up to hunt and kill demons. At least as far as I know.

Having your soul ripped out isn't what turns people into psychopaths. Research shows that it may be related to a defect in the brain. The book *The Psychopath Whisperer* is a great nonfiction read about psychopathy, including some chilling stories of children who I used as models for soulless Kenny.

People ask me if I believe in demons and Satan. If you check the afterword to my novel *The Portal* you can read my account of my close encounter of an evil kind. And while I made up that part about weak places in the fabric between Hell and Earth, that idea had its own real-world inspiration.

I attended a World Horror Convention in New Orleans one year. I woke up before dawn and took a walk around downtown outside my hotel. I didn't encounter anyone. But I was never at ease. It was as if there was something in the air, something in the ground that exuded evil. I've been in dozens of graveyards and never felt so ill at ease. Something in that city radiated darkness, and I've had other people tell me the same thing, completely unprompted. Sorry, New Orleans Tourist Board.

In the thanks department, the first and loudest go to editor Don D'Auria, whose splendid insight gave the manuscript the adjustments it needed to turn it into the story my characters, and you readers, deserved. Much gratitude also goes to the rest of the team at Flame Tree Press, who turn my data files into gorgeous books and sell them all over the world. Thank you to beta readers Somer Canon, Belinda Whitney, Teresa Robeson, Donna Fitzpatrick, and Deb DeAlteriis for sampling the sauce while it was still simmering and telling me if the spices were correct.

That's all the behind-the-scenes documentary I have. I hope you had a fun and scary ride with Drew through the world of demons and archdemons. I hope they leave him alone in the future, but they are pretty vengeful. We'll see if some other pleasant experience inspires me to put him and his family back in danger.

Russell James

FLAME TREE PRESS
FICTION WITHOUT FRONTIERS
Award-Winning Authors & Original Voices

Flame Tree Press is the trade fiction imprint of Flame Tree Publishing, focusing on excellent writing in horror and the supernatural, crime and mystery, science fiction and fantasy. Our aim is to explore beyond the boundaries of the everyday, with tales from both award-winning authors and original voices.

•

Other titles available by Russell James:
The Playing Card Killer
The Portal

Other horror and suspense titles available include:
Snowball by Gregory Bastianelli
Thirteen Days by Sunset Beach by Ramsey Campbell
Think Yourself Lucky by Ramsey Campbell
The Hungry Moon by Ramsey Campbell
The Influence by Ramsey Campbell
The Wise Friend by Ramsey Campbell
The Haunting of Henderson Close by Catherine Cavendish
The Garden of Bewitchment by Catherine Cavendish
The House by the Cemetery by John Everson
The Devil's Equinox by John Everson
Hellrider by JG Faherty
The Toy Thief by D.W. Gillespie
One By One by D.W. Gillespie
Black Wings by Megan Hart
The Sorrows by Jonathan Janz
Will Haunt You by Brian Kirk
We Are Monsters by Brian Kirk
Hearthstone Cottage by Frazer Lee
Those Who Came Before by J.H. Moncrieff
Stoker's Wilde by Steven Hopstaken & Melissa Prusi
Creature by Hunter Shea
Ghost Mine by Hunter Shea
Slash by Hunter Shea
The Forever House by Tim Waggoner
Your Turn to Suffer by Tim Waggoner
We Will Rise by Tim Waggoner

•

Join our mailing list for free short stories, new release details, news about our authors and special promotions:

flametreepress.com